THREAD AND DEAD

St. Martin's Paperbacks titles by
Elizabeth Penney

Hems & Homicide
Thread and Dead

THREAD AND DEAD

Elizabeth Penney

St. Martin's Paperbacks

This is a work of fiction. All of the characters, organizations, and events portrayed in this novel are either products of the author's imagination or are used fictitiously.

First published in the United States by St. Martin's Paperbacks, an imprint of St. Martin's Publishing Group.

THREAD AND DEAD

For information, address St. Martin's Publishing Group, 120 Broadway, New York, NY 10271.

www.stmartins.com

ISBN: 978-1-250-25797-0

Our books may be purchased in bulk for promotional, educational, or business use. Please contact your local bookseller or the Macmillan Corporate and Premium Sales Department at 1-800-221-7945, ext. 5442, or by email at MacmillanSpecialMarkets@macmillan.com.

Printed in the United States of America

10 9 8 7 6 5 4 3 2 1

for my lovely girls, big and little

Acknowledgments

Once again thank you to the wonderful team at St. Martin's Press, to everyone who helped me bring *Thread and Dead* to life. Much gratitude to my editor Nettie Finn especially, who provides gentle guidance and an incisive eye to my drafts. Thanks also to Holly Rice and Allison Ziegler, who helped launch the series with much wonderful PR, including mention in a national magazine and popular mystery publications.

In *Thread and Dead*, I feature a very interesting new business—growing seaweed in leased Maine waters. I want to thank Katie Flavin, who not only authored the informative *Kelp Farming Manual*, but also answered questions from me. I appreciate Katie for helping me get it right—and of course, any and all errors are all mine.

I'd also like to thank Jennifer Rodgers Lemaire and Sara McFerrin for their suggestions for items in Eleanor's attic. The cozy mystery community is so welcoming, and I especially want to mention the support of Dru Ann Love and Lori Caswell in promoting the series. Much appreciation to Jungle Red Writers, The Wickeds, Chicks on the Case, Writers Who Kill, and Maine Crime Fiction Writers, who so kindly featured my debut. And a special shout-out goes out to Shari Randall and the other authors in the Cozy Mystery Crew, who invited me to be part of their corner of Facebook. We have so much fun mingling with authors and readers. Please join us, if you're not already a member.

Last, but certainly not least, a heartfelt thank-you to those who read *Hems & Homicide*—and all your kind words. I'm so happy that you love Iris too.

CHAPTER 1

Quincy, please." I picked up my orange tabby "helper" for the third time and set him gently on the floor, then opened the box flaps. Inside was a collection of aprons I'd nabbed at an auction, colorful prints featuring vegetables and fruits—perfect for our new "garden bounty" window display. The Fourth of July theme had come down, and these new pieces were going up today, to celebrate our glorious, all-too-short Maine summer.

"Ooh, I love those," Grammie said, handing me a cup of freshly brewed coffee from our favorite place, the Belgian Bean. My grandmother, Anne Buckley, is my business partner in Ruffles & Bows, a vintage apron and linens shop in Blueberry Cove, Maine. Like me, she wore the signature store outfit, a white ruffled pinafore over a mid-century-inspired dress.

Our old-fashioned garb was not only comfortable, it suited the shop's décor as well. Located in what was once an ancestor's dry goods store, the space featured original tin ceilings, hanging light fixtures, and carved mahogany service counters and woodwork. We displayed stacks of crisp linens in antique cabinets and armoires and hung vintage aprons on rotating clotheslines. Ladder racks held tea towels, and potholders in every color dangled from cup hooks.

I took a sip of rich, dark coffee, then set the paper cup a safe distance away. "Look at this one." The half apron was pure confection, white organza embroidered with cherries and trimmed with red rickrack and bobbles.

"Gorgeous." Grammie rubbed the silky fabric between finger and thumb. "The variety of apron styles and themes never ceases to amaze me."

"Same here," I said. After being laid off as a designer for a home-goods catalog company in Portland, Maine, I started dabbling in online sales, driven by my interest in vintage fabrics. Now, several years later, I was still learning about aprons and household linens and their connection to women's history. The 1920s through the 1960s had seen a veritable explosion in personal expression when it came to aprons and kitchen linens. Most were handmade, often repurposing flour sacks and clothing fabric, and embellishments were common.

The shop phone rang and I grabbed it while Grammie continued to admire the new purchases. "Good morning. Ruffles and Bows, Iris speaking. How may I help you?" After almost two months in business, the greeting rolled off my tongue.

"Good morning to you as well," a sprightly yet scratchy voice said. "I'm calling to inquire about selling some antique linens. I understand you purchase inventory privately." By the formal phrasing, I guessed the caller was from an earlier generation.

"We often do," I said, reaching for a pad and pen. "Depending on our needs." This was my all-purpose disclaimer, in case the goods were ripped, stained, or otherwise undesirable. You wouldn't believe the rags some people thought were valuable antiques. "Who am I speaking with, please?"

"This is Eleanor Brady. I live at Shorehaven Cottage, six Cliff Road. Out on Cobscot Head. Do you know it?"

Did I know it? I hadn't been by there for years, but a vision of towers, gables, and gargoyles danced in my head. Shorehaven was the eclectic queen of so-called summer cottages built by wealthy tycoons during the late 1800s. The old Brady money came from railroads and shipping, as I recalled.

My palms began to sweat. Anything Eleanor wanted to sell was probably top-drawer. Despite the fact that wealthy families used the cottages only part of the year, the furnishings were usually high quality. Only the finest for the Bradys and their peers.

"Shorehaven is one of my favorite houses in Blueberry Cove," I said, almost breathless with excitement. "It's gorgeous."

A rapping on the front-door glass startled me, since we didn't open for a few more minutes. I looked up to see my best friend, Madison Morris, peering inside. With her was another good friend, Bella Ricci, owner of Mimosa Boutique. Both wore faded jeans and gauzy tops, held cups of Belgian Bean coffee, and carried leather totes. I gave them a wave and smile while Grammie went to let them in, Quincy at her heels. Maybe she would be the one to actually unlock the door, but he was the official greeter.

Back to Eleanor, who was chuckling at my previous remark. "We see eye to eye on the house, at least. My nephew calls it a hideous overgrown old ark, but I love the place. It's my home."

I disliked the nephew already. "Can you tell me a little bit about the linens?" I liked to be prepared for meetings with customers, so I could make an offer on the spot.

"Oh, I don't know." Her voice slid into vagueness. "I've got a closet full of bed sheets. And last week I found some old linens from Europe in a trunk. Embroidered and monogrammed. Never been used, far as I could tell."

My pulse jumped. Antique European sheets of good quality often sold for thousands, believe it or not. "I'm definitely interested," I said, trying to sound casual. But my fingernails bit into my palm. Hopefully another dealer wouldn't scoop me. "When can I come by?"

"Well, whenever you want. Another gentleman from Camden is coming out this afternoon. Oh, and there are aprons too. I think from the thirties. Do you want those?"

Did I ever! I held back a squeal. Patting my chest to calm down, I said, "How about this morning?" I had to grab that inventory before the other dealer even saw it.

We settled on a time, and after I hung up, I did a little dance in place, fists pumping. "Woo-hoo. We've got a hot one in the pipeline." To Grammie, I said, "Eleanor Brady, later this morning. European linens and antique aprons."

She gave me thumbs-up. "I haven't seen Eleanor for ages. I wonder how the old gal is doing. You'll have to say hello for me."

My friends were exchanging amused looks at my excitement. "I'm happy for you," Bella said. "I feel that way when I come across a great new designer." Bella had impeccable taste, which was why the Lobster Festival committee had put her in charge of the fashion show.

Since the 1940s, the five-day festival celebrating Maine's famous crustacean had included a parade, lobster dinners, and a carnival. In recent years, the organizers had added new events to expand the festivities—and further benefit the charities they supported. The official kickoff was the day after tomorrow, starting with the parade down Main Street.

"What's up?" I asked. "Are you here about the festival?" Grammie and I were in charge of keeping other retailers informed about the event. "Everyone has the festival poster and handouts for their in-store displays. And we collected all the raffle items and took them to the chamber office."

Madison consulted the clipboard she pulled out of her tote. "Great work. Another two items checked off the list." Madison, who had her own marketing business, was in charge of promoting the festival and coordinating the various teams and committees.

Bella smiled. "But that's not why we're here. Do you have time to talk for a minute, Iris?"

I glanced at Grammie, who nodded. "Go ahead," she said. "I'll take care of any customers." Since the clock had now struck nine, she went to the front window and turned the sign to "Open."

Picking up my coffee, I said, "Let's meet in the classroom." I led the way, flicking on the light in the adjacent space, once a smaller storefront. This fall, I planned to start offering sewing classes here, including stitching aprons from vintage patterns and up-cycling antique and used linens into projects. We took seats at the long table, Quincy jumping up onto a chair too. He liked to be in on the action.

"He's so cute," Bella said, rubbing his chin the way he liked it. He purred loudly. "How's your kitten, Madison?"

Madison had adopted Pixie, a tiger kitten, back in May. "She's adorable. Getting big." She pulled out her phone and showed us a couple of action shots.

Then Bella gave us a short update on her two children, Connor, eleven, and Alice, twelve, who were attending various summer programs. She was fairly recently divorced, so we deftly avoided mention of her obnoxious ex-husband. "The kids will be helping me during the festival," she said. "They look forward to it every year." She smiled at me. "And that brings me around to why we're here."

Madison passed around sheets of paper. "This is just a mock-up I threw together. It can change."

I picked up the page and studied it. At the top was a cartoon picture of a lobster wearing an apron, cooking utensils in his claws. "Put on Your Best Bib and Tucker. Enter the First Annual Lobster Bib and Apron Contest. Points for Creativity and Unique Designs! Big Prizes!" Like many of the festival events, this one benefited the children's playground.

"The contest will be part of the fashion show," Bella said. "The highlight, actually. We would love for you to be the only judge of that portion."

"I got Sunrise Resort to spring for a weekend for two as the grand prize," Madison said. The resort was one of her biggest clients.

"That's fantastic." I was already a judge for the rest of the show, so what was one more thing, right? But the weight of all I had going on this week pressed down onto my shoulders. The busy summer season at the store, which meant stocking fresh inventory was even more important. Helping with the festival. Dating Ian Stewart . . . well, that was in the extracurricular category.

I got a warm and tingly feeling whenever I thought about Ian, who I was seeing tonight. We were going to the Taste O' the Sea reception, a thank-you and dining preview for festival organizers and volunteers, then to dinner with Sophie Jacobs, owner of the Bean, and her almost-fiancé, lobsterman Jake.

But how could I say no to my friends? Plus judging an apron contest would help promote the store, since Ruffles & Bows was named as the sponsor. "All right, I'll do it."

"Thanks, Iris," Bella said with a grateful smile. "You won't regret it, I promise."

I sincerely hoped not. With a sigh, I got down to business. "Okay. Tell me how it will work."

An hour later found me at the wheel of Beverly, my '63 Ford Falcon, headed to Shorehaven Cottage and, fingers crossed, some gorgeous aprons and linens. Beverly had been a twenty-first birthday gift from my late grandfather, who had restored the old gal to perfection—and given her a name.

I drove through town, past the circa 1820 farmhouse where I lived with Grammie, and turned onto Cliff Road. Cobscot State Park was out here and I slowed as I went past the gate, noting the number of vehicles in the lot. The park was a popular place for hiking, picnicking, and investigating tidal pools.

Madison and Ian had talked me into going rock climbing here tomorrow, on the cliffs bordering the water. My stomach knotted in anxiety just thinking about scrambling up a rock face. I hated heights, even avoided climbing ladders, but they were convinced I would love it, especially at sunrise. An experience not to be missed, they claimed.

We would see.

Past the park, the road narrowed and trees pressed close, hiding any view of the shore. Not many people lived on this dead-end road and turnoffs were few. I slowed down, watching for the stone gateposts marking Shorehaven's entrance.

There it was, a sprawling brown-shingled heap sitting in a field overlooking the water. I eased Beverly down the drive, which was striped with weeds that brushed the undercarriage.

My heart sank as I drew closer. The once-grand ivy-covered house with its tall windows now presented an unfortunate aura of neglect. Shingles were missing here and there on the roof, and one gargoyle leaned forward on his perch, ready to do a header into the tangled garden below. A sawhorse blocked the crumbling stone portico, so I continued straight ahead, to a small graveled parking area ending in an iron fence smothered by holly bushes.

Eleanor had said to come to the side door, and to my right, I glimpsed a row of second-story windows beyond the fence. The entrance must be through that gate.

I climbed out of Beverly and shut the door gently. It was so quiet here, with only the muffled beat of the surf and the twitter of birds in the ivy disturbing the deep silence. If I squinted, I could imagine the house as it had been in its heyday. A terrible thought struck me. Maybe Eleanor *had* to sell things in order to do some repairs. The place was well on its way to falling down.

The buzz of an engine sounded from the road and I turned to see a red sports car zipping along. To my surprise, the driver braked sharply and turned down Shorehaven's drive.

As I stood frozen in place, my mind spun with conjectures while I watched the red car race toward me. Was the Camden dealer here already, hours ahead of schedule? Haggling was not my strong suit, and competing with another dealer even less so. I'd barely learned how to act during an auction.

The car ground to a halt beside Beverly, and a moment later a man climbed out. A tall, well-built man with tousled blond hair and chiseled features, wearing a white linen short-sleeved shirt and khaki shorts. Where had I been? I'd never seen an antiques dealer who looked like a male model. And he was far too young to be Eleanor's nephew, I thought.

He turned to face me, lifting his sunglasses. "Good morning," he said. He had a European accent.

I loved Ian but I was seriously swooning here. Wait,

what? Had I just said—even in my thoughts—that I *loved* Ian? Although I'd crushed on him back in high school, we had only been dating a couple of months. Clearly this European-sounding, sports-car driving man was throwing me off more than I'd thought.

And no, I wasn't going there, not yet. We'd agreed, after horrible breakups with former partners, to take it slow this time.

The newcomer was saying something, and I finally tuned in. "No, I'm not Miss Brady," I said. Only about fifty or so years younger. "I was just on my way in to see her. Are you here about the sheets?" I held my breath waiting for the answer.

He sent me a quizzical look. "Not exactly. My group is staying here. Miss Brady is our five-star host, the website said."

Oh, I got it now. Eleanor was renting rooms through one of those online services. Go, Eleanor. And phew, this man was probably not an antiques dealer.

"Follow me, then," I said, walking toward the gate. "She said to come in this way." I pulled on the handle, and the gate opened with a squeal that made me wince. Leaving it open, I stepped into the enclosure, my gaze falling on a large swimming pool with a tiled surround. Chaise longues and tables were placed here and there, and the blue-tinted water glittered invitingly.

Then I noticed an older woman stretched out on a lounge chair, dressed in a long white gown and lying with her arms at her sides. A net on a pole lay beside the chair, the type of thing used to clean pools. She wore an odd bonnet-type hat and her eyes were closed.

I stepped closer. "Eleanor?" I called. "Iris Buckley here. And—" I glanced over my shoulder.

He was right behind me. "Dr. Lukas de Wilde."

I wavered on my feet. Talk about the perfect name. I

had to somehow get this man and Bella, who was now ready to date, in the same room. "And Dr. Lukas de Wilde, your guest."

"The other three are arriving soon," he said. My romantic plot popped like a bubble. Until he added, "My colleagues." Not his "wife" or his "significant other." Plot still on, unless he *was* involved with someone, of course.

Eleanor hadn't budged. A fly circled her head and landed on her nose, then walked up the bridge. It left that prominent feature and crawled about her forehead. She still didn't move.

I found myself gripping Dr. de Wilde's muscular forearm. Had we arrived too late? Was Eleanor Brady gone?

CHAPTER 2

Dr. de Wilde glanced at me, consternation in his eyes. They were unusual, blue with a gold ring around the pupil. "Is she all right? Should we call for help?"

"Hold that thought. Let me take a closer look." Heart in my throat, I approached the lounge chair, studying Eleanor's bony chest for a hint of movement. Was that a slight flutter of lace? Encouraged, I took her wrist, noticing with a wince how fragile it was, almost like holding a baby bird.

In the shadow of the bonnet brim, Eleanor's eyes flashed open, startling me. Quite frankly, I was reminded of the creepy scene in a movie where a doll comes to life. I jumped back with a little cry.

"I felt someone touching me," she said, pushing to a more upright position. She waved at the fly circling her face again.

"That was me," I said. "I . . . we thought . . ." I decided to drop that line of discussion. I was sure she wouldn't enjoy hearing we'd been afraid she had passed. "Anyway, I'm Iris Buckley. From Ruffles and Bows." I waved a hand toward my companion. "And this is your guest, Dr. de Wilde."

Eleanor swung her body around and planted her feet on the tile surround. She cocked her head and gave

Dr. de Wilde a coquettish smile. "How nice to meet you."
She put out a hand. Thinking that she wanted to shake,
he stepped forward and grasped her fingers. But with a
grunt, she leaned forward and stood. "Thank you," she
said, dropping his hand and settling her long dress into
place. "You must excuse my appearance. I was cleaning
out the pool."

His amused eyes locked with mine and I had to stifle
a laugh. A more unlikely pool-servicing outfit I couldn't
imagine. Eleanor Brady was quite a character.

Eleanor craned her neck, peering past the professor
toward the drive. "Is the rest of your party here?"

"Not yet, Miss Brady," he said. "They're attending a
meeting at College of the Isles." The picturesquely named
local institution was renowned for its intensive study of
Maine's natural environment. "But I would like to check
us all in."

Glancing back and forth between us, the older woman
fluttered a bit, tapping one finger against her teeth. "Iris,
my dear, would you mind waiting here while I take care
of Dr. de Wilde? I have iced tea or cold water if you'd like
a glass."

"Iced tea would be great," I said, choosing a chair
under a table with an umbrella. "And please, take your
time." I leaned back against the thick cushions with a
sigh. There were worse things than sitting beside a pool
on a gorgeous summer day.

The pair went inside the house, Dr. de Wilde opening the French door for Eleanor to precede him. She re-
warded him with effusive appreciation for his courtesy.

What a beautiful spot. I couldn't see the water from
here due to the bushes and trees surrounding the pool enclosure. But the sound of breakers was a little louder and
accompanied by a steady onshore breeze. I started to pull

out my phone to check my e-mail and my calendar, but then I reconsidered. All that could wait.

"Here we are." Eleanor bustled back out through the French door, a small silver tray in her hands. It held one tall glass of iced tea, a sliver of lemon perched on the rim. Ice tinkled as she set the glass in front of me, along with a napkin, a tall spoon, and three sugar packets with the "Sweet on ME" design used by the Miss Blueberry Cove Diner, ME being the abbreviation for our state. Had Eleanor been reduced to stealing supplies for her guests? I sure hoped not. Maybe she'd bought a case, anticipating lots of renters.

"I'll be back in a jiffy," Eleanor said, patting my shoulder. "Soon as I get that nice young man settled in."

"I'm in no hurry," I said, ripping open a sugar packet. I used only one sugar in my iced tea, which took off the bitter edge without making it too sweet. Lounging and sipping tea, I imagined myself a summer visitor from a hundred years ago. This fantastic old cottage and the elegant lifestyle its residents had enjoyed made me long for a time machine.

That'd be one way to get out of rock climbing tomorrow morning. But since a time machine wasn't handy, I flipped mentally through the various excuses I could use. Like a forgotten dentist appointment (total lie, but seriously I preferred tooth drilling to rock climbing) or a sudden upset stomach (hopefully not from the Taste O' the Sea menu). Then, feeling guilty, I stopped myself. Ian really wanted me to go, and bailing on him at the last minute would be cowardly. He was too special—*we* were too special—for games or dishonesty. No, I had to pull up my big girl panties and deal.

Mindlessly pleating the sugar packet into tiny folds, I allowed myself to drift into a daydream. It might have

featured Ian kissing me for my bravery in climbing a cliff
with only a nylon rope to save me from death.

"Iris?" Eleanor appeared at my elbow, making me
jump. I hadn't heard her approaching. "Thanks for waiting so patiently. Would you like to see the linens?" She
had taken off the bonnet, revealing a head of finger-waved
white hair that made her look like an elderly flapper.

Oh yeah. Pretending to be very cool and casual, I took
a slow swallow of iced tea, set my glass on the tray, and
stood. I'd learned that it wasn't good business to let the
customer know how eager you were.

We entered the house through the French doors, arriving in a comfortable sitting room furnished with a mix
of wicker and upholstered chintz furniture. A marble-
and-walnut wet bar stood along the wall straight ahead,
while to my left, I glimpsed a formal living room through
open pocket doors. The woodwork and wainscoting were
carved, the plaster ceilings and moldings ornate. All of
it was magnificent if a little shabby, like the threadbare
Persian carpet under my feet.

Eleanor led me past the bar and into a huge entrance
hall dominated by a curving staircase. "Everything is upstairs," she said, taking hold of the bronze nymph topping
the newel post. With the other hand, she picked up her
long skirt so it wouldn't drag. Just like many a lady before
her, I couldn't help but think.

In the upper hall, we wandered past stained glass
windows casting vibrant colors onto the ivory-and-gold
wallpaper and carpet. Closed doors lined the corridor,
and near the end, we reached what looked like a built-
in cabinet. Bronze curlicue sconces with white globes
cast light on the scene as Eleanor opened double doors
with a flourish. Floor-to-ceiling shelves were packed with
folded sheets and pillowcases, most of them white, some

in tasteful pastels. A faint aroma of lavender and starch tickled my nose.

"I can see why you might want to downsize a little," I said with a laugh. Seriously, there had to be ten dozen sheets stacked in there, enough to stock a small hotel.

Eleanor chuckled in agreement as she tugged at a folded sheet. "Now that I've started renting rooms, I plan to keep a bunch. But even with three sets for each bed, I have far too many." She finally managed to extract the sheet and plopped it into my waiting arms.

The fabric was thick cotton, densely woven, and silky. Premium, in other words. "I like it. How many can I have?" I could sell pairs of this quality and vintage for close to a hundred dollars.

In the end, I took a dozen sets of white sheets and pillowcases—in plain white, with blue piping, and edged with lace. This purchase barely made a dent in the closet's contents, so I hoped to buy more if these sold well. Unless the other dealer snatched them up, of course. But I was stretching my budget already, buying this much.

"Do you have anything else for me?" I asked, hinting. Nice as the sheets were, they weren't the European linens Eleanor had mentioned on the phone. But maybe she'd changed her mind about selling. I wasn't the type to pressure a customer, unlike some of my competitors.

Eleanor put a finger to her lips, her eyes twinkling with mischief. "You mean the top-secret stash?" She gestured. "Come with me."

Leaving my sheets stacked on a window seat, I followed Eleanor down the hall and through a door to what must have been the servants' quarters. Here the wallpaper was faded and blotched with brown, the floorboards bare and worn. The small rooms were furnished with brass twin beds and not much else.

We ascended a narrow flight of stairs to the third floor. Eleanor pointed to a door on the right. "That's the nursery. My mother started out here as a nursemaid. Then she married my father and became mistress of the house."

I realized my mouth was hanging open and quickly closed it. I'd never heard this story, and my mind began to whir, thinking what a scandal an upstairs-downstairs romance must have been in the 1930s. Perhaps class distinctions weren't as rigid as, say, in England with its nobility, but they were there. *Still* were.

"Where was your mother from?" I asked, more to fill the silence than to pry.

"Belgium. She was an immigrant without family or connections. That's why she became a servant." Eleanor opened a door on the opposite wall. "This is the attic," she said, flicking on a light switch. Bare bulbs illuminated a long, slant-ceilinged space crammed with household goods and assorted junk.

"I've been slowly going through everything," she said, sidling past pieces of furniture and stacks of boxes. A wheeled rack holding garment bags squealed away when she pushed, coming to rest against a huge armoire. Who had carried *that* up here? "It wouldn't be fair to Craig if I leave a huge mess."

"Craig?" I picked my way across the room, jumping when I came face-to-face with a snarling raccoon. Stuffed, I realized after a few heart-pounding seconds. I'd never seen the appeal of taxidermy.

"My nephew." Eleanor was out of sight now and her voice was muffled.

Oh, the nephew. The one without the taste and brains to appreciate Shorehaven. Umbrellas in a stand knocked together when I bumped them with my rear. What was that among the handles? Seriously, a wooden leg?

"He's my only relative, so all this will be going to him,"

she went on. "I had two sisters and a brother—Craig's father—but they're gone. All of them, gone." She sounded forlorn, and I thought how lonely it must be to be the last one left of your family. "So anyway," she said, her tone brisk, "I was poking around up here and I found the linens I told you about. And some other things I need your professional opinion about."

Hinges squeaked, so I picked up the pace, eager to see the goods. Finally, a bit disheveled and definitely dusty, I reached Eleanor's side. She was sitting on the floor in front of a black metal trunk with tarnished brass trim. Heedless of my dress, I sat beside her.

A layer of tissue paper lay on top of the trunk's contents, and Eleanor carefully folded it back. "I remember looking in this trunk once, years ago. When I was a child. But Mama didn't like us playing around in the attic, so I forgot about it until now."

Under the tissue was a snowy sheet made from *fil de lin*, the finest of linen. Even before I pulled the piece from the trunk, I could imagine its *hand*—what we textile nerds called "fabric feel." The sheet was silky, light yet dense, nothing less than sumptuous. Details included handmade lace trim and an embroidered monogram with a *V* and an *S*.

"Who did this trunk belong to?" I asked, expecting her to mention a Brady ancestor, perhaps a bride who bought her trousseau in Paris.

Confusion shadowed Eleanor's eyes. "My mother." She picked up a handkerchief from an upper tray and showed it to me. This monogram was *C*, *d*, and *W*. "Claudia de Witte was her name. But I have wondered . . . how did an impoverished immigrant buy goods of this quality?"

Her question hung in the dusty air. How indeed? "Maybe they were gifts," I said. That would explain the other monogram.

"Maybe." Eleanor replaced the handkerchief. "But there's more." She scooted over to an identical trunk and opened the lid. Again, there was tissue paper that she folded back. "Look at this," she said, holding up a black-and-white plaid jacket trimmed with soft fur at collar, cuffs, and hem, and a matching skirt. She handed them to me. "Do you think they're valuable?"

The garments carried an aroma of cedar, which had protected the fabric from moths. I opened the jacket, gasping when I saw the label. *Chanel.* In addition to the iconic suit she was probably best known for, Coco Chanel had designed glamorous clothing like this outfit.

And there was more; a black-and-white satin evening dress, day frocks, a velvet wrap and mink stole, four pairs of dainty shoes, gloves, sets of gossamer undergarments. All designer-made.

"Oh yes, they're valuable," I said. "Not only designer, they're in excellent condition. I've seen similar garments go for tens of thousands of dollars."

"As I suspected," Eleanor said. "I never understood it," she added. "How did she go from this"—she waved a hand—"to this?" She opened a much more humble trunk and pulled out a bibbed apron trimmed with Battenberg lace at the shoulders and hem.

I want. Despite the beauty and value of the couture clothing, aprons and linens were my focus. "Can I look?"

She moved aside so I could pore over the contents of the trunk. A dozen aprons were inside, all styles worn by domestic help in the early twentieth century. They'd been immaculately taken care of, washed and starched, rips and tears mended with small, neat stitches. I didn't know which I loved more, the floral full apron from the 1920s or the V-bib trimmed with lace inserts. How about all of the above?

I clasped the lacy apron to my chest. "Can I buy everything in the trunk? And the linen sheets too." These purchases would take quite a bit of my reserve cash, but such rare items were worth it. Collectors on my list would be very interested.

Eleanor pursed her lips, a crafty expression in her eyes. "I'll let you. On one condition."

My eagerness deflated a tiny bit. Perhaps this purchase wasn't going to be the home run I'd hoped for. "What's that?" I kept my tone neutral and made sure to smile. *Never let them see you sweat.*

Eleanor turned back to the trunk of Chanel garments, reaching out a hand to stroke the suit's fur trim. "Can you sell these for me?"

The unexpected question surprised a laugh out of me. "I'm sorry, but clothes really aren't my area of expertise." Pricing the garments would require research into previous sales plus digging to find out which pieces were most collectible at the moment. And we'd need to find a partner to sell them, mostly likely an auction house that had the right connections and could command the highest prices.

She kept her eyes on the apparel as she said, "I want you to try and sell them for me. Everything in the trunk." Biting her lip, she darted a glance at me.

Reading mingled hope and fear in her eyes, I thought of this mansion, which was practically falling down around our ears. She needed the money, and despite my lack of experience in this department, I found myself saying yes.

"I won't give you any prices now," I said. "Let me do some research first. We'll need to find an auction house or a specialist in vintage clothing." Such a situation wasn't as clear-cut as me directly selling something and taking my share. But it didn't matter, since I was going to make this a pro-bono project. I didn't care if I made a dime from those designer clothes as long as Eleanor profited.

Eleanor hoisted herself to her feet by leaning on a nearby Victrola cabinet. "I appreciate your help, Iris." Her smile was warm. "But I didn't expect anything less from Anne's granddaughter. How is she?"

"She's doing well," I said. "I'm not sure if you knew, but Grammie is co-owner of my shop. It's wonderful working with her."

"I'm sure it is." Eleanor's face sagged with sorrow. "I was so sorry to hear about Joe." My grandfather, who died last winter. "He was a good man."

"He was." I paused briefly, thinking of Papa, then said, "I'll be back later with help to move these trunks." I wanted to keep the sheets and the clothing in their trunks until I had a chance to poke through. There might be labels or sales slips or other items that would add to an item's value. The aprons could go into a box.

"Maybe Lukas can help." She cocked her arm. "He has a nice set of muscles." She whistled, mischief gleaming in her eyes. Despite her advanced years, Eleanor had obviously retained a youthful and lively attitude toward life. Her fine features still held traces of beauty, and I could easily imagine her decades younger.

I giggled. "Only if he wants to. He is a guest, after all." The visiting professor might not take kindly to being drafted into service.

"Wait here, my dear," Eleanor said. "I'll be right back."

I spent the time drooling over the linen sheets and other textiles in the trunk. In this neck of the woods, such high-value items were fairly rare. Maybe I could even get a feature about vintage linens into our local paper, the *Herald*. Lars Lavely, their main reporter, owed me big time.

Footsteps echoed on the third-floor stairs—two sets. By the time they reached the top, I had both trunks shut and latched, ready to go. I had flattened cardboard boxes in my car and I'd bring one up for the aprons.

"My mother came from Belgium," Eleanor was saying as they entered the attic. "She immigrated in 1932."

"Really? What part?" Dr. de Wilde asked. He spotted where I was standing and began picking his way through. Then he stopped to move objects aside, clearing a path. "We're going to need room to get those trunks out."

"Antwerp," Eleanor said, helping him slide a stack of chairs over. "Are you familiar with it?"

As I joined them, he said, "Familiar with it? I was born and raised there."

"I've never been," Eleanor said. "Which is a shame."

As we moved furniture and boxes aside, Dr. de Wilde described the city, which now had a population of half a million. Antwerp had been an important port since the Middle Ages and was known for its diamond trade. "If you can visit," he concluded, "you should. It's a beautiful, cultured city. I go home as often as I can. Thankfully Brussels isn't far."

Brussels. My friend Sophie had gone to school for a semester at the Free University of Brussels. "I'm in for any trip to Europe." I said with a laugh. We each took a handle of a trunk and lifted.

With his help, a couple of near-accidents, and a few laughs, we got the trunks down two flights of stairs, out the front door—which had more steps—and loaded into Beverly's back seat, where they barely fit.

"Thank you so much, Dr. de Wilde." I grabbed two boxes and a roll of packing tape from the trunk, to pack the aprons and other sheets. "I literally could not have done it without you."

"No problem," he said. "And please, call me Lukas." Laugh lines crinkled around his eyes. "Carrying awkward and heavy objects down steep stairs together qualifies us for friendship, does it not?"

"Yes, yes it does," I agreed, returning his friendly gaze. "I hope I see you again during your visit. I'm Iris, by the way."

"Iris. So good to meet you." He shifted from one foot to the other. "Tonight I will be at the Taste O' the Sea reception. Are you attending?"

Conflicting thoughts competed for my mental bandwidth. Was he asking me out? *Surely not.* But now I had to make sure Bella did go tonight, since he was attending. Hopefully her sitter wouldn't cancel, but Grammie could sub in if so.

"I do plan on going," I said, adding, "with Ian Stewart, my boyfriend."

He didn't seem to react to the mention of Ian. Bad for my ego, maybe, but good news for my friend. "I'll see you there, then."

The crunch of gravel announced another vehicle arriving. We turned to see a navy blue Mercedes sedan easing down the drive. As the car drew closer, I saw the driver, who had gray hair and a bulldog jaw, scowling at us. Another renter?

Never taking his beady eyes off us, the newcomer parked the car next to Beverly and climbed out. He was on the short side and stocky—squat-bodied, almost. "What are you folks doing here?" he asked, jingling his keys.

Striving to return rudeness with civility, I said, "I'm Iris Buckley, owner of Ruffles and Bows on Main Street. Maybe you've heard of it?"

His answer was a grunt as he focused on Lukas. "And what's your story?"

Lukas ran a hand through his hair with a laugh. "I'm staying with Miss Brady. And you, sir?"

The front door flew open and Eleanor came trotting down the steps. "Craig. What are you doing here?"

My hackles went up. So this was the nephew, Eleanor's only relative.

Craig pasted a smile on his flabby face as his feet crunched across the gravel. "I just came by to see how my favorite auntie is doing. Mwah!" He gave her a loud, smacking kiss on the cheek.

Eleanor scrubbed at her cheek. "I hope you weren't bothering my friends."

Craig glanced over his shoulder at us. "Nope. Just getting acquainted." He slung a beefy arm around her shoulders. "Got a few things to talk about. Then I'll get out of your hair." Eleanor didn't struggle as he marched her back into the house, but something about the situation made me uncomfortable.

Maybe it wasn't any of our business, but I wasn't going to stand by while someone took advantage of that sweet woman. Not even a relative. On impulse, I said to Lukas, "Keep an eye on her, won't you? I don't have a good feeling about Craig."

The professor's voice was a low growl. "Neither do I. You can count on me, Iris."

CHAPTER 3

The Taste O' the Sea reception was held in the function room at the Lighthouse Grille, a sizable space embraced by a wraparound deck overlooking the water. Tonight, double doors were open to the evening air and guests were circulating inside and out after stopping by the bar. White-jacketed staff was setting up food on buffet tables along the wall.

"White wine?" Ian asked, knowing my preference.

I smiled at my gorgeous carpenter guy, thinking he certainly cleaned up well. Oh, he definitely looked great in jeans and a tool belt, but just as yummy in an open-collar pale green button-down and white chinos. He had a light tan, a hint of scruff, and dark hair that was still slightly rumpled and damp from his shower. As I said, yum.

"I'd love a glass of wine." As he shouldered to the bar, I looked around for my friends. Although Sophie and Bella weren't here yet, Madison was out on the deck, leaning on the rail and chatting with an attractive man who used a lot of hand gestures.

Once Ian returned with my wine and a bottle of locally brewed ale, we walked outside to join her. The man had wandered off and was talking to a group farther down the deck. "Hey, lady," I called as we approached.

She looked great in a flowing floral summer dress and strappy sandals.

She turned with a grin and gave us one-armed hugs, since she was holding a glass of wine. "Beautiful night, isn't it?" She turned and pointed at the cliffs across the bay, jutting rocks gilded by the sinking sun. "That's where we'll be tomorrow at sunrise."

I sipped wine, ignoring a stab of trepidation. I'd made the commitment to go, so I would power through. But that didn't mean I had to think about it too much. Changing the subject, I said, "I was out that way this afternoon. I bought the most wonderful stuff from Eleanor Brady at Shorehaven." Where I bought things was no secret in this case, since the provenance would greatly enhance desirability. People loved aprons and linens with a history, and anything from the Gilded Age summer cottages was snapped up.

"Shorehaven?" they said in unison with almost identical expressions of interest and envy. Everyone raised in Blueberry Cove knew that house. "Tell me what it was like inside," Madison added. "Was it amazing?"

"It was," I said. I described some of the features of the place and told them about my purchases. At the shop that afternoon, I had researched prices, which had further reinforced what great buys I had made. "You've got to see the European linen sheets, Madison. They're incredible." As for the clothing trunk, I'd taken that home. "And I'm going to try to sell a trunk of Chanel clothes from the 1930s for her."

"As in Coco Chanel?" Madison's mouth was an O. "Wow. I want to see those."

"And you shall." I turned to the doorway, where Rich Hammond, owner of the Grille, was standing. Rich had bought the restaurant from the original owners a couple of years ago when they retired, but despite initial apprehension on the part of locals, who hated change, he'd done a good job. The Grille had been beautifully upgraded while retaining its historic charm. The menu still featured traditional seafood but he had jazzed it up with world cuisine.

"We're about ready to begin, everyone," he said, clapping his hands together once. "If you'd like to come inside." As people filed past him, our jovial host slapped the men on the shoulders and offered women a cheek kiss or gentle shake, depending on how well they knew him. Madison and I got cheek kisses.

"How are you lovely ladies tonight?" he said. "We've got some really special items on the menu." He lowered his voice to almost a whisper. "Seaweed."

I felt my lip curl in disgust, but Madison said, "Awesome. Seaweed is a really hot trend." She nudged me with an elbow. "You're going to love it, Iris." Madison was always trying to get me to participate in her latest health kicks, whether exercise or diet.

"I'll stick with lobster," I muttered. As far as I was concerned, seaweed was that slimy green and brown stuff strewn about rocks and sand on the waterfront. Stinky and best avoided underfoot.

With a grin, Ian nodded in agreement. "Although in years past, lobster was fed to pigs and prisoners. It wasn't considered a delicacy."

"Don't confuse me with facts," I said. "I love lobster."

Inside the meeting room, a group of three men and three women hovered near the buffet table. With a lurch of surprise, I recognized Lukas among them. "Madison," I whispered. "See that tall man with blond hair? I met him today. Dr. Lukas de Wilde is his name."

She scanned him with sparkling dark eyes. "Holding out on me, are you?"

"I thought he'd be perfect for Bella." In months and

years past, I might have thought of Madison first, but not since she and Anton Ball, our police chief, had begun a tentative mating dance.

"He sure is," Madison decreed. She pulled me over to the wall, where the three of us stood to hear Rich's welcoming speech. "His friend tried to hit on me earlier. But I'm not sure he's my type." She nodded at a good-looking dark-haired man, who was now standing beside Lukas. He was fit and trim, if on the short side, with piercing brown eyes and deeply tanned skin. His hair was cut short and sleek, like an otter's fur. A gold watch glinted on his furry arm.

"Not bad, though," I said, to be fair. Although I was rooting for Madison and Anton to get together, I didn't want to be pushy about it. She shrugged in response.

The door to the main restaurant opened and Bella slipped in. She glanced around, spotted us, and worked her way around the room to where we stood. We merely mouthed greetings since Rich was beginning his welcome speech.

"This year we're doing something a little different," Rich said. "Oh, we've got the classics here, don't worry." He chuckled. "But College of the Isles is honored to be hosting a team of aquaculture experts this summer. A project called Farming the Sea."

I'd heard of aquaculture, which was a form of farming, only with sea animals or plants. It was said to hold promise in areas with declining fish or shellfish stock, like Maine.

Rich introduced the team. Lukas, who I'd already met at Shorehaven, was a professor at the University of Brussels. The man who spoke to Madison was Dr. Ruben Janssen, also from the university. A younger man with sandy curls was teaching assistant Theo Nesbitt. His fellow teaching assistant was Hailey Piper, petite and pretty, with long blonde hair, pointed features, and full, pouting lips.

"Hailey's local," Madison whispered. "Poor thing lost both parents to cancer a couple of years ago."

My heart gave a twinge of sympathetic sadness. I too had lost my parents, during a car accident when I was eight. Thankfully my wonderful grandparents had stepped in to care for me. I hoped Hailey had other family.

Lukas stepped forward. "Good evening, everyone." His gaze scanned the crowd, landing briefly on me with a smile. "On behalf of my team, I want to say how excited we are to be in beautiful Blueberry Cove." He paused for light applause. "In a time of high demand on our ocean resources, aquaculture offers much opportunity. Through environmentally sensitive techniques we can increase the supply of fish, shellfish, and yes, seaweed without further stressing the planet."

Dr. Ruben Janssen stepped forward. "And I'd like to add that seaweed has many uses. Including biofuel. Think of it, powering your automobiles with energy from the sea."

I imagined Beverly puttering down the road, emitting clouds of seaweed-scented exhaust. Would it only be sold at Shell stations? I bit back a snicker.

With a tight smile at his colleague, Lukas took back the reins. "Now I'd like to introduce you to Jamaica Jones and Patrick Chance, two local seaweed entrepreneurs. They'll tell us about the delights we're going to enjoy tonight."

The first thing that struck me about the farmers was their hair. Jamaica was dark-skinned, with long braids confined by a folded red bandana. She wore white overalls, a tie-dye tee, and red clogs, cute but practical. Tall and lean, Patrick rocked a man bun and was dressed in a plaid shirt over jeans and a thermal tee. He wore unlaced work boots.

"Hey," Patrick said with a wave. "We're real happy to be here and share our creations with you." He held up a packaged snack bar. "Including Seaseme Power Bars. Take one for dessert."

Jamaica darted him a look I couldn't quite decipher before adding, "The kitchen didn't know what to think when we delivered fresh seaweed and the recipes to make these dishes." She gestured to platters with flair, like a game-show host. "We have seaweed burger sliders, Asian deep-fried seaweed bites, and cucumber seaweed salad. Step right up, everyone. And enjoy." She delivered a final flourish with a grin and stepped away from the table.

People began to line up, picking up small plates and napkins and moving along. My friends and I joined the tail end. "Sophie and Jake still aren't here," I said to Ian. "Did Jake text you?" I checked my phone. Nothing.

"Maybe they got hung up." He waggled his brows at me.

I got his meaning immediately. Both of them worked hard—Sophie running the Bean and Jake out pulling lobster traps—and time together was precious. An inspiration to the rest of us, they had sizzling hot chemistry but were best friends too, with great communication and lots of laughter. I half expected to hear news of an engagement any minute.

"Probably so," I said with a laugh, turning my attention to the food. Scallops wrapped in bacon, check. Mini lobster roll, absolutely. Clams casino, you bet. All of it fresh and local. In fact, Jake had probably caught the lobster.

A familiar voice whispered in my ear. "Come on, you have to try the slider." Madison took two. "They might notice if you don't."

She knew how to get to me. I certainly didn't want

to hurt the feelings of the farmers, who were chatting with guests nearby. "All right." I gave in and took one. I skipped the other dishes, not quite adventurous enough yet to try them.

We found spots at one of the tiny round standing-height tables lining the walls. As Madison began telling us why seaweed was so nutritious, I sampled the lobster roll, half listening. My view was of the deck, and I saw Brendan Murphy, who worked at the Bean with Sophie, out there cleaning up empty glasses. This must be a second job for him, which wasn't unusual in the coastal economy.

Hailey Piper went out onto the deck and approached Brendan. He glanced up sharply, his shoulders stiffening. She moved closer, playing with a lock of her long hair, and he backed up. *Interesting.* Hailey was local, as was Brendan. Did they have a history? She continued to talk, throwing her head back in laughter, and even daring to put a hand on his arm. She must have broken through his reserve because I saw Brendan give one of his rare, beautiful smiles.

He made motions indicating he needed to get back to work, and she let him. But instead of coming inside, she moved to the railing to look at the view.

"I think I might go for seconds," Ian said, bringing me back to my friends.

I looked at his plate, which was empty. "Don't fill up. We're going out to dinner." This reception was supposed to take the place of appetizers, not be the whole meal.

"How did you like the seaweed dishes?" Madison asked Ian.

"Not bad," he said. "I might try another sample."

Traitor. I still hadn't even taken a nibble of mine. With a sigh, I bit the bullet, er, the seaweed slider. Lukas was out on the deck talking to Hailey now, and as with Brendan,

I could easily read the body language. The professor and teaching assistant were not happy with each other. Crossed arms, tapping feet, and scowls said it all.

Hmm. It wasn't bad. Kind of like a salty veggie burger. "It's good," I admitted to Madison, wiping my mouth with a napkin to nab a dribble of aioli mayo.

"Told you." Madison leaned close. "Do you know that man? He keeps looking over here."

I followed her gaze. Craig Brady was chatting with Dr. Ruben Janssen in the corner. She was right, he did keep darting glances my way. I waved and smiled and he averted his eyes with a frown. Lovely chap. "That's Eleanor Brady's nephew," I said. "I got the impression he wasn't very happy to see me at her house today."

Madison snorted. "He probably thinks you're taking advantage of her. Isn't that a concern many people have about their elderly relatives?"

"I suppose so," I admitted. "But actually, I was thinking the same about him. I get the feeling he bullies her."

"That's despicable." Madison scowled at Craig, who was fortunate he had his back turned. Her glares had the ability to strike fear into the biggest, baddest bully out there.

Bella joined us at the table. "Hey, ladies. How are you tonight?" She smiled over her shoulder at Theo Nesbitt, who was talking to Patrick, the seaweed farmer. "I would have been here sooner but I picked up a puppy dog." Theo glanced our way then averted his eyes, his cheeks reddening. The teaching assistant had sandy curls and the type of fair skin that showed every emotion. Right now he was mortified.

"Brave man," Madison cracked. "What is he? Twenty?"

"Twenty-two," Bella said, pursing her lips. "He just graduated from college."

I nudged Bella with my shoulder and looked at Lukas,

who was talking to Ian. "I was thinking more along those lines for you. Dr. Lukas."

"Dr. Delicious, more like," Madison said, deadpan. Her dry delivery set us off and we all giggled like schoolgirls.

"You are too much, Madison," Bella said. She looked over my shoulder, and suddenly the laughter left her as her brow creased in concern. "There's Sophie." She set down her wineglass. "Something's wrong."

I turned to see Sophie standing in the doorway, alone. Her hair was windswept and her eyes were red, as if she had been crying. Craning her neck, she searched the room until she spotted us, then rushed over to the table.

"What's wrong?" I asked in alarm. "Is it Jake? Is he okay?" Terrible scenarios ran through my head. Had his lobster boat sunk? No, I saw the *Maggie May* at harbor this afternoon. A car accident, maybe? I held my breath for the answer.

Sophie shook her head. "No, nothing like that." Her lips began to tremble. With an effort she swallowed and said, "We broke up. Jake and I are *over*." Her voice rose to a wail and she burst into tears.

The three of us exchanged glances of dismay and disbelief. "No way," Madison blurted. "You two are per—" She broke off, no doubt realizing that Sophie wouldn't want to hear how great she and Jake had been.

Bella swept Sophie into an embrace. "Oh, *cara*, I'm so, so sorry." She patted Sophie's back. "We are here for you, whatever you need."

I found a clean tissue in my bag and handed it over. "That's right, we sure are. Girls' night coming right up." Obviously dinner was off and I was sure Ian would understand. We could grab pizza and head over to my house.

"Great idea," Madison said. She lifted her glass. "But in the meantime, white or red?"

"A glass of red would be great." Sophie wiped her eyes with the tissue as Madison hurried off to the bar. "I'm so lucky to have such good friends." She balled the tissue and tossed it into a nearby waste can then ran her fingers through her hair.

Chatting and laughing, Lukas and Ian sauntered our way, appearing to be unaware of Sophie's emotional state. Since Ian and Jake were besties, I knew Ian would be upset about the breakup. I braced myself, not looking forward to him finding out. The ripple effects were going to be huge for all of us. We were such a tight-knit little gang.

Sophie froze when she noticed the men approaching, consternation and surprise warring on her face. Maybe she wasn't ready to talk to Ian.

Then I saw Lukas give her a tentative smile. "Sophie Jacobs. I thought I might see you when I came to this neck of the woods. Would it be bad of me to say I hoped we would run into each other?"

CHAPTER 4

Sophie ran fingers through her hair, over and over. "Lukas. I'm stunned. I had no—How long has it been? Eight years?" Her cheeks pinked, making her look even prettier.

The warmth in his eyes said volumes. Dr. Lukas de Wilde had been in love with Sophie once. Was he still? "You were twenty and I was twenty-three." He turned to us. "Sophie and I were at the University of Brussels at the same time."

"I was in an exchange program," Sophie explained. "Lukas was in the master's program."

Madison returned with a tray holding four glasses of wine. "What'd I miss?" she asked, sliding the tray onto the table and unloading the glasses.

A brief silence fell. Ian broke it. "Sophie and Lukas went to college together in Belgium."

"Really?" Madison took a sip of wine. "That's amazing. Did you know Sophie was living here?"

Lukas shook his head. "It is an example of, how do you say it? Serendipity." He smiled at Sophie. "We'll be here for the summer, Sophie, so I hope we'll have a chance to catch up."

"Hopefully," Sophie said, her voice faint. She picked up her glass of wine and drank half of it in one go. I couldn't blame her. Tonight had been one shock after another.

Perhaps sensing the tension around the table, Lukas said, "It was nice to see you all but I must excuse myself. Have a good evening." He looked at Sophie. "I'll be in touch."

"But how?" Sophie began to root through her tiny handbag for her phone. "I don't have your number."

"I'll come by for coffee soon." Lukas grinned. "I've been told the Belgian Bean makes the best in town."

"They sure do," Madison said. "Great food too. Good night, Dr. de Wilde."

After the good doctor strode away, Sophie stared after him, a shell-shocked expression on her face. And no wonder. First a devastating breakup and then, before she could take a breath, a former boyfriend reappeared. It was enough to make anyone's head spin.

Ian asked, "What's going on? I'm confused. And where *is* Jake? Did he cancel on us?"

Sophie bit her lip and shook her head, tears welling. "Jake isn't . . . going to make it tonight."

Ian's mouth opened in alarm, but before he could ask, I said, "He and Sophie broke up." I put a hand on his forearm. "Would you mind terribly if we take a rain check on dinner? We'd like to do an emergency girls' night instead."

He gave me a crooked smile. "Who am I to stand in the way of an emergency girls' night?" He picked up his beer bottle and drained it. "Besides, I need to go track down Jake and find out what's going on." He pecked me on the lips, gave Sophie a hug, and said, "Hang in there, kid." He then waved goodbye to everyone else and left.

"That man," Bella said, watching him leave. "He is fabulous."

"I think so too." Guilt rolled over me and I winced

I'd better downplay the gushing over Ian so as not to rub salt in Sophie's wounds. "Okay, girls. Want to head over to the farmhouse? I was thinking we could get pizza." Grammie and I lived on the old Buckley property, in the 1820 farmhouse she and my grandfather had restored. I sent Grammie a text to let her know we were coming— and gave her a heads-up on the reason.

"Sounds good to me," Madison said. Her thumbs worked the phone. "What do people want on their pizza? I'll pick up the order at Cheese Louise."

"Welcome, welcome." Grammie greeted us at the door with hugs. She gave Sophie an extra-long one I noticed. But that was Grammie for you, caring and supportive. My friends all loved her as if she were their own grandmother.

Madison carried two large pizza boxes into the kitchen and placed them on the center island. "I got one all veggie and one Greek with sausage. Dig in." Mouth-watering aromas of tomato, cheese, and oregano wafted toward us as she lifted the lids.

Grammie had already put out stacks of paper plates and napkins. For drinks, we chose from a selection of fruity seltzers and iced tea. The next few minutes were quiet except for the snap of caps and the murmurs of satisfaction as everyone took their first mouthfuls.

"I can't believe I'm this hungry," Madison said, reaching for a second slice. "After all that seaweed I ate."

Grammie gave a snort of laughter. "Seaweed? Since when is that served at the Grille?"

"Since tonight, I guess," I said. "Two local seaweed farmers had us test recipes the kitchen whipped up." I shrugged. "The seaweed burger wasn't bad. But I'm not giving up lobster any time soon."

Bella pointed a finger at me. "And the organizers of the Lobster Festival thank you."

Sophie put down her half-eaten slice of pizza. "Ugh. I forgot about the festival. Jake's on the food committee with me." She pressed her lips together. "I guess I'll just have to deal. I'm not going to let the other committee members down."

"What happened?" Grammie asked in a soft voice. "If you're ready to talk about it, that is."

Sophie thought about it while she scrubbed at her hands with a napkin. "I am. But let's wait until we finish eating." She gave us a sad smile. "I don't want to wreck anyone's dinner." This was typical Sophie, who lived to feed people well and often.

After we'd eaten our fill, we carried our drinks out to the back porch and settled on the rockers and the swing. Summer twilights in Maine are long and the sunset was still orange over the western hills. Crickets chirped, and a soft breeze carried the scents of cut grass and flowers from the garden. Showing off for our guests, Quincy chased a white moth through a patch of spiky red bee balm.

"What a beautiful night," Bella said with a sigh. "I wish I could bottle it up and save it for winter."

"You mean you don't like below-zero temps, howling winds, and six feet of snow?" Grammie asked in mock surprise.

We all laughed, except for Sophie, next to me on the swing. She sat head down, eyes fixed on her clasped hands. "It's all my fault," she whispered. "I really blew it." The rest of us remained silent, respecting that this was her story and she needed to share it in her own time.

Heaving a sigh, she went on. "We've been arguing more than usual lately, but little spats that blow over. I chalked it up to a super-busy summer. Tons of stress, both of us working seven days a week. But tonight"— she swallowed, hard—"tonight the spat kept going. We brought up all kinds of stuff. Like his lobster business, for example. He and his father used to be partners. His dad retired last winter, but Jake has nothing in writing that says it's solely his operation now."

"It needs to be for tax purposes, for one thing," Grammie said. "Or if Jake wants to get a loan or buy new equipment. Right now his dad would have to sign."

Sophie pointed a finger at her. "Exactly. But on the flip side, Jake apparently has a huge grievance with me. He says we're just treading water and he's over it."

"What does that mean?" Bella asked. "He wants to get married?"

Sophie ran a hand through her hair with a laugh. "He didn't actually *say* that, but I guess so."

"Is there a reason why you wouldn't want the same thing?" I asked delicately. We'd all been rooting for that to happen. Surely that company paperwork thing could be taken care of in a heartbeat.

She puffed out air. "I don't know. I mean, I love Jake, but whenever I think about putting a ring on it, I freeze up."

"It doesn't hurt to be cautious," Bella said. "I should have been. But no, I allowed Alan to sweep me off my feet. And smack, I landed right on my butt." Spoiled, en-titled Alan had expected Bella to put up with his cheating and other shenanigans. "However," Bella went on, "Jake is nothing like Alan. He's a good man."

"He is," Sophie said. She tapped her temple. "My head knows that. And so does my heart. But my legs, they want to run whenever I think about a permanent commitment." Her mouth turned down in a frown. "Ever since my first marriage."

This announcement was met with gasps and exclamations of surprise. Not that I thought I knew everything about Sophie. Far from it, since she had moved to town only two years ago. But why had she kept this major life event under wraps?

"It was quick, awful, and over," Sophie said, answering my unspoken question. "I was going to culinary school in Vermont when I met Wade." She shuddered. "He was . . ."

"Don't talk about it if you don't want to." I put my arm around her. "We get it."

Madison darted over and gave Sophie a hug. "We sure do. And listen, call me any time, day or night." The rest of us chimed agreement, including Grammie.

Sophie squeezed Madison hard then let go. "Thank you. I'm so lucky to have you guys." Her face scrunched up and tears began to flow. "I think I just made the biggest mistake of my life."

My heart went out to her. How I hated seeing my friend in pain. I'd been through a bad breakup before I moved home from Portland, and it had taken me months to get over it. In my case, ending the relationship had been for the best, but I just couldn't believe the same about Sophie and Jake. If there was a way to get them back together, I would find it.

After minute or two, Sophie wiped her eyes. "Sorry. That's enough for tonight." Her tone was brisk and resolute. "Let's talk about something else. Anything new and interesting?" She paused. "Besides Lukas de Wilde showing up out of the blue. Why don't we shelve *that* topic for now?"

Despite my curiosity about their former connection, I had to agree. Sophie needed time to process the evening's events. "I have an idea," I said. "Who wants to see the vintage Coco Chanel clothing I got from Eleanor Brady?"

"I do, I do!" Madison jumped out of her chair, making it rock wildly. We all laughed.

"I wish I had your enthusiasm, Madison," Grammie said. "Especially this time of night." Despite her words, she hopped right up, lithe as her granddaughter. Namely me. "I'll put on a pot of decaf and get out those cream-cheese brownies. For after we look."

The clothing trunk was in the living room, against one wall. My plan was to do the research at night, after shop hours. After washing my hands, I sat cross-legged on the floor beside it, ready to do the big reveal, while the others settled in on the sofas and armchairs. Grammie was the last to come in, after starting the coffee.

"All right," I said. "Are we ready?" At their assent, I threw open the trunk lid. "Ta-da." The first piece was the fur-trimmed jacket. I stood, holding it up in front of me.

Bella, our resident fashionista, gave a groan of awe. She reached out a hand. "May I?" Standing beside me, she pointed out exactly why the garment was so lovely—a figure-flattering defined waist, perfectly matched plaid fabric, and a sense of movement provided by the curved hem.

"It's a different shape than her later suits. They're more boxy." Sophie seemed as enthralled as the rest of us, and I was glad to have provided a distraction.

"Coco Chanel created some of the most glamorous dresses ever," Grammie said. "That suit reminds me of her costume work in Hollywood. Gloria Swanson wore Chanel."

"And so did Eleanor's mother," I said, with an ever-deepening sense of disbelief. "But she was a domestic worker." I shared Claudia de Witte's story, from immigrant to nursemaid to Walter Brady's wife. "I can't imagine how she got her hands on couture clothing. Eleanor doesn't know either, which meant Claudia kept secrets even from her daughter."

"How romantic." Madison's expression was dreamy. "The nursemaid married the millionaire."

"Maybe she wasn't always a nursemaid," Sophie said. "Did you think of that?"

"You're right. She might have come from a wealthy family." I picked up the matching plaid skirt and held it to my body, liking the way a bias-cut garment draped. "But that raises the question of why she moved down socially." Was it on purpose—or did she lack friends and connections?

Bella, who had been examining the jacket's interior, gave a loud gasp. "Look." She held up a large sapphire surrounded by diamonds in a teardrop setting. "I found this in the hem."

CHAPTER 5

thought they were weights at first, sewn in to hold the hem down." Bella handed me the sapphire then started working at the jacket seam again. "But the shape wasn't right. See?" She displayed a second star-shaped jewel, again a sapphire surrounded by diamonds, then a third.

"I bet Claudia took apart a necklace," Grammie said, taking the large sapphire from me. "But that begs a question, two questions actually. Where did she get the necklace, and why did she leave the pieces in the jacket?" She placed it on the coffee table.

"Either she was very wealthy, or"—I winced, hating to speak ill of Eleanor's mother—"or she stole it." The second theory might explain why she hid the stones rather than carry them openly and intact. I crossed my fingers, hoping Claudia had legitimately owned the necklace. By the looks of Shorehaven as it currently stood, finding valuable jewelry would be a welcome windfall.

Sophie held up a flower-shaped piece, the diamonds catching the light, then gently placed it next to the larger stone. "Could there be more jewelry in the other clothes?"

"Maybe." I picked up the skirt again and felt along the hem. "There's definitely something extra tucked in there."

In the end, we each took an article of clothing, finding a string of pearls in the black-and-white evening dress, diamond earrings and a bracelet in the frocks, and the rest of the necklace in the suit, which had six stars, eight flowers, and two large teardrop sapphires, plus connecting diamonds. After arranging the items on the coffee table, we sat around it to admire the collection.

Madison put a hand to her head. "I can't believe this. How long was this jewelry sitting up in Eleanor's attic?"

"Since the early 1930s," I said, snapping pictures of the pieces, including close-ups. I couldn't even guess at their value. "Eleanor definitely didn't know it was there or I'm sure she wouldn't have given me the trunk."

Grammie clasped her hands. "I can't wait to tell her. What a treat, finding treasure in the attic."

"In addition to the gorgeous vintage sheets and couture clothing Claudia owned, you mean?" I shook my head. "She was an enigma, that's for sure." And if Eleanor wanted to sell the jewelry, she'd need provenance, meaning a clear chain of ownership. Since I loved doing research, I would definitely volunteer to help. Plus I was itching to dig into the nursemaid's mysterious background. Was she a runaway heiress or an adventuress with a loose moral code? Either way, Claudia was hiding secrets.

The sun was well below the horizon when I reluctantly climbed out of bed the next morning. Quincy, curled warm in the blankets, lifted his head and eyed me incredulously. "Do ya believe it, Quince? When do I ever get up before dawn?" He merely blinked at me before snuggling back down with a groan.

The answer was never, since early morning and I were not friends. I staggered over to the dresser and pulled out nylon shorts in my favorite periwinkle blue, a white T-shirt, and underwear. The air was chilly now but would warm up after sunrise. Highs in the eighties were forecast today. I'd wear a windbreaker to start, and sneakers until I changed into climbing shoes. Madison had a pair that would fit me.

In the kitchen, I made a pot of coffee and toasted a sesame bagel. After filling a car cup and dressing the bagel with cream cheese and banana slices, I threw on the jacket and headed out to my car. In the still, damp morning air, my sneakers crunched loudly on the gravel and Beverly's engine started with a throaty roar. I winced, hoping I hadn't disturbed Grammie. She often had insomnia.

As I put the car into gear, my phone bleeped with a text from Madison. *Are you up?* I paused long enough to write back, *On the road, lady.* Well, I would be, in about sixty seconds.

Zipping along in Beverly this early, drinking coffee and taking bites of bagel, was a revelation. No other vehicles were in sight on this normally busy route, and an air of peaceful expectation lay over the rolling hills and slumbering homes. A fresh new day was about to begin. Anything was possible.

Maybe I should become an early riser. *Nah.* If Ian and Madison hadn't forced me out of the house, I would be cuddled up in bed with Quincy right now. A huge yawn burst from my chest at the thought.

Once I got to narrow Cobscot Point Road, the woods pressed close, forcing me to slow down to a crawl. I was cresting a small rise when a sharp whine and a bright light startled me. A scooter was coming fast, aimed right at me.

What on earth—with a jerk of the wheel, I swerved to the edge, my right tires hitting the sandy shoulder with a thump. Just in time. The tiny blue motorbike zoomed past like a demented hornet, with only inches to spare. All I saw was a helmeted rider hunched low over the handlebars.

Heart pounding, I braked and took a few deep breaths. After that close call, I was really awake.

Once my pulse slowed, I set off again, soon reaching the state park. In the parking lot, Ian and Madison were standing at the rear of Ian's truck, both with arms full of ropes and clipping things I couldn't begin to name. With a wave, I took the next slot, noticing a couple of other cars in addition to the truck and Madison's Mini Cooper. Probably other rock climbers or early walkers.

Holding my coffee, I got out of the car and went to join them. "Good morning," I said. "Or is it still night?"

Madison snickered. "Glad you made it." Then she sobered. "Seriously, you're going to love it."

"That's what you keep telling me." I moved closer to Ian, who greeted me with a kiss, a webbed contraption in his hands. "Hey, sweetie," he said, handing me the mysterious item. "Put this on."

I set the coffee cup down on the tailgate. "What is it?"

"A climbing harness," Madison said. She came over and helped me put it on, which involved putting both legs through loops and tightening it around my hips. "The rope is attached here," she explained, showing me a carabiner clipped in front.

My chest tightened and my pulse began to race as images flashed through my mind—climbing a sheer rock face, slipping, falling . . . splattering on the ground.

Madison must have seen the panic on my face because she patted me on the shoulder. "Don't worry, Iris. If you fall—and that isn't likely since it's a really easy route—the rope and harness will stop you immediately."

"I've fallen dozens of times," Ian said, which was comforting. Not. "Never got more than a scrape or two. Oh, there was the time I swung out and banged into the cliff. But that's why we have these." He handed me a neon yellow helmet.

I strapped it on, sincerely hoping it wouldn't be needed, then took the small pack he handed me next, which held drinks and snacks. He slung the ropes over his shoulder as Madison hoisted another pack with our shoes and climbing hardware. We set off for the cliff.

A path through the woods descended gradually to the rocky shore, offering occasional glimpses of the bay. The light was like gray powder, sifting lighter every moment, and along the watery horizon, the first hint of orange appeared.

At the bottom, I sat on a flat rock and took off my sneakers, then tugged the climbing shoes on. They were oddly snug and flexible, like heavy-duty ballet slippers. Madison and Ian consulted about the route, which from here looked like a jumble of jutting rocks, cracks, and ledges.

We are going to climb UP that. Panic rumbled in my belly and I froze, not able to make myself stand up.

Ian came over and hunkered down beside me. "You know, Iris, if you really don't want to do this, you don't have to."

I gazed into his eyes, which were warm with tender understanding. *What was I afraid of?* Both he and Madison were experienced climbers and they'd never put me into any danger. A burst of courage and determination rushed through me and I jumped to my feet. "I'm going to do it."

Ian ascended first, slotting climbing gear called nuts and cams into cracks, then clipping the climbing rope to them. This gear would hold us if we fell. Meanwhile, Madison belayed him, making sure to keep the rope taut. At the top, once secure, he set bolts for a top rope anchor—the safest form of climbing, she said. Once he was finished with the anchor, Madison lowered him.

"All right," he said with a grin. "Who's next?"

I didn't move. Madison stepped forward. "Me. Iris, I'm going to call out my every move as I go up, okay? Then you can copy me."

That made sense. "Perfect." I moved into a position where I could watch more closely. Behind us, the sun broke the horizon, spreading an orange glow over the sky and water. Sunbeams painted the cliffs gold and created stark contrasts of light and shadow.

"Isn't it awesome?" Ian asked me, watching the sunrise. He stood ready to support Madison as she climbed.

"It sure is," I said, taking in the spectacular scene. Islands solidified in the strengthening light, as did the old lobster boat puttering around offshore and the people moving around atop the cliffs, windbreaker hoods up against the chill.

"On belay," Madison said, her signal that she was ready to climb. After dipping her hands in chalk, she approached the cliff and, with several agile and assertive movements, was standing on the rock face. As promised, she called out every move, instructing me where footholds and handholds could be found. I began to see the small features that could support a climber.

Madison reached the top with a triumphant cry, then demonstrated how to descend, explaining how important it was to keep my feet on the rock, like walking backward down the cliff.

Now it was my turn. Madison helped me figure-eight the rope through my harness. I dipped my hands in chalk, hoping the dust would wick away the perspiration. As a last step, she pointed out a less-challenging route for me to try, to the right of where she and Ian had climbed.

"All right." I took a deep breath, flexing my fingers. "I'm gonna do this."

"One move at a time," Ian said. "Focus on where you're going to put your hands and feet next."

The first few steps were easy, big blocky rocks. *I've got this.* My hands found tiny ledges to cling to, and it felt perfectly natural to stretch out a foot, make sure it was secure, then push off and stand. Rinse and repeat.

"You're doing great, Iris," Ian called, echoed by Madison.

Halfway up, I paused for a moment to catch my breath and look around—not down. That would be a mistake. On top of the cliff to my right, someone in a blue wind-breaker was taking photographs. Of me? When sunlight hit his curly head, I recognized Theo Nesbitt, the teaching assistant. That's right, he was staying at Shorehaven. Maybe there was a path into the park from there.

My fingers were cramping. Time to move. "Use that crack right over your head," Madison called from below. "It's nice and wide."

I saw the feature she meant and reached for it. Soon my feet were resting on a nice ledge. Another three or four moves and I would be at the top. That knowledge gave me a burst of adrenaline and I moved fast.

When I stopped again to rest, I noticed Theo was gone. The sun was strong now, warming the rock under my hands, radiating toward my body. I basked for a moment, breathing deeply and looking around. Seagulls cried as they swooped overhead. On a shelf-like ledge down to my right, something fluttered. Squinting, I took a closer look.

Hair. The fluttering object was a length of long blonde hair. To my horror, a woman dressed in a T-shirt, shorts, and rock-climbing shoes lay sprawled faceup on the ledge. Even from this distance, I could tell she was seriously injured or dead. And I recognized her.

Hailey Piper.

CHAPTER 6

I shrieked, my fingers slipping painfully from their grip on the rock. My feet were next, one, then the other. I was falling. "Help!" I cried. "Help!"

"I've got you," Ian shouted. The rope jerked and I was dangling, having only fallen a couple of feet.

"Put your feet flat on the wall," Madison yelled. "Sit back in the harness."

Shaking all over, I managed to follow her instructions. Had I really seen Hailey Piper lying dead on the rocks? The sick heaving of my belly said yes.

Next Madison instructed me how to walk backward down the cliff as she gradually let out the rope. Under other circumstances I might even have enjoyed it, found it fun. But right now I felt as if I were watching myself from a distance. My real self was contracted and cold, shivering in a ball inside a shell that somehow managed to move.

Finally I reached the bottom, jumping the last few feet to land with a thump and a sigh. "What happened?" Ian asked. "You were doing so well up to that point."

I wrapped my arms around myself. "I saw Hailey Piper up there. She's lying on a ledge."

A crease appeared between Madison's slender brows. "Doing what? Sleeping?"

I shook my head violently, my teeth beginning to chatter. Why was the ocean breeze so cold? "No, she's dead. She must have fallen." An image of the young woman slipping off the cliff flashed through my mind.

"What?" Ian's voice was a bark. He leaned his head back and studied the rock face. "Show me where."

I pointed out the spot best as I could remember. From the ground, the top of the ledge wasn't visible. It looked like an outcropping.

Ian studied the terrain. "It's strange that I didn't see her. Or you, Madison. But we climbed over to the left, didn't we? And it wasn't quite light yet."

"That must be it," Madison stared at the cliff, frowning. "But I was focused on the climb, not looking around at the scenery."

"Theo taking a picture of me caught my attention," I said. "Or I might not have noticed." If I hadn't, how long would she have lain there without help?

"Come on, let's go," Ian said, bending to unlace his shoes. "It will be faster from the top. We'll leave the equipment up in case I need to climb down to reach her."

Galvanized into action, I helped them pick up and stow everything except the rope, which was dangling loose against the wall. Then the three of us charged up the path.

At the top, the anchor Ian had set earlier provided direction in finding Hailey. We trotted along the path a short distance and easily found the spot where she must have gone in. A series of blocky rocks and ledges made obvious lookout points. We made our way down the ledges, to a drop-off edged with stunted bushes and trees.

"There she is," I said. She hadn't moved. Which probably meant . . .

Ian studied the terrain. "I can free climb this. Call nine-one-one, okay?"

I grabbed his arm. "Use the rope. I don't want you to get hurt."

"It's all right," he said. "See those big rocks? They're more like stairs than a sheer cliff face."

Madison already had her phone out and was calling 911 to report a climbing accident. Without wavering, I watched Ian descend, as if my gaze could protect him. When he reached the floor of the ledge, I let out a huge sigh and collapsed onto a rock.

As he made his way to Hailey's side, a tiny red backpack next to a dwarfed pine caught my eye. Hailey's? Whoever it belonged to, it was tipped over, the contents strewn around on the pine needles. A candy wrapper danced in the wind, and without thinking I picked it up. One of Patrick's seaweed bars. I put a rock on top of it to hold it, figuring the police would want to reconstruct the accident.

Had Hailey fallen while trying to free climb? Or had she slipped from the top? I moved back a few steps with a shudder, imagining how a foot could slip on the pine needles.

My rear foot landed on something that moved backward, startling me even more in my fragile state. When I turned to look, I saw it was a cell phone. When I picked it up, it flashed on.

A text from Theo was on the screen. *See you soon.* Dated an hour ago.

"The police and an ambulance are on their way," Madison said. Her gaze landed on the phone I held. "What do you have there?"

"Hailey's phone, I think." Holding it gingerly by the edges, I set it next to the red pack. "And I think all this stuff belongs to her."

Madison frowned. "Why is everything all over the place? Did an animal get into her bag?" She glanced around the ground as well as up at the sky. Seagulls were pretty bold, and they'd been known to actually rip open a sealed bag of chips.

Ian whistled to get our attention. But when he had it, all he gave us was a headshake. No need to say more. My knees began to shake. "Oh, Madison." She gathered me into an embrace. I didn't know Hailey, but I was stricken by her tragic death. All that promise, gone in a moment.

The huffing of breath announced Ian's arrival. Madison released me and I hugged him, leaning into his warm strength. "How awful," I whispered. As I inhaled his distinctive Ian scent, I was grateful he hadn't fallen too. Why did anyone free climb? It was so risky.

He pushed back my hair and gazed down into my face, frown lines etching his tanned forehead. "I hate to say this, but it might not have been an accident."

I pulled back. "What do you mean?"

Ian plucked at my windbreaker sleeve. "She's holding a piece of nylon cloth in her hand. As if it ripped off someone's clothing when she fell." Madison gasped, a short, sharp sound of dismay.

A chill ran through me. "You mean she was pushed?"

He pressed his lips together and shook his head. "Hard to say for sure. But if she did slip and fall, and someone else was here, where are they now?"

Good question. I hadn't seen or heard anyone else while climbing. Except Theo, perched in another spot on the cliffs. *When I saw him, that is.* Had he witnessed Hailey's fall?

An uneasy silence fell over the three of us, while out in the bay, a boat engine rumbled, and above, squawking seagulls rode the air currents. The same wind that continued to ruffle poor Hailey's hair.

Madison's phone rang, a discordant jangle. "Anton," she told us. Blueberry Cove's chief of police. When she answered, he spoke loud enough that we could hear, asking directions to our spot. "I'll come meet you," she said. To us, she said, "I'll be right back." Still holding the phone, she hurried off.

Rustling sounded in the nearby bushes, followed by the thump of footsteps. Acting on instinct, I moved closer to Ian. Was it Hailey's companion, come back to the scene of the crime? Or misadventure?

The foliage parted and Lukas de Wilde emerged from the bushes. He wore a blue windbreaker and a pair of khaki nylon shorts, hiking sneakers on his feet. *A blue windbreaker.* I studied his garment for signs of damage, but it looked intact. "Farming the Sea" was embroidered in script on the chest.

"Hi, guys," he said. In any other circumstances, the colloquialism would have been charming in his accented English. "What is happening?"

I swallowed, not wanting to be the one to break the news. He looked so relaxed and peaceful, exactly like someone out for a carefree morning hike along the shore.

Ian crossed his arms, his gaze examining every inch of the other man's face. Last night it seemed that he and Lukas got along, were on their way to becoming friends, even. But today Ian was dead serious. "Did you see Hailey Piper this morning? Your teaching assistant?"

Lukas shook his head, confusion creasing his face. "Not since last night. Why?"

Ian winced. "I hate to break this to you, but she's met with an . . . accident." Ian pointed to where Hailey lay. "She didn't make it. And the police are on their way."

"I'm so sorry," I added.

With a cry, Lukas lunged forward, disbelief and horror warring on his features. At the edge of the cliff, he came to a halt, every muscle straining, eyes fixed on the young woman's body below. He rubbed a trembling hand

over his face. "Oh, no. This is awful. What are we—"
With a shudder, he turned away. "What happened? Did
you see her fall?"

"No," I said. "I was climbing the cliff when I looked
over and saw her. We're not sure how long she's been lying there."

Comprehension dawned on Lukas's face. "That's why
you asked me if I saw her. To figure out the timing. I wish
I could help you."

Ian nodded. "Yeah, I thought you might be able to fill
in some blanks. Like maybe you saw her talking to someone else."

Lukas's eyes narrowed at Ian's last comment, but he
didn't question it. "As I said, I didn't see her today." He
glanced at his watch. "I got up about forty-five minutes
ago and decided to take a walk. I haven't seen any of the
others yet."

"You mean Ruben or Theo?" I asked to clarify.

"That's right. Eleanor said breakfast starts at eight, so
I thought I had time for a nice stroll along the cliffs." His
grimace was rueful.

Voices drifted from the direction of the main trail.
I recognized Anton's deep, rumbling tones, joined by
Madison's higher-pitched voice. "Oh good, the police are
here," I said, my shoulders sagging in relief. We could
hand over responsibility for Hailey's death to their competent hands.

Two officers and two EMTs toting a stretcher accompanied Madison down the path. Besides Anton, the other
officer was Rhonda Davis, a young mother about my age.
She was married to a lobsterman, a good friend of Jake's.
Which reminded me, I really needed to check in on Sophie
this morning and find out how she was doing. But right
now everything beyond this clearing on the cliffs seemed
fuzzy and far away.

Anton's intense gaze flitted from face to face, taking us all in. He gave Ian and me tiny nods of acknowledgment before pulling out his badge for Lucas to see. "I'm Chief Ball and this is Officer Davis. You are?"

"Lukas de Wilde." Lukas ran a hand through his hair. "I am, er, *was* Miss Piper's supervisor." He pointed to the wording on his windbreaker. "She was working with me on the Farming the Sea project."

"Oh yeah," Anton said. "I heard about that." He glanced around. "Where is Miss Piper?"

Ian showed the officers and the EMTs where the stricken woman lay. Then Ian led the foursome as they picked their way down to the ledge. The three who remained above stood in silence for a long moment. Then Lukas spotted the red pack and started toward it. "Don't touch," I said. "I think it might be Hailey's."

Lukas stopped short. "Oh yes, it does look familiar."

I studied him closely, wondering if he really had forgotten. The memory of the heated discussion between Lukas and his assistant at the Lobster Grille flashed into my mind. His grief seemed genuine but that didn't mean the pair didn't have conflicts. But that begged the question of why he wanted to look at her pack. If he'd known it was hers, that is.

He moved a little closer to the edge, studying the cliff's terrain. "What do you think happened? Hailey was an expert climber."

I glanced at Madison, who said, "I guess that's up to the police to figure out."

"How did you happen to choose Hailey as a teaching assistant?" I asked, taking the opportunity to learn more about the young woman's background. "I understand she grew up around here somewhere."

"She did." Lukas cupped an elbow with a hand, resting the other on his chin. "Hailey and Theo were both exchange students in Belgium last semester. When Hailey applied for the position, her knowledge of Maine's ecology was a strong point in her favor." Regret and sorrow shone in his eyes. "What a tragedy. She had a bright future ahead of her."

Before I could probe further, Anton huffed his way back up the cliff. Although he was in great shape, his heavy uniform, duty belt, and boots made hiking difficult.

After he caught his breath, he said, "We need to do a technical recovery. Which means ropes and so forth."

"I can help," Lukas said. "I've been on rescue teams in the Alps." He gestured. "Ropes and pulleys and all that."

Anton shook his head. "I appreciate the offer, Dr. de Wilde." His firm tone discouraged any argument. "But as Miss Piper's supervisor, I'm going to need a statement from you ASAP." He turned to Madison and me. "And both of you as well. A team is meeting me at Shorehaven, so let's talk there."

Eleanor was setting a table on the pool terrace when we pulled up, Anton's unmarked vehicle in the lead, followed by Madison's Mini and me in Beverly. Today Eleanor wore a pair of white clamdiggers topped with a striped blue-and-white seersucker blouse—classic coastal wear. Squinting at us, she paused, clutching a handful of spoons, and watched as we parked beside Craig's sedan, got out and slammed the car doors in unison, and strolled through the gate. Lukas had ridden with Anton, in the cruiser. Ian was still with the recovery team at the cliffs.

When Eleanor's gaze focused on Anton, she dropped the spoons with a clatter. "I've been paying my lodging tax," she said. Her hands fluttered. "If you give me a minute, I'll get my checkbook and prove it."

He settled his hat more firmly on his head. "I'm not here about that, ma'am." He hesitated, then said in a gentle voice, "I understand Hailey Piper was staying with you?"

One fluttering hand went to Eleanor's mouth. "Hailey? Yes, she—" Then her eyes widened. "What do you mean, *was*?" Shock washed over her face.

"I'm sorry, Miss Brady," Anton said, pulling out a chair and helping her to sit. "But Miss Piper has met with an accident."

"An accident?" Eleanor began to wring her hands. "But she was fine a few hours ago. . . . I saw her leave the house."

"What time was that?" Anton's tone sharpened. He pulled out a tablet, ready to take notes, and sat at the table. At his gesture, the three of us also took seats.

"Sometime before dawn. Around four thirty, maybe?" She grimaced. "I'm up several times a night. I happened to look outside and I saw her going toward the shore path." She waved in the general direction of the shore. "I installed motion detector lighting in the gardens for the safety of my guests."

That impressed Anton, I could tell. "Did you see anyone else out there?" His face drooped in disappointment when she shook her head.

"No, I got back into bed and tried to sleep." Eleanor leaned forward, dropping her voice to a whisper. "Please tell me, what happened?"

Anton regarded her with compassion. "She fell," he said, his tone gentle again, "while climbing at the state park."

"Oh no," Eleanor cried. "That sweet girl." She burst into tears. "She was an orphan, you know. All alone in the world."

My heart ached at seeing Eleanor's distress. And poor Hailey. I pushed back in my chair. "I'll go make some tea." Wasn't tea with sugar good for shock?

Madison decided to go with me while Anton continued to question Eleanor and Lukas about Hailey's movements. Inside the door to the sitting room, Madison tugged at my arm to stop me, putting a finger to her lips. She tilted her chin toward the open pocket doors to our left.

Eleanor's nephew Craig, Dr. Ruben Janssen, and Patrick Chance, seaweed farmer with man bun, were seated around a table, cups of coffee in hand and papers scattered in front of them. "If I can free up some cash, I'll definitely be interested," Craig said. He picked up a piece of paper and handed it to Ruben. "But I do have a question."

While the trio was preoccupied, we quickly and quietly slipped past the open doors. Once out in the entrance hall, I released my held breath. "Whew. I really didn't want to talk to Craig."

"He is an ass, isn't he?" Madison said, her voice a whisper. "Which way to the kitchen?"

"Probably off the dining room." After a couple of false starts, we found the dining room at the end of the hall, adjacent to the formal living room. The pocket doors at that end were closed, so the men didn't see us slipping through the swinging door into the kitchen.

The old-fashioned kitchen was cavernous, painted pale green, and had tall windows overlooking an enclosed garden. The smell of something on the edge of burning leaked from the massive six-burner range. I grabbed a potholder and opened the oven door, then pulled out what looked like a breakfast casserole and set it on the stovetop. The cheesy eggs were studded with tomatoes, mushrooms, and green peppers.

"Yum, that looks good," Madison said, her belly giving an audible rumble. "We never got to have breakfast." We had planned to eat after finishing the climb, a cold meal of yogurt parfaits and muffins. "Maybe Eleanor will take pity on us."

"Hopefully." I eyed a pan of gently sizzling sausages with longing as I picked up a huge kettle. I carried it to the sink and filled it while Madison turned off the heat under the sausages and moved them to a platter, then found foil and covered the food to keep it warm.

After the water boiled, I made a pot of tea and Madison put mugs, milk, and sugar on a tray. "We make a good team," I said, picking up the tray.

"We sure do," she agreed, pushing open the kitchen door for me.

As we entered the hallway, Theo came thumping down the stairs. "What's going on?" he asked. "Several police cruisers just pulled up."

My instinct was to blurt the bad news but I choked back the words. Let Anton handle it. "I'm not sure," I hedged. But why *were* more cruisers arriving? I glanced at Madison, who appeared equally mystified. "We're taking tea out to Eleanor. She's on the terrace."

He decided to tag along, so I took advantage of the opportunity to ask him a question. "I saw you taking pictures up on the cliffs earlier," I said. "Did you get one of me, rock climbing?" Had he seen Hailey up there, maybe with someone? I was dying to know but didn't dare ask directly.

"Oh yeah, maybe," he said, glancing at my periwinkle shorts. "Your outfit looks familiar. I'll check and see if I got a good one."

Before this happened, I might have liked a memento of my one and only climbing adventure. Now I never wanted to think of it again.

Out on the terrace, Anton was talking to the new arrivals, a flock of men and women in blue. My heart thumped and my last hope faded when I noticed Detective Dennis Varney from the Maine State Police among them. If the state police were involved, that meant Hailey's death was considered suspicious. As in murder.

Spooked at this further confirmation of our worst fears, my hands shook when I set the tray on the table, making the dishes rattle. Eleanor glanced up at me with frightened eyes. Her fingers on my wrist felt like ice. "Hailey didn't just fall, did she, Iris?" she whispered.

Not trusting myself to speak, I shook my head. Lukas, sitting beside Eleanor, groaned softly and muttered under his breath. He pulled out his phone and began to tap at the screen. Notifying people about the situation, maybe? I didn't envy his situation. Beyond the tragedy of losing a young student, what would happen to his project now?

Theo, avidly watching the activity, pulled out a chair across from the professor, next to Madison. "What do you mean, Hailey fell? Is she okay?" His glance around the table was frantic as he looked to us for answers.

"No, she isn't," I said, since the truth was out now. "And I'm so sorry to tell you that." To forestall the questions brimming on his lips, I added, "The police will fill you in." *While cross-examining you thoroughly, I hope.* But I didn't say that part. Now that it was all but certain someone had sent Hailey to her death, I knew I couldn't trust Theo. After all, I'd seen him myself just moments before spotting Hailey's body.

Theo's face went pale. "Oh no. How awful. Poor Hailey." He slumped down in his seat, a hand to his face.

The group of officers dispersed and headed into the house, except for Anton and Detective Varney. The team was going to search for evidence under a search warrant, I guessed. Moving on autopilot, I poured Eleanor a mug of tea and added milk and sugar, whether she wanted them or not. As I set the mug in front of her, Anton and Detective Varney started walking toward us.

"Hold on!" a man shouted. One arm waving, Craig Brady crossed the terrace as fast as his short legs could carry him. Ruben watched from the doorway, Patrick hovering behind him like a shadow.

Anton and Detective Varney waited politely for Craig to reach them, although I could sense Anton's impatience in his stance. But his tone was perfectly polite when he asked, "How can we help you?"

Craig jabbed his finger at the house. "By telling me what's going on in my house."

Eleanor rose to her feet. "You mean, *my* house, don't you? They are here with a search warrant, and needless to say, I am cooperating fully."

"A search warrant for what?" Craig's bulldog face turned a nasty dark red. I was afraid he was going to have a heart attack right on the spot.

An officer opened a French door, one down from where Patrick and Ruben were standing. "Chief. I've got something," he called.

"Excuse us," Anton said. He and Detective Varney shouldered the obstructive Craig aside and hastened to join the officer.

They conferred inside the sitting room for a moment, and then Anton strode back across the terrace. We all watched him approach, Madison and I with interest, the others with frank trepidation. Eleanor took my hand again.

"Dr. Lukas de Wilde." Anton dipped his head in a brusque nod. "Will you please join us?" Despite the courteous words, it wasn't a request.

CHAPTER 7

Madison and I gawked at each other with open mouths, shocked by this turn of events. Did they really suspect Lukas of killing Hailey? I shifted in my seat in discomfort, remembering his disagreement with the young woman at the Grille. Had the animosity between them gone deeper than I knew?

Lukas stared at Anton for a long moment, his expression stoic. Then he pushed his chair back and stood. "Whatever I can do to help, Chief." He didn't look back as he followed Anton into the house.

Once the men disappeared inside, Theo let out a bark of disbelieving laughter. "Wow, that was intense." He ran both hands through his curls, making them stand on end. "Do they seriously think Dr. de Wilde had something to do with Hailey falling?"

A heavy silence fell over the terrace. Theo obviously hadn't connected all the dots about the fall being no accident and I wasn't going to enlighten him. Neither was anyone else, apparently.

After a moment, Patrick and Ruben sauntered over to Craig, who had plopped down at the table with us. "I'm going to head out," Patrick said to Craig. "Catch up later?" He patted Ruben on the shoulder. "Sorry to hear about your student. See you at the lab." To us, he said, "The lab is where we grow the baby seaweed before planting it out in the bay."

"Wonders never cease," Eleanor said faintly. "We used to try to get rid of seaweed, not encourage its growth."

"I hear you, Eleanor," Patrick said. "This morning I noticed you've got a great crop on the rocks down by your dock."

"You used a boat to get here?" I thought of the wooden lobster boat I'd seen chugging past the cliffs, heading this way.

"Of course," Patrick said with a shrug. "It's how I get around most days."

"I think we saw you when we were climbing," I said. "Is your boat pale green?" At his nod, my pulse gave a leap. He might have witnessed something important from the water. I made a mental note to tell Anton we had seen him near the cliffs.

Speaking of which, I glanced discreetly at my phone. When was Anton going to have time to take my statement? The shop was supposed to open in an hour. If I wasn't going to make it, I needed to give Grammie a heads-up.

"Oh my." Eleanor jumped up with a gasp. "I forgot all about breakfast. It must be burned to a crisp."

Madison gave her a reassuring smile. "Iris and I took care of it. In fact, we'd be happy to bring the food out here, if you'd like."

"What a great idea." I stood, happy for an excuse to go inside and maybe find out what was going on. "You just sit back and relax."

Eleanor sank back into her chair. "You really don't mind? There's plenty. Maybe those nice police officers would like something." As we headed off, she called, "Coffee is ready to go. Just flick the switch."

Lukas was being questioned in the formal living

room, and when Anton saw us enter the house, he came out, closing the pocket doors behind him. "What are you two doing?"

"Taking care of breakfast at Eleanor's request." Madison's tone was bright. "What are you doing?"

Anton made an odd sound, somewhere between amusement and annoyance. "I need to speak to both of you before you leave."

"How long will it be?" I asked. "If I'm going to be late, I need to let Grammie know."

"Another half hour, I'm guessing." Anton glanced over his shoulder. "After we're done talking to the professor."

I saw my opportunity. "You should talk to Patrick Chance. He went by the cliffs in his boat this morning. And I saw Theo Nesbitt on the shore path, really close to where Hailey fell. He took a picture of me rock climbing. Maybe he took one of the killer too." Maybe he *was* the killer, I added to myself.

The chief shook his head, a bemused expression on his face. "Iris," he started. Then he cleared his throat. "Thank you for that information. I'll take it under advisement."

"Oooh," Madison hooted. "I love it when you get all official." She clasped her hands in front of her chest as if swooning.

Anton's complexion now rivaled that of Craig's earlier. "I'll talk to you later," he finally said, before whipping the pocket doors open and stepping inside. They shut with a decisive click behind him.

"You're so good for him," I whispered to Madison as we scurried toward the kitchen. "He'll never get too pompous while you're around." We'd gone to school with Anton and while he was a very nice guy, he tended to take himself too seriously at times. We thought of it as our duty to prevent that.

Lukas strode into the kitchen while we were loading two trays. "Is that coffee I smell?" He beelined to the coffee maker and poured a cup. "Oh my, what a morning."

"So they didn't arrest you?" I blurted. "I was worried when they came to get you." I added a plate of buttered toast to my tray, which held the casserole and the sausages. Madison had dishes, silverware, and napkins.

His hand lurched and coffee splashed onto the floor. "What? No." He grimaced as he reached for a paper towel. "But they took my jacket into evidence."

We exchanged looks of confusion. Lukas was still wearing his windbreaker. "What do you mean?" I asked.

He pulled at the jacket. "This isn't my coat. I thought it was this morning when I grabbed it from the pegs near the door." Still talking, he bent to wipe the floor. "But they found mine in my room, complete with ink stain and a ripped pocket. Which meant something to the police, the rip that is, not the stain."

I knew exactly what it meant. The piece of cloth in Hailey's hand must have come from Lukas's jacket. "Was yours identical to the one you're wearing?"

Taking in what we were doing, Lukas threw away the paper towel then began to load mugs on a tray. "Everyone involved in Farming the Sea has the same jackets. The same size, even, except for Hailey and Jamaica's."

So had someone taken his jacket by accident or on purpose? Putting the ripped one in his room certainly seemed like a malicious act to me.

"I think someone is trying to frame you," Madison said, expressing my thoughts aloud.

His features creased in confusion. "Do you really think so? Maybe someone just found my jacket and put it back in my room."

Madison patted him on the shoulder. "You're so sweet, Lukas. Stick with us and we won't let you get railroaded."

She pointed to the tray of mugs. "Do you mind carrying that out for us?"

A few minutes later, while we were eating breakfast on the terrace, I remembered the jewelry tucked in Claudia de Witte's clothing hems. I opened my mouth to mention it before remembering that Craig was sitting right there at the table. I certainly didn't want him getting wind of the jewels. Then I had an idea. "Eleanor, are you free for dinner tonight? Grammie would love to catch up." I turned to Madison. "Let's make it a girls' night." Meaning we'd invite Sophie and Bella, too.

"I'm in," Madison said.

Eleanor's eyes lit up. "I would love to have a girls' night. Would you be able to come get me? I don't drive at night anymore."

I had no idea she was still driving, since I hadn't seen a car. Maybe it was parked in the small barn I'd spotted near the rear of the property. "We'd be happy to. How does six sound?"

Naturally Craig overheard the conversation. "I think it's about time for you to give up your license, Aunt Eleanor. I'd be happy to sell the Caddy for you." He grinned. "Or drive it. That sweet baby blue 1969 DeVille convertible."

Eleanor gripped her fork as if she wanted to stab him with it. "I am not giving up my license, Craig. Or Marilyn, either. How will I run my business without a car?"

Sweet. Her car was named Marilyn. I'd have to introduce her to Beverly.

"That's another thing, Auntie," he said. "I'm concerned about you overextending yourself by hosting guests." How obnoxious for him to bring it up in front of Ruben and Lukas, who were sitting at the table with us. Theo was inside, talking to the police. "In fact—"

Madison interrupted. "My mother doesn't like to drive at night, either. And she's only fifty." She glanced around the table. "Maybe you've heard of her. Dr. Zadie Morris. She's an orthopedic surgeon."

It wasn't like Madison to pull the doctor card when talking about her parents, but I understood why she was doing it. And by the frown on Craig's face, I guessed he got it too. Hopefully he would stop badgering Eleanor. He was treating her as if she wasn't a competent adult, able to make her own decisions.

"I have heard of Dr. Zadie," Eleanor said. "And your father is Dr. Horatio Morris, right? He's the best primary care physician around."

"Thanks, I think so too," Madison said, with a pleased smile. Madison was close to her parents, which was a good thing since she was living with them right now. Her older brother and sister lived in Boston, somewhere in the process of becoming medical doctors themselves. As Madison said about herself, she had broken the family mold by refusing to go into medicine. Ever since her first lemonade stand, sales and marketing were her passion.

As she and Eleanor chatted about Madison's parents, I took the opportunity to text Grammie. I told her I was going to be late—and why—and mentioned the possibility of dinner with Eleanor. She expressed sadness about Hailey, told me to take my time, and promised to pull out a frozen homemade chicken potpie for dinner. One of my favorites. I sent back heartfelt thanks illustrated with tons of pretty emojis. Grammie was wonderful.

Theo trotted back onto the terrace. "All done," he crowed, seeming relieved. He pointed at me. "Your turn, Iris."

After the morning's ordeal, arriving at the shop felt like coming home. Quincy greeted me at the back door with plaintive moans. "It's okay, Quince, I'm here." I set down my handbag and tote and gathered him into my arms nuzzling my nose into his soft fur. His purr rumbled in my ears.

"Iris. There you are." I looked up to see Grammie heading for me. She swept me into an embrace, cat included. "I'm so sorry." She didn't need to elaborate. Both of us shed a few tears for Hailey Piper. I'd been running on adrenaline, but now emotions were starting to break through.

I dried my eyes on a handkerchief, since Quincy objected to me using his fur, which was already quite wet. "Sorry, Quince," I said, blowing my nose. "Is there coffee? I could use another cup."

Traffic at the store was slow this morning, so I filled Grammie in about Hailey between customers. We also priced Eleanor's sheets and made up a display bed in the window. The tall walnut headboard looked wonderful with a pile of downy pillows, white sheets, and a rose-patterned duvet. Grammie had brought some pink and white beach roses from home and we put those in a vase, along with trailing ivy vines and sweet peas.

I ran a hand along the plump duvet, wishing I could crawl in for a nap. That would be a sight to greet visitors to town, the proprietor of Ruffles & Bows sleeping in the store window. Quincy, free of any such reservations, jumped onto the bed and curled up.

We both laughed. "That will drag 'em in," I said, only half joking. We already had customers who came by just to see the cat.

"Knock, knock." Bella entered the shop, a slim cardboard box in her hands. "I have posters," she sang out, setting the box on the counter.

Posters? For a second I had no idea what she was talking about. Then it sank in. The fashion show and lobster bib contest.

"Oh, he is so cute." With that exclamation, Bella

pounced on Quincy, who endured the attention with a smug smile. By her chipper attitude, I guessed she hadn't heard about Hailey's death yet, and for a moment, I was glad to pretend it hadn't happened.

I opened the box and peeked inside. The fashion show's poster was colorful and eye-catching, especially the outlined square at the bottom announcing the lobster bib contest. A stack of entry forms was underneath the posters.

"I've been passing the entry forms out all over town," Bella said. "We're going to get some great costumes, I can feel it."

Something bobbing along the sidewalk caught my eye. As the person reached for our door handle, I saw it was a huge stuffed lobster, worn on the head like a hat. "And here comes our first contestant, I'm guessing," I said. Our festival often brought out the wacky in people, and I had a feeling that the bib contest would only inspire new heights of zany.

CHAPTER 8

One of my favorite ways to unwind was helping Grammie make dinner in our cozy farmhouse kitchen, a glass of white wine close to hand and my ever-faithful cat watching for stray scraps to fall. What made it even better tonight was that we were cooking for the gang. Chicken potpie was in the oven, and I was slicing and dicing for a huge salad while Grammie stirred homemade cranberry sauce on the stove.

Someone knocked on the back door. "I'll go," Grammie said, turning down the burner and wiping her hands on her apron.

"I've got to get me one of those Mini Coopers," Eleanor was saying as she and Madison entered the kitchen. Madison had picked Eleanor up at Shorehaven. "Woo-hoo, can that baby crank."

"Madison," I said, shaking a finger in mock scolding. "Did you take Eleanor for a joy ride?" She loved showing people what her little sports car could do.

"Maybe." Madison gave me a knowing smile. She set a paper bag on the counter. "For our contribution, we brought fresh shrimp and cocktail sauce."

"Yum." I peeked inside and pulled out the tray of shrimp. "No seaweed?" I asked, tongue in cheek.

Madison poured two glasses of wine and handed one

to Eleanor. "Nope. But I do have sample energy bars from Patrick in the car. He wants our feedback."

I picked up salad servers and tossed the salad. "I can give him some right now. Yuck."

Madison laughed. "They're not bad, honest."

While we were chatting, Grammie had taken Eleanor on a tour of the downstairs, glasses of wine in hand. Vehicle tires crunching up the drive announced Sophie and Bella's arrival. When I'd called earlier to invite them, both had wanted to meet Eleanor—and see her face when we showed her the jewels found in her mother's clothing.

"I'll go let them in," Madison said. She grinned. "It will give me a chance to grab that box of energy bars."

"You're incorrigible." I pulled the lid off the shrimp platter and placed it beside a board holding cheese and crackers. We would have appetizers in here, standing around the island, and then eat the main course outside on the porch. The evening was warm and dry, perfect for dining al fresco. I grabbed plates, silverware, and napkins and set them on the counter by the porch door, ready to go out.

The trio soon entered the kitchen, Sophie laughing, I was glad to see. "No, I'm not going to make kelp waffles," she said to Madison. "I don't care how healthy it is." She held up a white paper bag. "Double-chocolate cheesecake brownies are more my style."

"Mine too. They'll be perfect with the espresso I brought," Bella said, setting down a tote. "Complete with Bialetti." Bella's prized Bialetti Moka Express was a classic stovetop espresso maker large enough to make six servings.

"We're certainly going to be bright-eyed and bushy-tailed tonight," I said, laughing. My phone bleeped with a text. Ian.

Hey, babe. Just got home. Long day. After helping

the recovery team at the cliffs, Ian had gone to his carpentry job up the coast. The poor guy must be pooped.

Same here, I texted back. *Dinner with the girls and Eleanor Brady. Then early night. Rest up yourself!* He and I still hadn't had our dinner date. Maybe tomorrow night. Then I remembered the Lobster Festival kickoff parade in the morning. I'd be busier than ever for the next week.

Across the room, Sophie blurted an exclamation. "Lukas just texted me."

"What'd he say?" Madison asked, moving to look over her shoulder.

"He wants to talk," Sophie read. "Tonight, at the Captain's Pub."

Bella tossed her hair. "Kind of short notice, isn't it?" Bella was very protective of her friends.

"Yeah, it is," Sophie admitted, sounding wary. "But part of me wants to get it over with. We never really talked after I left Belgium."

"You want closure, you mean?" Madison filled glasses of wine for Sophie and Bella. Her eyes flashed with a wicked expression I knew all too well. "I have an idea. Iris and I will go to the pub too. We won't interfere but we can hang out in case you need us."

Sophie picked up her glass and took a sip, thinking. "That could work." Her face cleared. "I'll do it." She set down her glass and sent a text.

Oops, spoke too soon, I wrote to Ian. *Will be at the Captain's Pub later, if you want to meet me. Will text when we head out.*

Sure. Sounds good. This was great. I would get to see my sweetie while providing backup for my friend. "All ight, everyone. Eat up." I put the phone aside and picked a shrimp by the tail, my mouth watering as I dredged rustacean through spicy sauce.

Grammie and Eleanor strolled back into the kitchen, laughing about something. While Grammie went to the stove, Eleanor stood by the island with her wine glass, beaming as she listened to us banter. "What a bevy of smart, beautiful women," she said, glancing around at us. "I haven't had this much fun in ages."

I put down my third shrimp tail and wiped my fingers. There wasn't any way I could make it all the way through dinner without telling her. "Eleanor," I said. "Remember that trunk of clothes you gave me to sell? We've got some very good news."

When we showed her the jewelry hidden in the clothing hems, Eleanor gasped, swore, and burst into tears. "I can't believe it," she said, accepting a second handkerchief from Grammie, who was sitting beside her on the sofa. "I had no idea. Where on earth did Mother get diamonds and pearls?" Confusion puckered her brow. "And why did she leave them in the attic all those years?"

"Do you know much about her background?" Grammie asked. On the coffee table, Claudia's jewelry winked and twinkled in the lamplight, mute testimony to a nursemaid's mysterious past.

"Not a lot," Eleanor admitted. "She never liked talking about herself." She balled up the handkerchief. "I'm starving. Why don't we continue this discussion over dinner?"

We didn't need to be asked twice, and within five minutes we were seated around the porch table, candles flickering. Grammie served heaping spoonfuls of chicken potpie onto each plate, and we passed around salad, dressing, and cranberry sauce. Quincy was on the floor next to me, enjoying a shrimp I'd cut up for his dish.

"Before we begin," Eleanor said. "I'd like to say grace, if that's all right."

"How nice," Grammie said. "Please go ahead."

We set our forks and napkins down and bowed our heads while Eleanor said a short and heartfelt prayer of thanksgiving. After she said amen, she gave a huge sigh. "I have to admit, until this . . . this miracle happened, I was really in a pickle."

"You mean with Shorehaven?" I asked, pouring tangy homemade Catalina dressing on my salad. I handed the pitcher to Madison, sitting on my right. "A house that big must require tons of maintenance."

"It sure does." Eleanor sighed again. "I'm sure you noticed that the old gal is getting a little shabby around the edges. Craig is always on me to sell but"—she blinked back tears—"Sorry, here I go again." She dabbed her eyes with the handkerchief. "The only way I want to leave that house is feetfirst. I was born there and I want to die there." She punctuated this last by banging her fist on the table. But softly, as suited a lady of her refined upbringing and good manners.

"I don't blame you a bit," Grammie said. "It's your home." She leaned forward, her gaze intent in the candlelight. "So what can we do to help?"

I held my breath waiting for Eleanor's answer, determined to do whatever she needed. She was such a sweetheart and an inspiration too. The expressions my friends wore told me they felt the same way. Eleanor now had a posse at her back—us.

"I'd like to know more about my mother," she finally said. "Who was she, really? What was her life like in Belgium? Why did she come to the United States?" She paused. "Was she running away from something, maybe?" She lifted a hand and let it drop. "Nothing seems to add up. Your average nursemaid doesn't travel with couture wear and jewelry."

"And oh, that clothing," Bella said, hissing in a breath. "Your mother had exquisite taste, that much is certain."

"Thank you, Bella," Eleanor said. "That means a lot, coming from you."

Madison turned to me. "You're our resident research expert. Any ideas?"

"Well," I said slowly. "We have a couple of challenges. Not that I mind those. First of all, we're looking for records and information from almost a hundred years ago. And second, most of our sources are probably in Belgium, which means a language barrier." Then I thought of a possible solution. "But maybe Lukas can help us," I said. "He's from Antwerp, he told me. He can look for information about Claudia and her family and translate it too."

"That is a great idea," Sophie said. "Lukas speaks French, Flemish, and German, as well as English. I'll ask him tonight." Sophie had been quieter than usual this evening, often seeming to be lost in thought. But she'd obviously been listening.

"Don't say why," I cautioned. "Until we know more, the jewelry should remain our little secret." Maybe I was paranoid, but valuables with a murky past often lured claimants out of the woodwork. Eleanor didn't need that complication.

Grammie helped herself to a little more salad then passed the bowl along. "Speaking of which, what do you want to do with the jewelry right now, Eleanor? I think it should go into a safe deposit box right away."

"Agreed," Eleanor said. "But not under my name." She cleared her throat. "It pains me to say this, but I don't trust Craig. He keeps trying to get me to sign over power of attorney." She bit her lip. "It's getting so bad lately, I'm thinking about changing my will."

CHAPTER 9

Later, on our way to the Captain's Pub in Madison's Mini, Eleanor's words about Craig kept echoing in my mind. I'd witnessed his attitude toward his aunt and hadn't liked it. But trying to get power of attorney? Pressuring her to sell her home? Surely that was verging into criminal territory. "And we're not going to stand for it," I said.

Madison glanced over at me and laughed. "What are you talking about?" She braked as traffic on Main Street slowed to a crawl. Blueberry Cove was jamming on a warm summer night, with groups of visitors strolling along the sidewalks. Restaurant doors and windows were open, their warmly lit interiors beckoning.

"Craig trying to get control of Eleanor's money," I said. "I knew there was a reason I didn't like him."

"He's a bully, plain and simple," Madison said. "I could read him like a book." She muttered under her breath as a car with out-of-state plates pulled out of a parking spot a little too slowly. Once they finally exited, she whipped the tiny car into the spot and shut off the engine.

"Good job," I said. We had ended up right in front of the pub, a clapboard storefront with an inset entrance. A hanging sign above depicted a bearded and wincing captain with an eye patch and a frothy mug of beer in his hand. Patrons on the day after, we often joked. Besides a selection of locally brewed beer, the pub offered great fried seafood, burgers, and chowder.

After locking the Mini, Madison paused to adjust her short jean skirt, worn with a loose white peasant blouse and tied espadrilles. She looked adorable, and judging by the admiring glances from passersby, they thought so too. As we crossed the sidewalk to enter the pub, I couldn't help but notice that I got a few looks as well in my retro print sundress topped with a light bolero sweater. I fluffed the full skirt, my heart skipping a beat. Maybe Ian was already here, waiting for me. He liked this dress.

But no, he hadn't arrived yet, I discovered when I scanned the packed room. The roar of chatter and laughter was almost loud enough to drown out the nasal wails from the guitar-strumming vocalist in the corner. Servers sidled through the throng, holding trays of drinks and steaming plates aloft.

"Sophie and Lukas are over there," Madison said into my ear. She tipped her chin toward a small booth where the couple sat. She tugged on my arm, guiding me toward the bar, where two stools had opened up.

Madison ordered glasses of wine, and we perched and sipped, people watching since it was too loud to chat where we were seated. Over at the booth, Sophie and Lukas looked pretty intense, both leaning across the table as they talked. After ten minutes, I texted Ian. *At the pub. See you soon?*

The answer came back immediately. *Sorry. Dad asked me to help him. Be right down.* Ian's parents operated the Farmhouse B&B here in town, and he lived for free in the garage loft apartment, in exchange for doing chores and repairs around the inn.

No prob. Ian's helpfulness was a wonderful trait. Plus there was nothing hotter than a guy wearing a tool belt adored competent men.

Sophie half rose in her seat, waving her hand in a gesture indicating we should join them. Grabbing our glasses of wine, Madison and I made our way over to the booth. By the time we reached them, Sophie was sitting beside Lukas, leaving the other bench seat for us.

Hmm. Seems like the convo had gone very well. "Hey," I said, sitting on the outside so I could watch for Ian. "How's it going?"

Sophie and Lukas stared at each other for a moment, as if deciding who should go first. Then Lukas cleared his throat. "Everything is wonderful. We, ah, how do you say it? Cleared the air." He nodded in emphasis. "All is good now."

"We met the second day I was at school," Sophie said. "And after that we were pretty inseparable. But then . . . with the pressure of exams plus his graduation and my return to the States looming, well, we had a huge fight. We were pretty young and certainly not ready to settle down." She winced. "I left Belgium without saying good-bye."

I hated to admit it, but this sounded somewhat similar to Sophie's situation with Jake. Things got too intense, tempers flared, and they broke up. What if Sophie and Lukas had made a huge mistake years ago? Should I be glad they'd found each other again, instead of sad about poor Jake? But, personal feelings aside, I wanted Sophie to be happy, whether she ended up with Jake or Lukas. Or neither.

"It was very sad," Lukas was saying. "I sent an e-mail or two . . ."

Sophie screwed up her nose in a grimace. "I never got them. The college changed our e-mail addresses. And I wrote a letter but—"

"I moved and it never got to me." Lukas smiled at

Sophie. "But here we are. And we have another chance. Maybe," he quickly added, no doubt picking up on her deer-in-headlights expression.

"Another chance to be friends," Sophie said firmly. Her voice brightened with a change of subject. "Anyway, I wanted you two to tell Lukas about the research project we discussed earlier."

Everyone looked at me. Oh yes, Eleanor's mother. "Eleanor wants to learn more about her mother's background," I said. "We thought since you're also from Antwerp, you might know some sources over there. And help us translate them."

"Sources like what?" Lukas asked, spinning his empty beer glass a quarter turn at a time. "Family genealogy, that kind of thing?"

"Exactly," I said. "She knows Claudia emigrated from Antwerp but that's it. Vital records can get quite sketchy when you go back almost a hundred years." I knew that from my own family-tree research. Birth certificates, an important source of information, were often nonexistent or destroyed. Ellis Island immigration records were helpful but names were often misspelled and other information omitted or inaccurate.

"I'd be glad to help," Lukas said. He pulled out his phone. "What is her name?" He typed as I told him. "And she came here in what year?"

"In 1932," I said. "Then she got a job as nursemaid for the Brady family. After Mr. Brady's first wife died, she married him and had Eleanor."

"Quite a story," Lukas said. "Like a fairy tale."

Complete with fabulous jewelry and clothing. But I didn't mention those details. "Thanks, Lukas. I'm going to try some ideas at this end." Including Ellis Island and steamship records.

"I hope we can help her," Lukas said. "She's a wonderful woman." His face darkened. "And I hope they figure out what happened to poor Hailey. What a tragedy."

Me too. As Hailey's professor, Lukas might know something important related to her death. I racked my brain, trying to decide how to best question him. I wanted to know more about the confrontation they had on the Grille's deck, for one thing.

"You know who didn't show up for work today?" Sophie said. "Brendan."

At first her comment seemed like a total sidebar. Then I remembered. Brendan had dated Hailey. "Does he do that often?" I asked. I knew from talking to other small businesses that unreliable help was a big issue.

"No." Sophie made a noise of disgust. "Never. I tried calling him but it went right to voice mail. But I guess I'm going to cut him some slack. He's probably upset over Hailey."

"He's so cute," Madison said. "I love seeing him buzz around town on that little blue scooter."

A blue scooter? "You know what—" I clamped my mouth shut, thinking better of mentioning my almost-accident with a blue scooter on Cliff Road. Had Brendan been driving? If so, what was he doing in that particular location so early? Had he been with Hailey? My stomach turned over. Had he killed her? I hadn't thought to mention the incident to Anton during my interview. I really should do that right away, even though I hated to implicate the young server.

They all gave me a funny look, so I quickly said, "I forgot what I was going to say. But Lukas, you must be devastated about Hailey. After all, she was part of your team."

"I really am," Lukas said sadly. "She was so young. And brilliant, really."

Inhaling a deep breath, I went ahead and asked the question that had been bothering me. "But I couldn't help but wonder though, why you two were arguing on the deck during Taste O' the Sea? I hope it was nothing serious, and that you ended things on good terms." A flash of heat made the top of my head tingle. I'd tried to lead into the topic subtly, but wasn't at all sure I'd succeeded.

Lukas lounged back in his seat, a puzzled expression in his eyes as he toyed with a napkin. "I wasn't aware we had a witness, but since you asked . . ." I flushed in mortification when he paused to make his point. "Hailey was a very ambitious young lady. She and Theo are—were—competing for a prestigious and lucrative fellowship at my university. When you saw us, she was attempting to downgrade his work to me. Trying to put herself into first place." His jaw clenched. "I don't like such ploys and I told her so."

"I'm sorry I brought it up," I mumbled. But in a way, I wasn't. I now knew that Theo and Hailey had been rivals. And he'd been on the cliffs that morning. Another piece of information to give Anton.

Lukas made a gesture that dismissed the topic. "It's all moot now. And for the record, I'm never influenced by the antics of students. I have a very logical and systematic method of determining who comes out ahead."

"Oh yes, you do," Sophie said, lightening the mood. "Remember those Frisbee competitions?" She and Lukas began to reminisce.

I glanced around the room. Where was Ian? Once he showed up, I would suggest we get out of there before I put my foot in my mouth again. The last thing I wanted to do was insert myself into a police investigation. Earlier this year, I'd found myself digging into not one but two murders, mainly because my own sweet Grammie was a suspect. Hopefully Anton and his team would quickly figure out if someone *had* pushed Hailey off the cliff, as they suspected, and identify the culprit. The person wearing the ripped jacket.

Dr. Ruben Janssen walked up to the booth. "Hey, hey, hey, Lukas. Here you are, with three very lovely ladies. How do you rate?" He winked at me. "Some men have all the luck."

Lukas greeted his colleague with a roar of joy. "Glad you could make it. Next round is on me." He and Sophie slid out and started toward the bar.

"Dewar's on the rocks," Ruben called after him. "Make it a double."

Madison pushed me gently. "Iris, please let me out." Ruben moved to let me stand and Madison slipped out from behind me. "I'll be right back," she said. "Ladies room."

Ruben bowed with a sweeping gesture. "Have a seat."

I thought of making an excuse and escaping like everyone else, but I found myself sitting again while he took a seat opposite. Had he gotten along with Hailey, unlike Theo and Lukas? Then I scolded myself. *Be good, Iris.*

He studied me with twinkling eyes, his tuft of dark hair and rosy cheeks reminding me of a good-humored elf. "I'm having fun tonight," he said. "Are you?" He seemed to have successfully suppressed any sorrow about Hailey's death, if indeed he felt any. He reached out a hand, attempting to take mine.

No. I snatched back my hand but decided to play nice. He was Lukas's friend, and Lukas was Sophie's friend. "This is one of my favorite places," I said.

He leaned back and studied the room. "When Lukas said he wanted to do a project in Maine, I wasn't very sure about it. But he was right. There is much opportunity here." He slammed his fist down on the wooden table. "And we will make the most of it."

"In seaweed, you mean?" I asked. The street door opened, allowing a raucous group to enter. No Ian, though.

A crafty light shone in his eyes. He leaned across the table, dropping his voice to a hoarse whisper. "We have discovered the secret. We are going to power the world with seaweed." He chuckled. "I will fill your tank with the most efficient renewable energy the world has ever seen." He wiggled his brows up and down.

This last part was actually starting to sound interesting, but curiosity got the best of me. I had to know. "So," I said bluntly. "That was awful. What happened today?" Ruben stared at me in confusion. "With your student."

"Oh. Yes." His features twisted in dramatic sorrow. "Such a wonderful young woman. So bright, a promising future. She was in my advanced biochemistry class last semester."

"We happened to be out there, climbing. I was the one who found her." I shuddered and paused, letting that sink it. "I saw Lukas and Theo on the trails too. Taking a morning walk. Were you with them?"

His brows knit together, his expression sober. "No, I was in my room. Working. I get the most done before breakfast, I find."

Truth or lie? Not up to me to determine, I reminded myself. The front door opened again and this time Ian strode in, looking around for me. "Sorry, Ruben," I said, leaping up. "Got to go." He watched me like a pouting child as I hurried off.

I caught up with Ian near the bar, tugging at his arm so he'd see me. "Hi," I said, leaning close.

He put an arm around me. "Sorry I'm so late." He glanced at my empty hands. "What are you drinking?"

I'd left my wine glass behind at the booth. "Wine. But Lukas is buying a round." I tipped my chin toward the professor, who was leaning against the bar, talking to the bartender, Sophie standing next to him.

Ian jerked in surprise. "What's that about?"

"You mean Sophie? Nothing." I hoped. "They used to date in college." I slid my arm through his. "Come with me a minute."

In the back hallway near the restrooms, I threw myself into his arms.

"Hmm. To what do I owe this warm greeting?" he murmured.

"Just you being you," I said, kissing him again. The tension rolled off my shoulders as we snuggled close. What a long, terrible day it had been. At that moment, I was so grateful to be alive, an attitude I resolved to remember.

The back door to the parking lot opened with a rattle, and we pulled apart. A tall, familiar figure sloped in. Jake Adams. *Uh-oh.* "Hi, Jake," I said, my voice more high-pitched than normal. "What are you up to?"

Standing with his hands in his jeans pockets, he shrugged. He was wearing the battered brown leather jacket Sophie loved, open over a T-shirt. "Not much. Thought I'd stop in for a quick beer." He made as though to sidle past us, but I stepped into his path.

"Wait," I said, putting my hand up. "Don't go in there."

He halted, frowning at my upraised hand. "Why not?" Then understanding flashed over his features. "Is Sophie here? And she doesn't want to see me?" He craned his neck to stare into the main room.

"It's not that, man," Ian said. "At least I don't think so." He gave me a helpless look. "It's just—"

It was up to me to rip the bandage off, I guess. Not fun. "She's with someone, Jake." His eyes flared in alarm. "No, not on a date or anything. But I wanted to warn you. So you wouldn't be blindsided." Or Sophie, either.

Jake rubbed a hand over his face, his expression bleak. "I guess it's really over, then. I better get used to it."

I exchanged a look of alarm with Ian. "No, it's not, Jake. Lukas is an old . . . friend, from college. He doesn't mean anything to her." *I hope.*

Ian clapped his best friend on the shoulder. "Buck up, man. It's not over until it's over. Fight for her."

Jake stared at the doorway to the main room, chewing his bottom lip. I sensed he was tempted to take Ian's advice and go talk to Sophie. But then he pivoted on his heel and headed for the back exit. "I can't do it, guys," he called over his shoulder. "Later."

The door slammed behind him. To my fanciful ears, it was as though he was also slamming the door on his relationship with Sophie.

CHAPTER 10

In my experience, nothing was more corny yet heartwarming than a hometown parade. Ten minutes 'til ten the next morning found Grammie and me standing outside Ruffles & Bows, waiting for the kickoff of the Lobster Festival. On both sides of the street, visitors and locals were setting up folding chairs, and children wearing face paint ran around, bouncing in excitement. Once the parade ended, the rest of the festival would officially start at the waterfront park, with games, music, vendor booths, and the first big batches of lobsters and clams steaming away.

I spotted Madison strolling down the sidewalk toward us, cup of Belgian Bean coffee in hand and the strap of a leather tote over her shoulder. I raised my own mug of Bean to her in salute.

"How was the rest of last night?" I asked when she reached us. After seeing Jake, Ian and I had skipped out of the pub. We'd taken a ride out to the lighthouse in his truck and—well, enough said about that. But our time together was nice enough that I still had a glow.

After handing Grammie her paper cup, Madison rifled through her tote. "I didn't stay that long. Not after Dr. Ruben started putting the moves on me."

I hooted a laugh. "Seriously? He tried to hold my hand but I wouldn't let him."

"Thanks for letting me know," Madison said. "I almost said yes to a lunch date." She must have felt me staring, because she said, "What? You-know-who hasn't exactly asked me out yet." She was referring to Anton. The pair had been circling each other for a couple of months now. The suspense was killing the rest of us.

"Dr. Ruben?" Grammie asked. "Who is that?"

"He's one of the professors staying at Eleanor's," I explained, realizing she hadn't met Ruben or Lukas. "Part of the seaweed group. Apparently he's decided that he's God's gift to the women of Blueberry Cove."

Still rooting in her bag, Madison snorted in response to my comment. Then she pulled a booklet out of her bag. "Aha, found it." She flipped through, then, holding the booklet with one hand, took back her coffee. "I want us to do this."

I studied the page over her shoulder, seeing that it listed various events taking place during the festival. "Which thing? Not the three-legged race."

"No, not that. We haven't entered one of those since my growth spurt." Madison was about six inches taller than me, which had made for interesting times when we hobbled along together. "The cardboard boat race."

A block away, the whooping of sirens echoed and a whirl of blue and white lights reflected off storefront windows. The parade was finally starting.

Anton, as police chief, was naturally in the lead, sitting proudly at the wheel of the police SUV. When he passed Ruffles & Bows, he slowed even more, smiling over at us, well, at Madison. Grinning, she gave him a cheery beauty-queen wave in return. If he didn't ask her out soon, I was going to play go-between and do it.

The fire engine behind Anton gave an earsplitting blat, so he sped up. Behind the fire truck, a color guard of local veterans marched in formation. They got a huge hand and cheers from the spectators.

Once the color guard gave way to a truck pulling a Coast Guard fast response boat, I responded to her suggestion. "The cardboard boat race? Why?" In this admittedly amusing event, people rowed across the harbor in crafts made of corrugated cardboard. Naturally they often fell apart, dropping their passengers into the freezing-cold water.

"Because it will be fun." Madison turned to look at Quincy, who was watching the parade from the safety of the store's front window. She blew him a kiss and he touched his nose to the glass in response. "I think we should build a catboat. Shaped like Quincy."

"Oh, a catboat. Funny." Actual catboats were small sailboats with the mast up front. "And I have an idea." I pulled at my apron skirt. "The sail can be an apron."

Madison snapped her fingers and pointed at me. "Perfect. We're going to win." She grinned. "The grand prize is a spa day for two at the Sunrise Resort." The Sunrise, the plushest, most expensive hotel around, had a fantastic spa. They were also one of Madison's marketing clients.

"That's not a conflict of interest or anything?" I smiled at a group of children dressed like mermaids and pirates going by on a float. How cute.

"No, they're not putting on the contest," Madison said. "Plus there are tons of prizes." She handed me the booklet.

"Oh yeah." If we didn't get the spa day, I saw we might win an oil change from a local garage or a pest-control assessment. We'd definitely have to flip coins for those. I gave her the booklet back. "I'll do it."

"Yay." Madison clapped. "I'll enter us later. We can start working on the boat tomorrow." She waved at the Captain's Pub float, the servers all wearing eye patches and captain's hats, male and female alike.

"Sounds good." I took a sip of coffee, almost choking when I saw the next float going by. It held a giant—I mean ginormous—bright red lobster made of foam, metal wiring, and clay. The thing had to be over ten feet long and three or four feet high. The kids around us went ballistic with excitement although one little girl cried. Probably imagining herself snatched up in one of its huge claws. The lobster's revenge, a Maine coast version of Godzilla.

"Miss?" a voice said. "Are you Iris Buckley?" I turned to see a tall, balding man standing at my elbow.

"I am," I said. "And this is my store." I gestured toward the storefront. "How may I help you?"

He handed me a piece of paper, one of the lobster bib contest applications all filled out, I noticed. "I was wondering . . . is there electricity at this event?" He chuckled. "I mean, for us contestants to use."

"Um," I said, to stall. What a strange question, considering this was an apparel contest. I glanced at his name before folding the application and putting it into my apron pocket. "I'll check on that for you, Mr. Buxton."

"Great." He gave me two thumbs up. "My cell number is on the form. Text me."

"Sure thing." I couldn't wait to see what he came up with.

"Look," Madison was saying. "It's Eleanor."

Indeed it was Eleanor, riding in Marilyn's back seat and wearing a huge sunhat attached with a scarf and huge sunglasses, like an old-fashioned movie star. Lukas was at the wheel, dashing in a chauffer's hat. From the attic maybe? Eleanor gave the pageant wave to admirers on both sides of the street.

"Aww," I said, seeing a line of vintage cars trailing after Marilyn. "I should have entered Beverly in the parade."

"Definitely next year," Madison said. "We'll all dress up in period-appropriate outfits."

"Is that Dr. Ruben?" Grammie asked. "He's quite handsome."

"No, that's Lukas," I said. "Sophie's old college boyfriend. He's the other professor on the seaweed project."

Grammie's brows rose. "Wow. Where can I sign up for a class?"

Madison and I exchanged delighted glances. "Grammie, you're too funny," I said. I drank the last of my coffee. "I think it's time to go in and get to work."

Down the street, the blat of trumpets and tubas announced the end of the parade, the marching band from the high school. A last police cruiser tailed the youngsters, keeping everyone safe. The onlookers began to fold chairs and chatter about what to do next. Children fought over candy thrown to them by parade participants.

"Same here," Madison said. "I've got a client meeting in ten minutes." Hitching up her tote, she said goodbye and dashed across the street.

Inside the store, Grammie puttered around, dusting and rearranging some stock. I used the store computer to check our website. Several orders had come in for Eleanor's basic sheets so I pulled the sets from inventory to be packaged for mailing.

Customers drifted into the shop, usually in pairs or groups of three or more. The colorful summer prints were getting a lot of attention, including from a trio of twenty-somethings who were trying them on and giggling.

A pretty blonde wearing a cherry half apron over her

shorts admired her reflection in a mirror. "I love this, but what if Geoff expects me to wait on him hand or foot or something?"

"The apron," intoned a tall brunette, sliding her hands into the pockets of a lemon and lime bib apron that looked super with her coloring, "is a symbol of feminine oppression."

"Seriously, Tiff, how true," said the third, who had caramel curls. "My grandmother wore one like, all the time." She fluffed the ruffles on the white taffeta hostess apron she was holding up. "But this is so, so pretty."

Grammie, who was straightening stock nearby, popped around the corner and said in a deadpan voice, "And sometimes an apron is just an apron."

The young women burst into laughter and, with a few nudges and whispers of encouragement among themselves, each bought an apron. They left the shop with tissue-stuffed Ruffles & Bows bags and smiles on their faces.

At lunchtime, I went down to the Mug Up Deli to pick up an order to go. Usually we brought lunch, either sandwiches or leftovers, but this morning we had been in a hurry. On the way, I passed the Bean, noticing a blue scooter parked outside in the alley. Brendan must have made it to work. Seeing the tiny vehicle reminded me that I needed to tell Anton about my near-accident yesterday. Just in case it did have a bearing on Hailey's death.

Before I forgot, I stopped right there and called his cell. It went to voice mail, so I left a message. Then I continued on to the Mug Up.

As I opened the door, Bella was coming out, holding a paper sack. "Great minds," I said after we exchanged greetings. "I'm here to get lunch too."

"Town is crazy today and the festival barely started" she said. "We've been slammed in the store, plus thi▪

have been coming in for the fashion show." Clothing stores around the area were contributing outfits, both to help charity and for a mention in the program.

"I've gotten a couple of entries for the lobster bib portion." I remembered Mr. Buxton's query. "Is there power available for the contestants to use?"

She cocked her head, giving me a quizzical look. "I'm sure we can arrange something. But what—"

"I have no idea." My phone rang so I waved goodbye and ducked into the deli. "Hey, Anton." I said. "I know you're super busy but I need five minutes." I glanced around to be sure no one was listening. "It's about Hailey."

"Tell you what, let me grab lunch and I'll come up to the store." The sound of carnival music and passing traffic in the background clued me in that he was down at the festival.

I looked at the deli counter, which was miraculously experiencing a lull. "How about this? I'm at the Mug Up and I'll buy you a sandwich." I hesitated. "That won't be construed as bribery of a public official, will it?" I was joking.

He bellowed a laugh. "As long as you're not guilty of something, we'll be all set."

After we hung up, I hurried up to the counter to add a loaded roast beef sub to our order. I also grabbed another bag of salt-and-pepper kettle chips, mine and Grammie's latest addiction.

Back at the store, I barely had time to set out the food on the side room table before Anton walked in. "I'll keep an eye on the front," Grammie said, taking her lunch to the counter. Quincy, torn between her tuna melt sub and my usual classic Maine Italian with ham and cheese, chose to follow Grammie. I wasn't surprised. He loved tuna.

We dug into lunch for a couple of moments, crunching

in silence. "Thanks, Iris," Anton said. "It's been a busy couple of days."

"Everything under control down at the festival?" Thousands of visitors were expected, which meant our small force would be stretched thin. Traffic alone was a nightmare.

"Yeah, we called in additional officers from other towns," Anton said. "They all appreciate the overtime." His dark eyes locked with mine, and I sensed his thoughts shift from our chitchat to the much more serious issue of Hailey's death. "What was it you wanted to talk to me about?"

I put my sandwich down and wiped my hands with a napkin. No sense in beating around the bush. "On my way to the park yesterday morning, on Cliff Road, a blue scooter almost hit me head-on. It was coming from the direction of the park and Shorehaven." I paused to inhale, knowing that I was putting a nice young man directly in the investigation's crosshairs. "I believe it was Brendan Murphy, who works at the Bean. He used to date Hailey. And he owns a blue scooter. It's there right now, you can see it."

Anton popped a chip into his mouth, his gaze never leaving mine. "You saw his face?"

This was the weak spot in my story, but I was glad to have one. Maybe it wasn't Brendan driving. I shook my head. "No, he was just a blur when he went by, he was driving so fast. But how many blue scooters are there around here? And I saw the two of them talking at Taste O' the Sea the night before. Maybe they reconnected."

Anton pulled out his phone and made some notes. "I'll certainly follow up on that." His lips twisted in a rueful grimace. "We don't have much else."

My pulse leaped. "You mean besides the jacket? I think that was planted in Lukas's room."

He leaned forward, lowering his voice so custom

walking into the store wouldn't hear. "And why do you think that?"

"He was wearing a blue jacket when I saw him at the cliffs. After we"—I swallowed—"found Hailey. Would he have really gone back after killing her and changed to a different identical jacket? If my jacket ripped like that, I would have thrown it in the ocean or something."

Anton considered this. "Unless he wanted to implicate himself and then throw us off the trail by claiming he was framed."

I put a hand to my head. "Ouch. Maybe you can get some kind of DNA off the coat and figure out who else was wearing it." Then I thought of something. "Was there any DNA under her fingernails?"

"To answer your first question," he said, "the jacket was stored next to a lot of others, so any hairs or skin cell samples are probably worthless. And no, there was nothing under her fingernails, unfortunately."

"I appreciate you telling me this much," I said. "I won't blab it around, promise."

He shrugged. "I trust you to be discreet. And to be honest, we never know where a break in the case will come from." The rueful expression returned. "Not that I have so much experience with homicide, thankfully."

Last spring, when helping solve not one murder, but two, I'd discovered that I had a knack for investigating. Not that I should put it to use or anything. But while we were on the topic . . . "I learned something interesting last night," I said. "While chatting with Lukas at the Captain's Pub."

A crease appeared between his brows. "Iris," he said in a stern voice.

"I wasn't snooping," I said hastily. "At least not much," qualified. "But anyway, it's too late now." I took a deep breath. "When I was at the Taste O' the Sea, I saw Hailey and Lukas arguing on the deck. Last night, he told me that she and Theo were competing for a fellowship, and Hailey was trying to criticize Theo's work. Lukas didn't like that."

"And?" Anton's tone was bland, which made me think that I had overreacted to this information.

I shrugged. "Not sure. Just thought I'd mention it, in case it's relevant. Theo was on the cliffs that morning. I saw him." After a beat, I added, "Ruben said he was in his room. But he might have been lying." *Shut up, Iris.* In a lame attempt to cover up, I said, "Ruben asked Madison out to lunch."

Anton's hand jerked, making his iced tea splash, but he quickly recovered. "Look, I appreciate you passing all this along, but please, don't play detective, okay? It's one thing to observe something, but to question people . . . not a good idea."

I formed a Girl Scout salute with three fingers. "I'm not, promise. And I really hope you figure it out soon. Her poor family. They must be devastated."

Sadness flickered in Anton's eyes. "Both of Hailey's parents are gone. Cancer, within months of each other a couple of years ago. We haven't been able to find any other relatives."

"Oh, how awful," I blurted. Clapping a hand over my mouth, I looked over my shoulder, hoping the customers hadn't heard me. But they were chatting with Grammie and not paying any attention to us. "I knew she was an orphan, but I was hoping she had someone who cared."

"We do," Anton said softly.

"I know," was my reply. Of course Anton and his team were committed to bringing Hailey's killer to justice. It was their job. And they were good at it.

Then a burst of resolve made me sit up straight in

my chair. Hailey also had us, I realized, Grammie, my friends, and me. We'd make sure she wasn't forgotten. And if we could do anything to help solve her murder— without interfering with the investigation, of course— then we'd do it. Hailey didn't deserve anything less.

CHAPTER 11

The aroma of sizzling bacon greeted me when I lumbered into the kitchen early the next morning, still wearing short-sleeved summer pajamas. Grammie, who was standing at the stove flipping pancakes, laughed. "You two are quite the pair."

I glanced behind me at Quincy, who was padding along, looking as tired and slothful as I felt. "Neither of us got much sleep." Sometimes the racing thoughts and worries I managed to keep at bay during the day attacked me at night. Last night it was all about Hailey. Who killed her? Was it Brendan? Theo? Even Lukas? Would we ever find out? As a result, I was restless and up three times in the night, disturbing my poor cat.

Yawning, I staggered to the coffee maker and poured a cup. "Madison and I are going to run over to Eleanor's this morning. She found some things that belonged to her mother. Maybe they'll help us with our research."

Grammie used tongs to remove strips of bacon from the pan and place them on a paper-towel-lined plate. "I hope so. The whole thing is quite the mystery."

I pulled out the kitty kibble and filled Quincy's dish. "Not to be mercenary, but a good backstory will help us sell the Chanel clothing and everything else too." I'd learned that customers loved buying things with a story behind them. Claudia's history would only add to the cachet of linens and aprons from a historic summer cottage, which I'd already factored into the prices. Every time someone used a pair of those sheets or tied on an apron, they could dream about staying in a romantic summer cottage on the coast. Or in the case of the European sheets, a castle, maybe?

"And that will help Eleanor," Grammie said. "The auction houses are going to love it." She put two steaming hot pancakes onto a plate and added bacon, then placed it on the island, next to butter and Vermont maple syrup. "Here you go." At the sound of Madison's Mini roaring up the drive, she pulled out another plate.

I went to let Madison in, and we pulled up stools to the island to devour breakfast. "I'll drive this morning if you want," she said around a mouthful of pancake. A tiny piece of bacon accidentally fell from her fingers to the floor, where Quincy pounced.

"Sure." I chased syrup around my plate with a piece of pancake. "We go right by here so you can drop me off after."

After we helped Grammie clean up, Madison had another cup of coffee while I showered and dressed. Today I was in a floral mood, so I wore a full-shirted frock with a pale lavender print. Matching flats completed the outfit.

On the way out to Shorehaven, I filled Madison in regarding my talk with Anton. The prohibition against blabbing didn't extend to my inner circle, I was pretty sure—and almost definitely not to his crush.

"It's got to be someone either staying at the house or with easy access," Madison said as she expertly changed gears, sending us flying around corners and over hills. "And obviously someone who knew which jacket belonged to Lukas."

"You think the killer used his on purpose?" I asked,

thinking that such a move showed premeditation. "That would be truly fiendish."

"More fiendish than pushing a young woman off a cliff and leaving her there?" She flipped on the signal and braked, then turned onto Cliff Road.

"Good point," I said, my stomach clenching with anger. "We need to know more about the people involved." One benefit of working on Eleanor's research project was that it gave us an excuse to go to Shorehaven and talk to Hailey's colleagues. Listening to myself, I realized I'd made the decision to investigate. Well, to help, I clarified, without treading on toes or angering a killer, as I'd promised Anton.

"Um, there is one more thing," I said as we slowed to enter Shorehaven's drive. "I kind of let it slip that Ruben asked you out."

She shot me a glance. "But I said no."

"Yeah, and I didn't mention that part. Not on purpose. There wasn't a good time, since we were really talking about Hailey. Now I feel bad." And I did. While part of me wanted to let Anton squirm, let him worry about Madison dating someone else, it wasn't really my MO to play games. Nor Madison's.

Madison sighed. "Tell him I said no, okay? While I wish he would go ahead and ask if he's going to, I'm not going to try to make him jealous." Then she grinned. "Not on purpose anyway."

I laughed. "Oh, he reacted all right." I pulled out my phone and sent a quick text to Anton. *She said no.* He'd get it.

Several cars were parked in front of Shorehaven, including a lime green VW, a white SUV, Lukas's sports car, and Craig's Mercedes. I groaned to myself. Hopefully Craig's presence wouldn't derail our plans today. We needed to speak privately with Eleanor.

"Ruben drives the SUV, which is a rental," Madison said. "And how do I know this? We had to wrest the keys away from him the other night so Theo could drive. After that double Scotch."

"Good times," I said, picturing the scene. "I didn't see Theo at the pub."

"He showed up later," Madison said, parking the Mini beside the VW. "With Jamaica." As she turned off the engine, she nodded at the lime green bug. "I think that's her car."

I realized I hadn't seen or spoken to Jamaica since the tasting at the Grille. "I'm glad she's here. I'd like to know more about her seaweed farm. Plus maybe she knew Hailey."

"Maybe so," Madison said. "Since they were all working together." She lowered her voice. "Iris and Madison, on the case."

I laughed as I grabbed my tote out of the back. "Come on, partner. Time to get to work."

Lukas and Jamaica were seated on the pool terrace, drinking coffee and looking at what looked like a marine chart. They both looked up when we walked through the gate. Today Jamaica wore blue overalls and a white T-shirt, a blue-and-white bandana constraining her braids. "Good morning," Lukas said. "How are you today?"

We returned his greeting and then I asked Jamaica, "Is that the plan for your seaweed farm?" I marveled at the idea that someone could choose an area in the bay and call it a farm.

"It is." She ran a finger along a rectangle out in the water. "I'm going to be a thousand feet off shore out here." She pointed to a rectangle on land, the representation of a building. "That's Shorehaven. But all you'll be able to see from the cliffs are orange mooring balls. And lobster buoys when the lines growing seaweed are in."

"In order to get lease approval from the state," Lukas said, "the farm needs to be away from any navigational channels. It also can't infringe on essential habitats."

"And then there's the sea bottom to consider so the moorings hold," Jamaica said, "plus current, nutrient availability, and depth." She laughed. "It's been a process. Especially since . . ." Her words trailed off but she didn't clarify.

Despite all the miles of shorefront and acres of water edging Maine, I could see that finding a good site might be complicated. But I had another question. "Ruben and Patrick mentioned something about a lab. Are you growing test-tube seaweed?"

I meant that as a joke and thankfully they laughed. "Kind of," Jamaica said. "We collect spores from mature seaweed and release them into a tank, where they settle on tubes wound with twine. They grow in a tank until they are ready to be transplanted." She smiled at us. "If you'd like to see the process in person, you're welcome to come check it out."

Madison and I exchanged glances. "I would love that," I said, and Madison nodded in agreement. Jamaica's invitation was another opportunity to learn more about Hailey. Plus I was starting to find seaweed farming interesting, even if I still didn't want to ingest any of the end product. "When would be a good time?"

Jamaica thought for a moment. "How about tonight, around five? We're hosting a Business After Hours with the Chamber of Commerce."

"Does that work for you, Madison?" The store closed at five, so I could make it.

Madison checked her phone. "I'm free. This afternoon, I was planning to start building our boat at the store. So we can go together from there."

That's right, we had the cardboard boat race coming

up. Another adventure I'd somehow agreed to. But I left that for now and said, "I'd like to bring my grandmother along, if that's okay. I know she'll be interested."

They agreed that Grammie was a welcome addition to the event and we left them to get back to work. Eleanor had said on the phone to come right in, so we entered the house through the French doors that led to the sitting room.

Voices drifting from the kitchen gave us an indication where to find Eleanor. "Have a seat, Auntie Eleanor," Craig said, his voice booming in the high-ceilinged room. "I'll find your glasses for you."

"I can't imagine where they went . . . but I need them to read the cookbook." In contrast to her nephew, Eleanor sounded weak, almost frail.

"Aha," Craig cried as we entered. He backed out of the refrigerator. "They were in the butter keeper."

Eleanor put a trembling hand to her face. "What were they doing in there?" She took the wire-rimmed eyeglasses from him and put them on. "I don't remember putting them inside the refrigerator."

I rapped on the doorjamb, to warn them of our arrival. "Good morning. Craig. Eleanor."

Craig looked as if he were inhaling the aroma of sour milk. "Hello. What are you doing here?"

"Um, er," I said eloquently, not wanting him to know the real reason.

Madison stepped in, thankfully. "Iris's grandmother wants your recipe for seafood chowder." That had come up during dinner, when Eleanor said she made a lovely soup with fish, lobster, scallops, and clams.

"That's right, I did promise dear Anne that recipe." Understanding replaced confusion in the older woman's eyes, I was glad to see. She began to leaf through the cookbook on the table, which was annotated with hand-written notes.

Probably bored by this discussion of cooking, Craig said, "I'm heading out, Auntie. Business to attend to."

"Goodbye, Craig," Eleanor said, her eyes not leaving the pages she was leafing through. She muttered under her breath as she searched.

He lingered in the doorway, scowling, as if he wanted to say more, but Eleanor kept her back resolutely turned. I gave him a big grin, hoping to irritate the man, who infuriated me. With a grunt, he flapped his hand in a wave and left.

Once he was gone, his footsteps receding and the French door closing behind him, Eleanor swiveled in her seat. "Now I remember. You're here to see the compact."

She hadn't specified the item but I said yes, we were. "Anything to help us figure out Claudia's background will be useful," I said.

Eleanor rose. "Come with me." She tapped the cookbook. "I'll write out the recipe and give it to you later."

She took us up the back stairs, which were right off the kitchen, handy for the servants who would have used them. We emerged in the upstairs hall. "My room is this way," Eleanor said, leading us in the opposite direction of the guest wing.

As I'd experienced the last time I was there, roaming Shorehaven felt like stepping back in time. With the old-fashioned wallpaper and antique furnishings and fixtures, I could easily believe that nothing had changed since Eleanor's childhood. Her room was more of a suite, with bedroom, sitting room, and en suite bathroom. Open French doors led to a balcony furnished with comfortable lounge chairs.

"My mother spent a lot of time out here," Eleanor said

stepping outside. "She used to sit and read or do hand sewing. But she spent a lot of time looking at the view."

"I don't blame her," I said, taking a deep breath of fresh, salty air. The view really was spectacular, south toward Blueberry Cove's harbor and east to islands in the bay. Beyond them was the Atlantic, three thousand miles of ocean ending at the shores of Europe. Had Claudia thought about her home when she sat out here? Why hadn't she ever returned? In those days, a trip to Europe might not be easy but it was far from impossible. And the Bradys had plenty of money, so it wasn't due to lack of funds.

After enjoying the view for a few minutes, we went back inside. Eleanor rummaged through a carved high-boy's small jewelry drawer and withdrew a gold compact engraved with Claudia's initials. "I forgot I had this," she said, handing it to me. She grimaced. "It seems that I'm forgetting all kinds of things lately."

I prayed it wasn't anything serious. "What does your doctor think?" I asked gently.

She shook her head. "Dr. Morris said I was fine at my last checkup a couple of weeks ago. I'm only on one medication. And vitamins. Aren't they supposed to help your memory?"

Only one medication, at her age. That was impressive, since many seniors had multiple prescriptions. I guessed Dr. Morris was Madison's father.

"Don't hesitate to go back," Madison said. "Or call. Dad says he always wants to hear from his patients."

"I'll do that, dear." Eleanor rummaged through the drawers again. This time she handed us a black-and-white postcard of a marching band dressed in berets and sashes. The watching crowd was a sea of white boaters. "That's postcard from the 1920 Olympics in Antwerp," she ex-ained. "Mother would have been ten."

Evidence that suggested Claudia had grown up in Antwerp. As for the compact, the weight alone spoke to its value, as did the European gold hallmark—750—which meant 18-karat gold was used. This, like the clothing and sheets, was another object that would not normally belong to a working-class girl.

"And this," Eleanor said, "is my mother." The sepia-toned photograph showed a young Eleanor, about four years old, sitting between her parents. Walter was handsome, with dark, side-parted hair and a small moustache. Claudia had blonde wavy hair worn off a wide brow and killer cheekbones. Eleanor was a perfect mix of them both.

"You were so cute," Madison said. "And your mom was a beauty."

Eleanor smiled at the photograph. "She sure was, inside and out."

I took quick snapshots of the items with my cell phone. "Lukas is going to help us research your mom's background," I said. "He's from Antwerp, plus he knows French and Flemish. I hope that's okay?"

After I handed them back, Eleanor placed the compact and the postcard in the drawer and shut it gently. "That's wonderful. He's such a nice young man." She pursed her lips. "Despite what the police might think."

She must be talking about his jacket, which the killer wore when pushing Hailey off the cliff. "Well, I have it on good authority that they aren't making an arrest yet," I said. "There isn't enough evidence."

Eleanor smoothed the bureau scarf, which was fine linen edged with lace. "I wonder how long it will take." She turned to face us. "The whole thing is very disturbing. At least they finally finished searching the house. I thought Craig was going to have a heart attack, he was so furious at the intrusion."

I had a realization. "You mean Hailey's room isn't off-limits anymore?"

"No, they released it," Eleanor said. Her brow furrowed. "They told me I could pack up her things any time I want." She shivered. "But I haven't been able to make myself go in there. I guess I'm a wimp."

"I don't blame you a bit," I said. Packing up a victim's clothing and effects wasn't a task any rational person would *want* to do. "But Madison and I will help you." And take the opportunity to look for clues. I was sure the police had already removed anything obvious or important, like her laptop, but we might find something to help us figure out who killed her.

"Would you do that for me?" Eleanor sounded grateful. "I really can't thank you enough."

"We have time to do it now," Madison said. "If that works."

Eleanor agreed that now was perfect and led us to the other wing. Decorated in blue and white, Hailey's room featured a canopy bed, an armchair reading area by a fireplace, and a private bathroom.

My belly clenched at the sight of the bed, the covers pulled back on one side and one pillow still indented. Untouched since that fateful morning. But by all appearances, she had slept alone, which eased the tension in my belly a trifle. Maybe Brendan was off the hook.

I glanced around the rest of the room, noticing discarded clothing hung over a chair and shoes scattered across the carpet. An empty area on the desk surrounded by books and folders spoke of where a laptop had once sat.

Eleanor turned on the light in the bathroom, which had only one tiny, high window, revealing a few toiletries on the vanity and used towels hanging over the shower curtain rod. "As the only woman, she got the one guest room with an attached bathroom. Sometimes men can be slobs."

"You've got that right," Madison said. She opened a closet door and pulled out a suitcase. "We'll pack everything inside this. How's that?"

Eleanor sucked in a breath. "I can't tell you how much I appreciate your help." She blinked rapidly against the tears brimming in her eyes. "Maybe I'm a foolish old woman, but I'm just devastated over Hailey's death. Such a waste."

I hugged Eleanor briefly, her bones delicate and bird-like in my arms. "I understand perfectly. That's why Madison and I aren't going to let this go. The truth needs to come out."

Eleanor dashed tears away with the back of her hand with a tiny laugh. "I'm so grateful to you both." She darted at me, then Madison, pecking us on the cheeks. "I'll be downstairs if you need me."

Madison picked up the suitcase and set it on the bed, open like a clamshell. "She is such a sweetheart. I wonder if she would adopt me." She laughed to indicate she was joking. Madison had two sets of wonderful grandparents already.

"Seriously," I said. "I love her too." I glanced around with a sigh, not exactly looking forward to our task. "I guess we'd better get to work."

Working together, we cleared the bathroom and folded Hailey's clothes, checking each pocket for clues. We didn't find much, only a crumpled dollar bill in one jacket pocket and a receipt from the Bean tucked in her jeans. Then we tackled the desk. The folders and books were related to the aquaculture project, which made sense. I flipped through a notebook but only found scribbles from lectures about seaweed.

"Wow," Madison said, picking up the books to pack them. "She certainly was a dedicated student."

"Seems that way," I said. "But remember, her personal life and entertainment are probably on her devices. Even any novels she was reading." In the interest of being thorough, I got down on my hands and knees and looked under the desk. There, in the back, I saw a small rectangle and reached for it.

It was a matchbook. I backed out from underneath, gripping it in my fingers. "Look at this, Madison." The cover depicted a line drawing of a stone castle with turrets. I read the gold embossed script below, "Château de Mount-Gauthier. In Rochefort, Belgium."

"Fancy," Madison said. "Maybe she stayed there."

Something didn't sit quite right. "On a student's budget?" I pulled out my phone and looked it up, learning that the hotel was an exclusive resort and spa. It was also totally gorgeous, perfect for a romantic getaway. On impulse, I snapped pictures of the front and back of the matchbook. Yes, I was grasping at straws, but we hadn't found anything out of the ordinary in here. Except for maybe this matchbook.

The sound of a door shutting followed by footsteps in the hallway caught my attention. I peeked out through the partially open door to see Lukas striding down the hallway. Maybe he could shed light on the matchbook.

"Hey, Lukas," I called. "Can I talk to you a second?"

He stopped and pivoted on his heel, waiting until I caught up to him. I showed him the picture of the matchbook on my phone, enlarging it. "Do you know if Hailey ever went there?" She might well have found the matchbook somewhere and picked it up.

A crease appeared between his brows. "I don't. But"— muttering the name of the hotel, he tapped a finger on his chin—"something about the place rings a bell." His frown deepened. "But I can't remember what, exactly." After a few more seconds, he nodded. "Tell you what, let me think about it. Okay?"

I watched him continue down the corridor, hoping that he would recall where and how he'd heard about the resort. Until then, we were exactly in the same position as before. Nowhere.

CHAPTER 12

Four o'clock that afternoon found me helping Madison build our cardboard boat. She'd located a couple of huge cardboard boxes somewhere and managed to get them to the store in her Mini. Then we'd taken over the side room as we measured, cut, and glued a little boat barely large enough to hold us both.

"This is really going to work?" I asked with skepticism as Madison slathered glue onto a cross-brace. She set it in place and I helped push it down to make the glue hold.

"Long enough for us to finish the race," she said, which wasn't really reassuring. "We're going to cover all the seams with duct tape, which will help." She grinned. "Don't worry. I watched tons of videos, plus talked to last year's winners."

While she cut another brace to size, I looked again at the plan she had sketched. Wrapping-paper rolls would form the mast, and I had a plain apron we could use as a sail. To carry out the catboat theme, a cardboard cat's head and tail would adorn the craft fore and aft. And, instead of a solid color, we planned to paint the boat cream with orange stripes, like Quincy's coat. It would be eye-catching and cute, that was for sure. I just wasn't sure it would float.

As if he knew he was the inspiration for our work, Quincy sat regally nearby, watching. I reached out and fluffed the soft fur under his chin. "What do you think of our boat?" I asked him. He butted my hand with his head, purring in approval. We didn't have time to take him home before the lab tour, so he'd be staying here until later.

Out in the main room, Grammie was waiting on the few customers we had. Although we'd seen some new faces, the festival was the main draw in town this afternoon. Who could blame people? The weather was spectacular. I'd rather be outside myself.

"Hold this, will you?" Madison asked. She pushed another brace into place and squirted glue while I held the piece steady. "After the tour we'll come back here to tape and paint." The race was tomorrow afternoon so we were really cutting it close.

Grammie appeared in the doorway. "Iris, you have company." She moved aside to reveal Lars Lavely, local reporter for the *Blueberry Cove Herald*.

Great. Of course Lars had tracked me down. Hailey's demise was big news for a publication that usually featured committee meeting minutes and photographs of children eating ice cream cones. Sweet small-town stuff, but not exactly hard news.

"Hey, Lars," I said. "What brings you by?" I said that to make him work for it.

The reporter, who was short and bearded with dark-rimmed hipster glasses, sauntered into the room without answering my question, a knowing smile on his face. "Madison. Glad you're here too. I can talk to both of you." Without invitation, he pulled out a chair and sat.

"Make yourself at home," I said, allowing a hint of sarcasm into my tone. In general, though, I wanted to stay on good terms with Lars. Playing nice had gotten us some good coverage in a paper that everyone read, locals and visitors alike.

Naturally he wanted quotes about our discovery of Hailey. We made our statements about the actual event as bland as possible, trying to be discreet and not sensationalize the event. Lars could do that all by himself.

"So, did you see anyone else up there that morning?" Behind the glasses, his eyes were alight with reporting fervor.

The part of me that always answered questions—am I well-trained or what?—wanted to share seeing Theo, Patrick's boat, and then later, Lukas. But I refrained, not wanting to point fingers in the newspaper. It was up to the police to disclose that type of information. "There were a few walkers on the cliffs," I said. "But I didn't see Hailey with anyone. Remember, the sun was just coming up. Not the best visibility." Madison echoed my evasion. "And make sure you say how shocked and saddened we are," I added. "It's a real tragedy."

With a disappointed shrug, Lars made a final note. "Well, I guess that's it." He pushed back his chair and stood. "Got to go. On deadline."

"Don't let us hold you up," I said, warming the words with a smile. Phew. That ordeal was over.

Lars rushed out, brushing past Grammie with a nod. "Iris, I just put out the closed sign," she said, "and I'm going to cash out. Let me know when you're ready to go."

"We'll only be a few more minutes," I said. The last task right now was to make the mast. For the sail, I'd starched the apron until the skirt was stiff, so it'd stand straight out. We couldn't rely on wind to make it look like a sail. In fact, I was hoping it wouldn't be windy during the race. Swells and a headwind would make paddling much more difficult.

We taped the mast together and then I tied the starched

apron onto it, using the sash strings. The white semicircle looked pretty cool, even if it wasn't the typical triangle shape used for sailing.

"Not bad," I said, setting the contraption aside carefully. "Is there a prize for originality?"

"There's one for creativity." Madison looked pleased as she surveyed our work. Then she studied her hands. "I'd better wash up before we go. I'm all sticky."

"And I'd better feed you, Quince," I said to my cat. We kept food and dishes here at the store for occasions like this one. After a short period of getting used to the routine, he enjoyed being at the store, with a rotation between his favorite napping and people-watching spots.

Since we were returning to the store after the tour, we rode together in Beverly to the lab. The facility was located on the edge of town, an old mill building that had once produced woolen cloth from sheep dotting the Maine hillsides. College of the Isles and a local development organization had turned the defunct mill into business incubators. And now a couple of spaces were dedicated to seaweed, according to the sign.

"Sea's Best," Madison read. "And Sea Gold. Huh. I got the impression Jamaica and Patrick were in business together."

"Me too." I found a space to park and pulled in. This time of day, the parking lot held only a few vehicles. I recognized Jamaica's bug and Ruben's rental SUV, but a battered blue pickup truck was unfamiliar to me.

As we climbed out, an old Volvo wagon pulled in. Sophie. "Hey," she called, climbing out. "Here for the Business After Hours?"

"We are," I called back, stopping to wait for her to reach us. A few more cars pulled in while we waited. They were getting a great turnout.

The four of us pushed through a glass door into a dim

lit lobby where an empty desk sat. Corridors stretched in both directions, with posted signs indicating where the different enterprises could be found. Straight ahead, an open door revealed a brightly lit conference room. I spotted Lukas with a plastic cup in his hand, talking to Theo.

"I think we're meeting in there," I said, walking that way.

Inside the conference room, people milled about, drinking fruit punch and eating cheese and crackers and grapes from a big platter. No seaweed dishes in sight, surprisingly. I said as much to Jamaica, when she joined me at the table.

Tossing her braids with a laugh, she lowered her voice. "To be honest, cheese and crackers were quick and easy." She glanced around. "The chamber kind of sprung it on us last minute."

More people pushed into the already crowded room, and I recognized faces from the Taste O' the Sea event at the Grille. Local dignitaries, most of them, here to learn more about two of the town's newest enterprises. I'd have to say that seaweed growing ranked among the most unusual, too.

I looked around for my friends and saw Sophie standing next to Lukas, smiling at something he was saying. Guilt panged. I hadn't had a chance to talk to her since seeing Jake at the pub. And now certainly wasn't the time. I'd have breakfast at the Bean tomorrow, I decided. I'd corner her there.

At Ruben's whistled signal, I stuffed a cracker holding Brie into my mouth and washed it down with punch. Time to get started.

First, we all took seats and watched a short film. This took us through the seaweed life cycle and explained the process of farming the plants. Instead of gathering plants the wild, which had been done for centuries, spores were carefully harvested from mature plants and germinated in a lab under strict and sterile conditions. Once large enough, they were set out in the water on lines that held them in place as they grew. After six months or so, the lines were retrieved and the plants harvested for further processing.

After the video ended to sporadic clapping, Ruben said, "We're going to split into two groups for the tour. Jamaica and Patrick have almost identical lab setups, and since the rooms aren't large, that will work better."

I ended up in Jamaica's group, along with Grammie and Madison. We followed the seaweed farmer down a hallway, where she unlocked a door. "How did you get into seaweed farming?" Grammie asked.

Jamaica pushed open the door to let us enter. "I studied marine biology in college, and I've always been interested in how we can make our oceans more sustainable. I also grew up on a small farm in Vermont, so you could say it's in my blood. What I'm doing now brings everything together for me."

Seaweed farming did sound perfect for her. I glanced around the lab with curiosity. Tables were set up with microscopes and other mysterious equipment that Jamaica told us was used to extract seaweed spores. Gurgling tanks full of seawater incubated them as they sprouted and grew. Right now the seaweed babies were just brown fuzz on the growing tubes.

"Everything has to be sterile, including the water," Jamaica told us. "We can't allow any contamination or it will ruin our crop." She explained how the seawater filling the tanks had temperature, pH, light, and filtering requirements. "It goes from this"—she showed us a spore, which was almost invisible—"to this." She held up a full length of slippery kelp, about fifteen feet long. Everyone oohed and ahhed.

"I think it's amazing," Grammie said. "We've always regarded seaweed as a nuisance, but now it's a real moneymaker."

"Well, we hope so, Mrs. Buckley," Jamaica said. "That's what we're aiming at. Maybe in a few more years, there will be dozens of us growing weed in the water." She gave us a sly smile, knowing how her words sounded.

"That's a whole new topic," Theo called out to laughter. "Check with us next year."

The tour broke up then and everyone milled around, either leaving the building or grabbing more refreshments. I asked someone for directions to the ladies' room. The one closest to the front door was occupied so I went to the end of the hall, past the nurseries.

No one was in this area now, and motion-sensitive lights flared on as I walked down the hall. It was kind of creepy at night, all the doors shut and my shoes squeaking on the waxed tiles.

The restroom was unisex, with room for one, so when I heard voices outside the door, my first thought was that it was other people wanting to use it. But when I opened the door after washing my hands, I saw two figures partway down the corridor, not right outside.

Jamaica and Patrick. Something about the intensity of their body language made me hesitate, Jamaica's folded arms and Patrick's hunched shoulders.

"It's really not cool, Patrick," Jamaica said. "It's half mine."

Patrick made a nasty scoffing sound. "You should've thought about that before—"

"Before I bounced your ass?" Jamaica's brows rose. "Business doesn't have anything to do with our *former* relationship."

The scowl on his face said he didn't agree. "Get an attorney then. See how far that gets you."

"I plan on it." Jamaica stabbed a finger toward him. "You're not going to get away with stealing my work."

Behind me, the automatic flush finally decided to do its job—loudly. I winced when they both glanced my way at the noise. Pretending I hadn't been listening, I stepped out of the bathroom and let the door shut with a thunk.

The pair gave each other one last glowering stare before Jamaica whirled around and went into her lab. Patrick stalked down the hallway ahead of me, heading toward the main area. Trotting at his heels, I wondered if I should try to talk to him. After witnessing his hostility toward Jamaica, who I liked, I really didn't want to. What if Hailey had gotten on his wrong side too? I shuddered slightly at the possibility.

"Hey, Patrick," I called, deciding I needed to take advantage of this opportunity. He stopped dead and turned around, regarding me with a blank expression as I caught up. "I've been wanting to talk to you."

He crossed his arms, a cynical expression on his face. "Really? About what?"

Half-formed sentences flitted through my mind as I tried to settle on an approach. Mr. Prickly certainly wasn't making it easy. "Are you doing okay?" I moved slightly closer, my voice soft. Maybe an appeal to his better nature would work. He had met Hailey, right? Anyone who had would at least feel sad about her untimely death.

"I don't know what you mean." His gaze darted to Jamaica's lab door. Did he think I was talking about the two of them?

"I was there . . . I found her. Hailey. When I was climbing." I wasn't faking the shock and sadness in my voice.

He reared back slightly. "Huh. I didn't know that." Arms still crossed, he regarded me with narrowed eyes. "That must have been rough."

"It was," I agreed. "But the terrible thing is, no one

saw it happen. But people were around." I made my eyes wide. "Theo was taking pictures. And I saw your boat. Did you notice anything while you were on the water?"

"My boat?" He thought about denying he was there, I could tell by his expression. But maybe he remembered telling me he had arrived at Shorehaven by water. "Oh, yeah, I was out there in my boat that morning. I visit my seaweed site every day. So does Jamaica."

Jamaica? I hadn't even considered her a possible suspect. "Was she out there that morning too?"

His dark eyes gleamed with an expression I couldn't decipher. "I'm pretty sure I saw her. But back to your original question, no, I didn't notice Hailey on the cliffs. I was busy navigating. Lots of rocks around there."

"I'm sure," I said, thinking of the ledges near the cliffs. "Oh well." I started walking again, this time with Patrick by my side. He kept glancing at me, his mood seeming to have lightened.

"You said you saw Theo up there." His voice was almost a whisper.

My senses sharpened. Where was this going? "I did. He was taking pictures. Along with other people watching the sunrise. It's a great spot for that."

His lips curved in a satisfied smile. "I bet." He lowered his voice even more. "You are aware that Theo hated Hailey, right? She was trying to push him out of the program."

CHAPTER 13

While I stood there, frozen in my tracks, Patrick gave me a jaunty wave and sauntered off. His revelation had been calculated to throw suspicion in a new direction, and I had to admit he had succeeded. All by itself, maybe not, but it matched what Lukas told me at the pub. Hailey had attempted to undermine the other teaching assistant's work, which, in the competitive academic world, was a gauntlet toss. Some healthy jockeying for position was to be expected, sure. I'd experienced it myself at college when other designers competed with me for awards. But still, there was an ethical line and it was beginning to seem that Hailey had crossed it. And most damning of all, Theo was aware of her tactics. According to Patrick, anyway.

A chill ran down my spine. Means, motive, and opportunity. Theo had all three. An unwelcome image formed in my mind: the confrontation on the cliffs, a struggle ending in a fierce push. Hailey flying backward, clutching at Theo's jacket as she fell. The scenario was plausible. But had it actually happened? Had Theo meant to kill her or had it been an accident? And maybe, just maybe, he was innocent and this was all in my head.

"Iris?" Grammie called. "Ready to get going?" She

and Madison were standing near the front entrance, looking impatient.

I shook off my dark and tangled thoughts. "Yes, I'm ready. Madison and I have more work to do on the boat tonight." Right now, that was the last thing I wanted to do, but the paint needed time to dry before the race late tomorrow afternoon.

Back at the shop, Grammie drove off in her Jeep, heading for home. Before we got started, Madison tuned to lively rock music on her phone while I made chai tea. With those mood-changers, I was able to push aside thoughts of Hailey's murder, for the most part. A couple of times I was tempted to tell Madison about my encounter with Patrick, but I couldn't bring myself to raise the topic. The subject was a like a gloomy pit I was dancing around, trying to pretend it wasn't there. One word about it and I'd slide back inside.

Using Quincy as our model, we painted the cardboard boat in orange and buff stripes with white sections at the chest and feet. It was going to be really cute. Unfortunately, our muse was quite uncooperative and kept trying to walk on the freshly painted cardboard. After he tracked kitty prints across the wooden floor for the second time, I gave up.

"He's going to have go outside," I said, getting up and chasing the cat, who naturally ran into the main room. I finally nabbed him as he was getting ready to leap up onto an antique patchwork quilt. "No, you don't. You're coming with me."

Leaving Madison to wipe up the latex paint prints— again—I carried Quincy out to the alley behind the store, where Beverly was parked. "Sorry to do this, Quince," I said, feeling guilty. "But you're making a mess."

This time of night, the alley was in near total darkness, lit only by a light over my back entrance and a streetlight down at the end. On both sides, three-story buildings loomed over this narrow passageway used mainly for trash and deliveries. Not wanting to linger, I hurried over to Beverly, parked a short distance away.

Despite struggling with a very unhappy cat, I managed to get the rear passenger door open. "I'll give you a treat if you go nicely into your cage," I said. He hated that thing, but I didn't like transporting him loose in the car.

Keeping Quincy tucked firmly under one arm, I unlatched the cage then positioned us to do the "one two three, cat inside and door is latched" maneuver I'd perfected.

Bang. A nearby trash can fell over, the lid rolling away with a rattle. Startled, I jerked upright, hit my head on the metal doorframe, and dropped Quincy. Ignoring my throbbing head, I lurched forward and grabbed him before he could dart off. He had the bad habit of running toward trouble.

A scraping sound came from the same direction, as if another trash can was being pushed along the pavement. Narrowing my eyes, I squinted into the black shadows behind the adjacent buildings. Was it a raccoon? They loved getting into trash. Or worse, it might be a black bear. Once they got a taste for human garbage, they could become quite the nuisance.

Then a footstep rang out. Or what I imagined was a footstep. "Is someone there?" I called, my voice wobbling.

Silence. The hair on the back of my neck rose and I had the prickling sense that I was being watched. Not wanting to linger any longer, I bolted for the back door, leaving the car passenger door wide open.

Madison looked up with surprise when I dashed into the side room, panting. "I thought you were taking him out to the car." She dabbed a bit of white paint at the end of the cardboard tail, matching Quincy's.

Still holding onto the cat, I collapsed onto a folding chair. "I was. But something was out there. It knocked down a trash can."

She made a final dab and set the brush across the can. "An animal?"

I'd heard footsteps. Or had I? With every minute that ticked by, my memory became hazier. "Maybe." At her wide-eyed look, I amended that. "I mean, yeah, most likely." Who would hang around in the back alley, anyway? It wasn't a very pleasant place even in broad daylight.

Madison eyed the two of us, huddled together in the chair. "Why don't I finish up while you keep him under control? There isn't much more to do."

I snuggled Quincy, burying my nose in his soft fur. "Sounds like a plan." Hopefully by the time we left, whatever—or whoever—was lurking would be long gone.

Lit by shafts of bright sunshine, the alley was more dingy than menacing the next morning. But as I rolled Beverly to a stop in my usual spot, I noticed the tipped-over trash can still lying on its side. No scattered garbage as you might expect, though. No spilled bags, even. Hmm. Why would an animal try to open an empty can?

The truth hit me like a splash of cold water. Someone *had* been loitering back here last night. Part of me was relieved, to be honest, to know I hadn't overreacted. But who would do such a thing? And why?

After locking the car, I trotted over to the fallen can. Maybe my spy had left something behind. But no, the entire area was surprisingly pristine, without a gum wrapper or a glob of discarded food in sight. I checked the other cans. They were all empty, which meant the noise hadn't been someone making a late-night garbage run.

Decidedly unsettled, I set the tipped can upright and put the lid back on. There wasn't anything worth reporting to the police, plus what would they say anyway? Avoid dark places alone. Even if accompanied by an attack cat.

The thought of Quincy defending me made me smile. Grammie was bringing him down later, when we opened. Right now I was headed to the Bean for breakfast—and hopefully a heart-to-heart with Sophie.

Naturally the Bean was packed, the usual summer morning crowd augmented by festivalgoers. I stood at the rear of the line, using the time inching forward to think about the day ahead. Business as usual—sell aprons, meet new customers . . . oh yeah, and sail a cardboard boat in the icy-cold harbor.

By the time I reached the front of the line, my mouth was watering, teased by the aromas of baking waffles and maple syrup.

"Hey, Iris. Great to see you." Sophie stood ready to take my order. "What can I get you?"

My original plan had been a modest muffin with coffee. But the words that came out of my mouth were, "Belgian Benedict, with two eggs and extra hollandaise. And my usual large coffee." I glanced over my shoulder at the line snaking behind me. "I was hoping we could catch up this morning, but I guess I wasn't thinking. You're slammed."

"We are," Sophie said, entering my order into the computer. "But grab a seat and I'll take my break." She tipped her chin to a two-top where a couple was getting ready to leave. She made a shooing motion. "Quick, grab that table. You can pay later."

I hovered with a sheepish smile as the couple cleared dishes, gathered belongings, and finally departed, then plopped into one of the seats. Grabbing a restaurant seat during Maine's busy season was almost a contact sport.

To kill time while waiting for breakfast, I picked up a copy of the *Blueberry Cove Herald* that someone had left neatly folded on the wide windowsill.

The question of whether Lars had made his deadline yesterday was answered the moment I viewed the front page. SLIP AND FALL—OR WAS IT? screamed the headline. A picture of the cliffs and a headshot of Hailey adorned the text.

Great. Not for the first time, I reflected that Lars was wasted in Blueberry Cove. Surely the tabloids paid better. Despite the cheesy headline, the article was solid, if not providing anything conclusive about Hailey's death or information beyond what I already knew. He characterized his mention of me as the "local business owner stunned by a grisly discovery while enjoying a sunrise climb in the park." Madison was the "supportive friend," and Ian, "the intrepid expert climber who helped with rescue efforts."

"Breakfast is served." I looked up to see Sophie standing beside me with a tray. She set my breakfast and two cups of coffee on the table before taking the opposite seat.

"What's new in the weekly rag?" she asked, picking up her mug and sipping. When I showed her the article, she winced at the headline. "Lars is something else."

I folded the paper and put it back on the windowsill. "That's one way of putting it." Picking up my utensils, I made the first cut into the Belgian Benedict, allowing creamy sauce and egg yolk to flood the deep, crunchy waffle underneath. I took my first mouthful. The flavor was incredible, a blend of sweet and savory balanced by salty ham. Every cell in my body rejoiced.

Sitting with elbows propped as she cradled her cup, Sophie grinned. "I love watching you eat."

"Really?" I was more gobbler than graceful diner.

"Yep." Sophie took a sip. "You really enjoy your food. And that's why I cook."

I cut off another portion. "Please accept my gratitude

for your efforts. This is one of the best things I've ever eaten."

Her grin widened. "Give me a good review on social media, will you?"

"Five stars it is," I promised. After a couple more bites, I said, "I saw Jake at the pub the other night. Ian and I were in the back hallway when he came in."

Sophie set down her cup, her face paling. "The night I was there with Lukas?"

I nodded. "I told him Lukas was only a friend. But he wouldn't go in and talk to you. He left."

She stared out the window unseeing, fretting her bottom lip with her teeth. "How'd he seem?" she finally asked.

"Not good." Might as well be honest. "He's devastated, Soph. I think you should talk to him."

Hope and fear warred in her gaze. "You think so? What if—" She broke off, swallowed, then shook her head. "No, he's the one who pulled the plug. He should come to me." With that, she pushed back her chair and stood. "I've got to get back to work." She tapped the table. "Breakfast is on the house."

"What? No, I'll—" Before I could finish my sentence, she was halfway across the room, moving through the tightly packed tables and bodies like the pro she was.

I slumped back in my seat. That didn't go as well as I hoped. Both of them were stubborn, that was for sure. After a second, I shook off my disappointment. This breakfast was too good to waste.

Up at the counter, Theo Nesbitt was paying for his order. Here was a welcome change of direction. When he turned around to scan the room for a seat, I waved him over. *Come into my web, little fly, said the spider.*

"That looks good," I said as Theo settled into the seat

across from me. He'd ordered a waffle with maple link sausage on the side.

"Sure does." He swirled the ball of butter around with his fork, then opened the container of maple syrup and poured. "This is one of my favorite places to eat in town."

"Mine too," I said. Sitting back, I drank coffee while he took the first few bites. Not nice to interrogate someone on an empty stomach. Trying not to be obvious, I took a closer look at Hailey's competitor.

Theo was unimpressive at best, pale and weedy with a lingering air of adolescence. Although he must be in his early twenties if he'd already graduated from college. Not terrible looking, but his eyes were slightly protuberant and his dirty-blond curls were limp and too long.

Was I sitting across from a killer? It was hard to fathom, although murderers came in all sizes and shapes. Some were charming, even—and intelligent. And many were adept at hiding the truth about themselves and their crimes.

Faster than I thought possible, Theo devoured the waffle and sausages. He sat back, resting a hand on his stomach and gave a gentle belch. "Whoops. Sorry."

With a smile and a shrug, I signaled that I wasn't offended. My nerves tensed. How to bring up Hailey? Maybe beating around the bush was the best method. "So tell me about your career plans," I said. "What you're doing with the seaweed farmers is really cool."

Ripping open small packets, he added three sugars to his coffee. "Yeah, it sure is. My plan is to learn all the cutting-edge techniques I can and then work developing the seaweed industry in New England." He picked up the cup and took a slurping gulp. "With all the issues around fishing, seaweed is a great option for diversifying."

Another familiar face, Brendan Murphy, emerged from the back and began clearing a nearby table. Some customers didn't realize we were supposed to bus our own dishes. I gave him a wave. Fly number two, if I could catch him.

"Where are you from?" I asked, turning my attention back to Theo.

"New Bedford, Mass." His mouth twisted in a wry grimace. "So I've seen the struggles up close and personal. Relatives of mine are commercial fishermen."

"I hear that." New Bedford was one of the region's major seaports, and as a Maine native I'd certainly watched the ups and downs of the fishing industry with interest. Much of our coastal economy hinged on availability of the lobsters, clams, and haddock our visitors enjoyed. "Tell me about the fellowship you're hoping to win."

His gaze dropped and he began to fiddle with the utensils on his plate. "Yeah. Well. Since I'm the only one in the running now, it's more of a shoo-in." He sighed. "Just have to work on the finances."

He didn't seem happy about winning by default. Interesting. "Was Hailey also hoping to get the fellowship?" Lukas had said so, but I wanted to hear it from Theo.

"Uh-huh." The fiddling continued. "She had a pretty ruthless attitude about it too. But why should I be surprised? After what she did to me last semester . . ."

"Which was?" I lifted my cup to my mouth only to find it almost empty. Darn it. I certainly didn't want to interrupt Theo right now. Getting up for a refill might squash the conversation.

Theo sighed deeply, his bony chest lifting and falling. "I made the mistake of helping her out. She was having trouble in one of our science classes so I agreed to tutor her."

"And?" I felt like I was dragging the story out of him.

He leaned forward across the table, his features tense with suppressed anger. "And she cheated. She stole my work and turned it in as her own. And get this: she ended up with a better grade than me. And some extra perks." His voice rose to an offended squawk.

Brendan appeared at my side with a coffeepot. He must have noticed my cup was empty. "Refill?" I nodded yes and as he poured, he said to Theo, "Hailey wasn't a trustworthy person. But I guess you figured that out, huh?"

"How'd you know Hailey?" Theo asked, staring up at the other young man through his tangled locks.

"I used to date her." Brendan lifted the pot with a flourish. "Many moons ago." He held it out to Theo. "Want some?" At Theo's nod, he dispensed hot coffee into his cup, then sauntered off to another table.

I'd never seen Brendan do the refill circuit, ever. Maybe he'd volunteered on purpose, to talk to Theo about Hailey. Which meant he was eavesdropping while clearing the tables. Understandable. If I heard Ian's name bandied about, I'd listen.

"I really didn't want this," Theo said with a laugh, pushing the cup away. "But I hated to be rude." He scraped his chair away from the table. "I've got to run. They're expecting me at the lab." He picked up his dirty plate. "Want me to take yours?"

"Sure," I said, setting my plate on top of his. "Thanks. I'll clear your cup for you."

I watched as the teaching assistant ambled away, detouring to the bus pan to dump the dishes and silverware. Our conversation was a start at least. No confession yet but what he'd told me only strengthened the motive piece of the equation.

Hailey had obviously been a thorn in Theo's side for months, trying to best him at every turn. No doubt his mild demeanor and willingness to help had made him an easy target, and once he caught on, he was justifiably upset. But some people didn't express their anger well. They allowed it to fester inside until it exploded, often with disastrous results.

As a rationale for Theo's guilt, this theory was plausible—but far from ironclad. No wonder the police hadn't made an arrest yet. There were plenty of suspects but little real evidence pointing at a specific person. According to Brendan, Hailey wasn't trustworthy. Who else had she damaged with her schemes?

CHAPTER 14

Across the room, Brendan called to another employee, "I'm going to take my break now." He set down the empty coffeepot and whipped off his apron while heading toward the kitchen door.

Should I? I hesitated then decided, yes, I should. I cleared the cups, pouring the leftover coffee into a container used for that purpose. Then I hurried out of the restaurant.

As I guessed, Brendan was smoking a cigarette in the side alley, a narrow slice of space between the Bean and the adjacent building. "Hey," I greeted him. "I've been hoping to catch up with you."

In the midst of inhaling, he cocked a brow. "And why is that?" he said after releasing a stream of smoke. He seemed if not exactly cagey, cautious.

I moved closer, avoiding a puddle of something dubious. As with Theo, I decided to take an indirect approach to the topic of Hailey. "You almost hit me the other morning. On Cliff Road."

His eyes flared in surprise as he took an instinctive step backward. "That was you?" He took a hasty drag. "I'm sorry, I know I was driving too fast."

"No harm done," I said. "But you really should be

careful on that scooter." The vehicle in question was tucked up against the wall, near the kitchen door.

He kicked at a stray clump of asphalt with his toe. "I usually am. So dumb. I was upset so I drove a little crazy."

"Upset about Hailey?" I held my breath, wondering if he would answer or blow me off. This line of questioning was pretty personal and I barely knew Brendan.

But he must have needed someone to talk to, because he nodded and said, "Yeah, Hailey. My kryptonite, I call her. We went out in high school and hooked up a few times since. Whenever she was around. Summers mostly. I was pretty tired of the sitch, but I didn't say no when I ran into her the other day." Still holding the cigarette, he scratched the end of his nose. "Should have, that's for sure."

I remembered Hailey approaching Brendan while he was clearing tables on the Grille's deck. But not wanting to be seen as a nosy creeper, I didn't mention it. "She was a beautiful girl," I said instead. "And she had a powerful personality."

He took another drag. "Yeah. All true. But she could flip on a dime. And when I went out to Shorehaven the other night, at her invitation no less, she was on a tear about something. Not fun. Finally, after drinking with her into the wee hours, I crashed on a couch downstairs."

"Good call." Driving a scooter impaired was far too dangerous. I waited a beat before asking, "What was she upset about?" Again, not my business. Hopefully he would bother to answer.

Brendan made a sound somewhere between a laugh and a grunt. "The usual. Someone wasn't giving her what she wanted." He waved the cigarette. "Who, I'm not sure. Or what. She didn't really say plus we were drinking . . ." He took a final drag then dropped the butt, stubbing it out with his shoe before carefully picked it up and tossing it into a can labeled SMOKES.

"Did you see her the next morning?" What I was really asking was whether he had gone for a sunrise stroll with her, lost his temper, and pushed her off the cliff. Or alternately, whether he had seen her with someone else, aka the killer.

Instead of answering, he pulled out his cigarette pack and extended it to me. When I shook my head, he shook out another and lit up, the onshore breeze forcing him to cup his hands around the flame.

Was he stalling? Brendan had the fair skin of a natural redhead, and a telltale flush was creeping up his neck. But when he blinked furiously, I realized he had tears in his eyes. "No," he said, his voice husky. "I got out of there soon as I woke up. I didn't see Hailey." He cleared his throat. "But if I had, maybe . . ."

My stomach sank with a thud. Maybe she would still be alive.

"Both Theo and Brendan had good reason to resent Hailey," I said to Grammie a little later, while we were getting ready to open the store. "But I'm having a hard time seeing either of them as a killer."

"That's because you're soft-hearted." Grammie slid a new roll of register tape into the dispenser. "You don't want to think anyone could be that evil." That task complete, she turned on the iPad that served as our point of sale system.

"Very true. I sure don't." I slid the last bunch of store bags into their standing slot beneath the counter, and as I straightened, a sticky note on the counter caught my eye. "Oh yeah. I've been meaning to research auction houses for Eleanor's clothing and jewelry. Maybe I'll have a chance today." My plan was to identify the houses most likely to show interest—and work hard to get her the most money.

"By the way, I took her jewelry to the bank," Grammie said, placing the cash drawer inside the register. "It's now safe and sound in a deposit box."

"That's a relief." I went to the coffee station and measured coffee into a filter basket. We offered coffee and tea to customers, inviting them to sit in the side room if they wanted. Quincy padded over to nudge my ankles, excited by my proximity to his snack tin. "Hold on, you. I'll give you a treat in a second."

A rapping on the front door caught our attention. A short, plump woman with a brown bob pressed the edges of both hands and her face into the glass, peering inside. "Now there's an eager customer," Grammie said.

Since Grammie was busy logging onto the point of sale system, I went to answer the door. We weren't officially open for another five minutes but I wasn't going to be a jerk and make the customer wait. "Good morning," I said after unlocking the door, which now had nose and lip prints. "Come on in." I turned the hanging sign to OPEN.

She thrust a piece of paper at me. "Oh, I don't need to come in. I just wanted to give you my entry form."

"For the lobster bib contest?" I guessed, accepting the entry.

"Exactly." She glanced both ways before leaning close and whispering, "Are we restricted as to the materials we use?"

What an odd question. "Um, no, I don't think so," I said. "As long as you can wear it."

She thrust a fist into the air. "Yes. Thanks so much. Ta-ta." She bounced off down the sidewalk.

"Tell you what, Grammie," I said, looking over the form. "This contest is really attracting some interesting people." Including Mr. Buxton, who I owed a text regarding electricity at the event. After giving Quincy his treat, I found the right form in the file folder and sent the message. Then I tucked the folder away for safekeeping.

My cell phone rang in my apron pocket. Sophie. Oops. I was so eager to talk to Brendan I hadn't paid my check. "Hey, Sophie," I said. "I still owe you for breakfast."

"No, it's fine. I told you it was on the house." Dishes clattered in the background and she turned away from the phone for a second. "Sorry. I'm back. I was wondering if you have lunch plans. If not, Lukas and I want to come by. He said he has news about Eleanor's mother. And I'll bring Niçoise salad bowls and iced tea."

"Yum. Love Niçoise." My heart jumped at the news of Lukas's progress. "That's awesome Lukas found something already. See you then." After I disconnected the call, I gave Grammie the update.

"Oh, excellent," she said. "I hope Claudia's story will help when you contact the auction houses."

"Me too. From what I've seen, an interesting provenance can definitely boost interest and prices." I wandered over to the spinning clothes rack to rearrange the display. The hostess aprons were selling fast, leaving empty spots that I filled with colorful kitchen linens. Time to look for more inventory, another task that never ended. Not that I was complaining.

The bells on the door jingled and the first customers of the day strolled in. Grammie and I turned to them with smiles. Quincy greeted them with a meow. Showtime.

In between customers, I managed to get online and research auction houses. In addition to the big New York names—Sotheby's and Christie's—there were smaller houses around New England that offered high-quality items like Eleanor's. I made bookmarks, planning to contact each house to gauge interest, find out about their fees, and get estimated appraisals. We'd need to send photos of each item at some point, but I could at least get the ball rolling.

Just before noon, Madison strolled into the store, carrying a duffle bag.

"Doing a lot of shopping?" I quipped. "Oh, and did you get my text? News at one, with Dr. Lukas de Wilde."

Madison dropped the duffle in the side room with a thud. "I did. And I'll be staying for that." She hunkered down and unzipped the bag, then pulled out a black and bright blue garment. "This is your wetsuit, to wear during the boat race."

I took the neoprene suit, which looked far too small, and held it up against my torso. It had short sleeves and legs that went to mid-thigh. "Seriously? You want me to wear this?" With my curves compressed inside it, I would resemble a sausage.

"It will help keep you alive in cold water, should we sink," Madison said. She tossed shoes and gloves made from similar materials out of the bag. "Booties and gloves."

"We're going to look so good, uh-huh." I rolled my eyes.

"Don't worry," Grammie said. "No one will see it under the life jacket."

"True," I said. "Uh-oh. Do we have life jackets? And what about paddles?"

"All taken care of. They're in my car." Madison took back my outfit and put it in the duffle, then stowed it in the corner. She went over to check the catboat, making sure the paint was dry and the seams were intact. "The boat is looking good."

I had a sudden thought. "How are we getting the boat down to the harbor?" Neither of our vehicles was large enough. And I couldn't see us carrying it through the streets, one on each end.

"On it," she said with a grin. "Ian is coming to get it later with his pickup truck."

"Good call." My heart skipped a beat at hearing Ian's name. We had plans after the race to attend a clambake and listen to music. It would be the first opportunity I'd had to attend the festival. I'd basically been consumed with Hailey's death and helping Eleanor, both of which were priorities, of course. But maybe it wouldn't hurt to take a night off with my guy and eat some lobster.

A customer in the main room was looking around for help, so I excused myself and went to assist her. She ended up buying three sets of sheets from Shorehaven for gifts and a martini-themed hostess apron for herself. As I rang up her sale, she asked, "Do you sell that apron you're wearing?" She put the glasses on a chain around her neck on her nose and took a closer look.

She was referring to the white pinafore we wore as a shop uniform. Grammie and I had designed and sewn them. "I haven't yet," I said. "But if you're interested, I can do a custom order." I hadn't before, but custom work might be a nice addition to what we offered. Exactly when I would have time to sew, I had no idea.

"I would really like that," she said. "I have three granddaughters who would look darling in them. Maybe you could embroider their names? Ava, Aria, and Anna."

"Oh, what cute names. We certainly could. If you give me your contact information, I'll send you a quote. I'll need their sizes."

"Wonderful," she said, writing her name, e-mail address, and the girls' sizes on an order form I handed her. Two, four, and six. How cute. "I would like them for Christmas, so no big rush."

"Perfect." I should have time to sew three small aprons before then. Maybe after fall foliage ended and visitor traffic died down—until ski season. The so-called shoulder seasons of late fall and early spring in Maine seemed to be getting shorter every year. More and more people were visiting year-round.

A couple of minutes later, the customer left with a big smile on her face and a promise to return. "I really love our business," I said to Grammie. "It's so much fun to make people happy." Especially since we were sharing our passion for beautiful aprons and linens.

"I feel the same way," Grammie said. She showed me the impressive tally of sales for the morning. She winked at me. "They seem to be very happy indeed."

The front door burst open and Sophie bustled in, holding a huge paper bag, Lukas on her heels. He reached out to stop the door from shutting to allow Bella, who was behind him, to enter.

"Bella." I swooped her into a hug, inhaling her light but sophisticated perfume. "I didn't expect to see you today."

She laughed. "I managed to sneak out for a bit. My new employee is working out really well, I'm happy to report."

Sophie made a face of mock hurt. "I don't get any sugar?"

"Of course you do." Her arms were full so I hugged the whole package. "I'm so lucky, I get to see you twice today."

"Three times," she said with a laugh. "I'll be cheering you on later, during the race."

"Oh no." I put a hand to my head. "Is everyone I know going to be watching?"

"Yes," Grammie and my friends said in unison.

Lukas looked confused, so while Sophie set down the bag in the side room and began unpacking our lunch, Madison showed him the boat, with Quincy's help.

"I can see you were the inspiration," Lukas told Quincy, bending to give him a chin rub. "Good job."

"Yeah, he helped all right," I said, exchanging a smiling glance with Madison. "We had paint paw prints all over the store." I put out a stack of paper bowls, forks, and napkins next to the colorful and tempting platter of tuna, green beans, hard-boiled eggs, tomatoes, olives, greens, and potatoes. The dressing was a mustard and herb–infused oil and vinegar. A pan of fluffy homemade dinner rolls and local butter rounded out the meal.

Grammie added tall pitchers of iced tea and water to the table, and we lined up to fill our bowls and tall cups. Then we sat around the long table and dug in, with Grammie and me keeping an eye out for customers. Fortunately we were in one of those inexplicable lulls in foot traffic and were able to eat without interruption.

I chased the last bite of tuna around my bowl. "So, tell us what you found out about Claudia, Lukas. We're dying to hear."

Before replying, he finished chewing and dabbed his mouth with a napkin. "That salad was so good. Thank you, Sophie." He balled up the napkin in his fist as he said, "I've got good news and bad news." As we all continued to stare at him, he shifted in his seat and said, "Claudia de Witte was from a noble and wealthy family, well established in Antwerp for generations. She was engaged to marry Baron Xavier Delberke."

Madison slapped her hand on the table. "Sounds like good news to me. Well, except for the engagement. Wonder what the story is there."

Claudia's ownership of couture clothing and expensive jewelry now made sense. She came from a wealthy family. But why had she kept her past hidden? Why had she worked as a nursemaid, one of the lowest rungs on the domestic worker ladder? In fact, why was she employed at all?

Grammie said slowly, "So what's the bad news, Lukas? Was she running away from her fiancé?"

He pressed his lips together, then sighed deeply, as though working up to what he had to say. "No, it's worse. Claudia's father, Baron Adrien de Witte, was killed during a robbery. In 1932, the same year Claudia left Antwerp."

Left or fled? Were the diamonds Claudia hid stolen? Did she have anything to do with her father's death? My delicious lunch now sat heavy in my stomach. Putting a hand on my belly, I groaned. "I can't tell Eleanor about this. Please don't make me."

The uneasy silence that fell over the table told me no one else wanted to volunteer to break the news.

"I think we need to keep digging before we say anything," Grammie said. "Maybe it's a coincidence. We don't even know if Claudia was in the country when her father died."

I felt a spark of hope. "Good point, Grammie. Lukas, do you know the actual date Baron de Witte was killed?"

"Let me double check." Lukas pulled out his phone and scrolled through. "May first, 1932. According to the newspaper article, the butler found Baron de Witte suffering a head injury in his library. His safe was standing open and empty." He looked up at us. "Baron de Witte was involved in the diamond trade. But there aren't good records of what he was keeping in the safe."

Diamonds. Like the ones from Claudia's necklace. "Where do we go from here?" I asked. "How can we find out when she arrived? We don't even know which ship she was on." I thought of the trunk, which didn't even boast a shipping label.

"I have some ideas," Grammie said. "Some friends of mine have been tracing their ancestors through the Ellis Island website. They told me that some manifests from ocean liners are also online now."

"Maybe we can find her name on one of the lists," Madison said. "At least we have the year to work with."

Madison's optimism eased my fears of reaching a dead end. I was usually the one gnawing at sources like a dog with a bone, but the stakes in garment history were usually pretty low. Learning the truth about Claudia was far more important. I just hoped we'd be happy with the answers.

CHAPTER 15

A couple more feet. Come on, come on." Dr. Horatio Morris, Madison's father, gestured as Ian backed his truck down the boat ramp. He put a hand up. "Halt. You're there."

As the tall, lean physician hurried to help Ian unload our boat, I glanced around at the chaotic scene. Onlookers and other paddlers milled about, preparing for the start of the cardboard boat race under the direction of someone using a bullhorn. The creative boat designs included a dragon, a Viking ship, a race car, and a big yellow duck.

"This is fun," Dr. Zadie Morris said into my ear. "I'll be rooting for you and Madison." Although not as tall as her husband and daughter, Zadie was also trim and athletic. She wore the standard summer uniform of Capri pants, T-shirt, cotton sweater tied around her shoulders, and sandals on her feet.

"Thanks. Madison is hoping we win the grand prize." I rolled my eyes. "Fat chance. I'll be happy to make it across the harbor without swimming for it." The thick life jacket was biting into my waist, so I pulled it into a better position. The wet suit wasn't too uncomfortable, though, despite my fight to tug it on. An hour later, I had almost gotten used to wearing something resembling a rubber swimsuit from the 1920s.

"That's it," Madison said, directing her dad and Ian as they carried the boat to our spot in the lineup. "Put it right here." They set the boat gently onto the cement ramp, the bow in the water. Once the race started, we'd push off and climb inside—volunteer pushers would give us a boost to send us on our way.

"Is that an apron you used for a sail?" Zadie asked, lifting her sunglasses for a better look. "The whole thing is very clever. A real catboat." She turned to smile at Grammie, who was coming to join us.

"The design was all Madison," I said. "And the apron is to promote the store." We'd painted S.S. RUFFLES & BOWS across the stern (even though we were using human power, not steam). The thought of steamships made me think of Claudia again. I planned to start researching tomorrow. Right now I had to survive a boat race.

Ian came up beside me and gave me a kiss on the lips. "Good luck, babe. I'll be waiting with a couple of cold ones after."

"Awesome. I'm looking forward to the clambake." Down on the rocky beach, people were already tending the seaweed-heaped underground pits holding lobsters, clams, and corn on the cob.

"You look cute, by the way," he said, pushing back a strand of my hair. His arm was warm around my (very corseted) waist.

"Thanks." I snickered, plucking at the skintight neoprene. "I hope I can get it off later. It's welded to my body."

"All right, teams," bellowed the man with the bullhorn. "Are you ready?"

Paddles in hand, the teams gathered around their boats. Grammie and Zadie retreated to stand with other spectators while Horatio and Ian prepared to push us.

Both wore shorts and water shoes so they could wade in up to their knees.

"Three . . . two . . . one . . . GO!" the caller yelled.

Gripping the side of the boat, I stepped into the water, the icy temps immediately freezing my calves. But my toes were still warm in the booties. Amazing.

"Get in," Madison called, holding the boat steady.

I more or less fell in, almost braining myself with my paddle, then struggled to a seated position and crossed my legs. Ian and Horatio held the boat for Madison to climb inside, in the back. As the more experienced paddler, she was going to steer us.

With a mighty shove from our pushers, we glided out into deeper water. So far, so good. No leaks.

"Paddle," Madison said. "On the left."

I dug the paddle in, working feverishly to move us toward a course marked by yellow buoys. We had to weave our way through them and then across the harbor to another landing.

Shouts and screams erupted to my right and I looked over to see a boat taking on water and sinking, forcing half a dozen people to drop into the water. Worse, they were blocking other boats right behind them, almost like a traffic jam.

"Bummer," Madison said. "They must have had too many people."

"I hope that was it," I said, still not confident that the cardboard boats would hold up long. To check how far we'd gone, I glanced back at the shore. From his position next to Grammie, Zadie, and Horatio, Ian waved. I waved back by lifting my paddle. A short distance from Ian, a figure in a blue windbreaker was snapping pictures of the scene. When he lowered the camera, I saw it was Theo. He started weaving through the crowd, headed toward the other side of the harbor. He probably wanted to take pictures of the winners, I figured.

"Paddle on the right," Madison called. We were on a collision course with another boat, and with laughter and deft movements of our paddles, disaster was averted.

Now, finally working together in a rhythm, we circled the first of the buoys. "One more down," Madison said, as behind us another boat floundered, the crew unable to coordinate their movements. Then they started laughing, which made them even more helpless.

"Yahoo!" I called when we deftly whipped around the next buoy, bringing us into the lead. I glanced at the shore to see if Ian noticed. He did, giving us a two-handed victory shake. Then I saw Theo, strolling along a deserted dock—and a figure in a black hoodie right behind him, walking with hood up and head down. What was that about?

"Look out, Iris!" Madison called. We were about ready to hit the next buoy.

"Sorry," I called back, paddling furiously to correct. "I got distracted."

We finally made it through the gauntlet of buoys and were on our way across a stretch of clear water to the landing area. People were gradually filtering over there, eager to see who would win the race. I looked for Theo but didn't see him. But the person who had been following him was now heading swiftly up the dock toward Main Street. How strange. I hoped Theo was all right.

A cold trickle of water brought my attention forcibly back to the boat. With a thrill of alarm, I noticed a trail of water seeping in from the front corner. In fact, I was now sitting in a puddle. I would have noticed sooner but the wetsuit had insulated my rear. "Madison. I think we've got a leak."

"No way," she scoffed. "We taped this boat up good."

With a chuckling gurgle, water started coming in on my left. "Uh-oh. We just got another leak."

Madison made a disgusted sound. "You're right. It's coming in back here now."

I started paddling faster, hoping we could make land before the boat took on too much water. But the trickle soon became a stream of ice-cold salt water, and right in front of my eyes, the pieces of the boat started to come apart. "We're not going to make it, Madison."

"I see that. Help!" she shouted, waving her paddle. "We're going under."

I copied her, waving my arms. On shore, people starting pointing and talking to each other. Ian put both hands around his mouth to yell, "Hang on! Help is coming."

The water was lapping around my waist. It felt like sitting in a cold bathtub. But oddly enough, I wasn't freezing cold. The wetsuit must be helping.

A motorboat engine started over by the docks and soon a skiff nosed out into the harbor. I recognized Jake's red brush cut at the helm. "Yay, Jake is coming to save us." He buzzed toward us, not too fast since he didn't want to make a wake and swamp the other boats, which had passed us. It was every team for itself out here in the dog-eat-dog world of cardboard boat racing.

Jake's engine throttled down as he came alongside us. With his help, we managed to climb into his boat. In my case, it was more like rolling over the gunwale and plopping inside like a beached porpoise. The cardboard boat came into the real boat with us. We couldn't leave it in the water, like floating garbage. I held the mast with the apron still attached, now a flag of surrender.

"I don't understand why it fell apart," Madison said as the boat hummed back to the docks. "I built it just like they said." Judging by what Madison told me, many videos had gone into the building of that boat.

"Me neither." I shifted to a more comfortable position, the water inside my suit squishing about. I couldn't wait to change. Dry clothing would feel heavenly.

As we approached the shore, the crowd began to cheer and clap. To ham it up, I waved our apron flag. "The mariners return," I called. "Saved from the deep." More cheering greeted my cry. I waved the mast again and grinned, thinking we might make it into the newspaper. They always printed two pages of shots from the festival, plus more on their social media pages. Cameras clicked away and I spotted Lars in the crowd, but I didn't see Theo anywhere, which was surprising since he'd seemed to have his camera at the ready.

Ian moved toward the shore, ready to help us disembark. "What a disaster," he said, gripping the bow of Jake's boat and tugging it onto the shore. "You were doing so well."

"Don't remind me," Madison said with a groan as she jumped out of the boat into the water. "That spa day was within our reach. But now it's been snatched away."

Grammie and Madison's parents hurried up. "My heart was in my mouth," Grammie said. She gave us both a hug, careful not to touch our soaked lower bodies.

"I could tell the boat was sinking," Zadie said, also embracing us. "I was worried hypothermia would set in and you would drown."

"That's why they were wearing wet suits and life jackets, dear," Horatio said. "Plus there was a harbor full of boats ready to come to the rescue." He nodded at Jake. "Like the gallant Jake."

"True," Zadie said. "But a mother is always going to worry." She put a hand on Madison's shoulder. "Is there anything I can do for you right now?"

"No, Mom, we're fine," Madison said, shaking her head. "I'll see you at the clambake in half an hour or so."

Grammie gave me another squeeze. "See you there, Iris."

I kissed her cheek. "Sure thing, Gram. Save me a few clams." We both adored fresh Maine clams.

"What do you want to do with the cardboard?" Jake asked after Grammie and the Morrises walked away. "I can drop it off in a dumpster."

"Nice of you to offer, Jake, but it's our mess and we'll take care of it," Madison said. She grabbed one end, and indicated for me to take the other. Ian stepped into the water to support the sagging middle, and the three of us awkwardly conveyed the whole shebang to dry land.

"Thanks for saving us," I said to Jake. Gosh, he was cute with his freckles and wide smile crinkling his eyes. How could I get him back together with Sophie?

"Any time, ladies, any time," he said with a dip of his head. "Want to give me a push?" he asked Ian, who gave the skiff a mighty shove, sending it out into deep enough water to start the engine.

After Jake roared away, Madison and I stared at the heap of soggy paper that had been our prize-winning dream. Wanting to better understand what had gone wrong, I bent down and examined the front corner. Hmm. That was odd. "Did you put another piece of tape on the seams?" I showed her the spot, where a second piece of tape was curling away from the one underneath. It looked different than the roll I remembered using, actually. It wasn't as wide and the color was slightly different.

Madison frowned. "No. We only put on one layer of tape. I don't know where that came from."

I pulled off a piece. "Look. It's definitely different.

Not as wide." But the color was a close match, which was why we hadn't noticed it.

Our eyes locked and I could tell by Madison's expression she was thinking the same thing I was. But it was Ian who spoke. "Someone messed with your boat," he said, his eyes flashing with anger. "They wanted you to sink."

CHAPTER 16

Said aloud, his statement staggered me, in fact it literally made me unsteady on my feet for a moment. Who would do such a thing? And why? "It was a warning," I whispered. Had to be. Someone wanted us to stop poking into Claudia's past or Hailey's death. I couldn't picture the other contestants bothering to sabotage a competitor. The prizes weren't that great, though the spa day was pretty cool.

I inhaled deeply, grateful to be on dry land. Despite the unpleasant experience of getting dunked in cold water, we had been in full view of the shore at all times. Wet suits and life jackets meant the chance of drowning had been pretty slight. But not impossible, I reminded myself. What if one of us had panicked?

Madison's brows knit together as she glanced at the people standing nearby. Stepping closer to us, she lowered her voice. "The boat was fine when it left the shop. How and when did someone get to it?"

Ian rubbed his chin. "Must have been while it was in the back of my truck." He gestured toward the waterfront park. "The public lots were full so I had to park down behind the library. Near the dumpster."

I knew the spot, having used it myself when I couldn't find a place. A thick screen of bushes hid the dumpster from view. But obviously someone had seen him drive down there and then had taken advantage of the opportunity to tamper with our boat.

A cold sensation trickled down my spine—and it wasn't water. What would they do next? Something worse? I gritted my teeth, warmed by a flare of anger at the idea of someone hurting my friend. *Try and stop us*, I mentally told the perpetrator. We certainly weren't going to quit investigating now. This was war.

Madison nudged the ruined boat with her toe. "Ian, can you bring your truck around and load this up? I want to take a closer look after it dries out."

"Sure thing," Ian said. "Where do you want me to take it?"

I thought of returning the boat to the store but I didn't want the wet mess cluttering up the side room. "How about my barn? I'll ride over to the house with you and get changed there." Home would be a more comfortable place to wrestle out of the wetsuit than the public changing room.

While Ian trotted off to get the truck, the contestants who had completed the race started paddling back to the launch point, where the prizes were going to be announced. The crowd began to thin as spectators started drifting away.

I remembered Theo with a jolt. Where was he? He hadn't come over to the landing to watch the end of the race. "Have you seen Theo?" I asked Madison. "I thought for sure we would."

She gave me a funny look. "No. Why are you asking?"

"I noticed him over at the launch, taking pictures. Then he walked in this direction, but went out onto that dock." I pointed. "Someone wearing a hoodie was following him." Who wore a hoodie on a warm day like this, anyway? The same person who ruined our boat? "Something happened to him, I just know it." My last words rose to almost a shout, and several people glanced my way in curiosity.

Madison sent me a concerned look. "Settle down, Iris. I'm sure he's fine." When she saw my mouth open in protest, she added, "Okay, we'll go look for him."

"I'll go," I said. "Someone needs to wait here with our boat for Ian to get back." I eyed the pile of cardboard ruefully. "Or what's left of it." If we left it unattended, someone would probably throw it away.

Madison chewed her bottom lip. "All right. But if you're not back in ten, we're gonna come looking for you." They'd have to. We didn't bring our phones onto the boat, for fear they'd get wet. Mine was in my bag, in the rear of Madison's Mini.

I began backing up, raising a thumb in victory. "So you agree with me. Something might be wrong." When she nodded, I turned and began to trot, my booties squishing with every step. The wet suit was generally not suitable for running—too tight and it chafed my legs. But I race-walked as fast as I could, along the landing and then down the dock where I'd seen Theo.

We were at the working end of the harbor, and fishing boats and other commercial craft lined this dock, rocking gently at anchor. The wide dock also held barrels and boxes and other large items that blocked my view. My stomach clenched as I checked every boat, object, and even the water around the boats for a sign of the teaching assistant. What if he'd fallen in and no one heard his cries for help? Or what if he was crushed between the dock and the hull of a boat? Dangers were everywhere on the waterfront, especially for the inexperienced and unwary.

I was almost at the end when I saw him, sitting up with

his back toward me. My heart leaped, the relief making me weak in the knees. I wasn't going to find another dead body, not today anyway.

My booties slapped as I ran the rest of the way. "Theo. You're okay."

With one hand pressed to the back of his head, he turned to look at me. "Sort of. Someone hit me." He gestured with his other hand. "And stole my camera."

His camera. Was it the target of an opportunistic thief? Or did someone believe he had incriminating photos on the card, namely to do with Hailey's death?

I gently moved his hand away. "Let me take a look." The skin was barely broken but he had quite a lump. "You need to get checked out. Let me have your phone." I held out my hand for it, then realized. "They didn't take that too, did they?"

He shook his head then winced. "No. Just the camera." He felt around in his jacket pocket and pulled out his phone.

I touched the screen and it lit up. When I saw the screen background, I almost dropped it and had to move my hands fast to save it. Hailey and Theo, heads together, both grinning. "Okay," I said, hoping he hadn't noticed me fumbling with his expensive device. "What's your password?" He told me and I called 911 for an ambulance and the police.

While I did this, Theo sat with slumped shoulders, as though relieved someone was taking charge. After I hung up, I hesitated a second and called Ian. He and Madison needed to know what was up. "Hello?" he answered, wary.

"It's me," I said. "I had to borrow a phone. Mine's in the car."

"Where are you, babe?" he asked. "I'm just pulling down to the ramp and I only see Madison."

I filled him in quickly. "Why don't you two drive up and park at the head of the dock? The police should be here any minute." A siren wailed in duplicate—in my ears and through the phone, on Ian's end. "Here they come."

Moments later, the dock shook as medical personnel and officers thundered to the rescue. I was glad to see Anton in the lead. "What do we have here?" he asked when the group reached us.

"Theo has a head injury," I said. "Someone hit him on the back of the head and stole his camera."

Anton gave an order to the EMTs, who began to check Theo over, taking his blood pressure and examining his injury. "Did you lose consciousness?" one asked.

"Maybe for a minute," Theo said. "I don't really know. I was trying to take a picture when, *wham*, the next thing I know I'm down on the dock."

"Did you see who did it?" Anton asked. At Theo's response, he pressed his lips together in exasperation.

"I saw someone," I said. "That's why I'm here. I was worried about Theo."

Anton took my elbow and moved me aside. Rhonda joined us. "Can you give us a description, Iris?"

I shook my head. "Not really. The person was wearing a black hoodie." I explained how I'd seen Theo on the shore and noticed the person walking behind him. "It didn't look right to me. So when he didn't show up at the landing, I came looking for him."

The chief glanced at the teaching assistant, who was answering questions for the EMTs. "Good thing you followed your instincts." His gaze roamed over my outfit. "Where did you see all this from?"

"I was in the cardboard boat race," I said. "But Madison and I sank."

"Madison?" Anton's eyes lit with a fervor I'd seen there before. "Is she okay?" Rhonda rolled her eyes, then winked at me. She'd noticed his interest in my best friend as well.

"She's fine. In fact, here she comes." Madison and Ian were walking down the dock. "We want to talk to you later. We think someone sabotaged our boat."

Anton had half turned and was watching Madison. "We can do that." He gave her a wave and started up the dock.

Rhonda and I looked at each other and smiled. "Is there anything else you can tell us?" she asked me.

I looked at Theo, who was laughing at something one of the EMTs said. It looked like he was going to be fine, thankfully. "Not really," I told Rhonda, hoping I could leave. I was starting to get clammy and cold and was dying to change my clothes. "They left Theo's phone, so I wonder if they were targeting just the camera. For the pictures Theo might have taken."

She got it. "You mean related to Miss Piper's death? I'll make sure to mention that to the chief." She nodded at me. "You're free to go."

After saying goodbye to Theo and promising to check in for an update later, I hurried up the dock. "Ian," I said. "We can leave." Anton had rejoined his team but Madison was standing stock-still on the dock, a bemused expression on her face. "What's up, Mads? Ready to head out?"

She shook herself. "Sure am." She gestured up the dock. "After you."

On the way to Ian's truck, I gave them the update about Theo. Then we rode together to the public parking lot, where I retrieved my tote from Madison's car and made a plan to meet up at the clambake in an hour.

I could tell there was something on Madison's mind but I didn't want to question her in front of Ian. I'd wait until we were alone.

Much longer than an hour later, Ian and I strolled hand in hand through the festival, on our way to join our friends. At my house, we'd taken advantage of the opportunity to hang out and talk and, yes, smooch a little. The porch swing is perfect for that, by the way.

"You're late," Madison said with a smirk as we strolled up to the picnic table where she was sitting with Grammie, Sophie, Bella, and Bella's children. She held up an envelope, flipping it back and forth. "Guess what? We won a prize."

"For what?" I said hello to the others and smiled at the kids, who were eating hot dogs and French fries. "We didn't even finish."

"For most creative," Madison handed me the envelope. "Here. You do the honors since our boat was inspired by your cat." She scooted down the bench to allow us to sit down.

"Plus using that darling apron as a sail?" Bella put in. "A real stroke of genius."

"Why, thank you," I said with a little bow before sliding onto the bench. "I impressed myself when I came up with it."

"Why don't I go get us something to drink?" Ian suggested, remaining standing. "I take it the clambake isn't quite ready?"

Sophie patted her stomach. "Ten minutes, they said. I can't wait. It smells so good." She was right. The aroma of steaming lobster and clams drifted our way from the nearby pits and my own belly gave an excited rumble in response.

"Clams? Yuck." Connor, Bella's eleven-year-old, wrinkled his nose. "They're disgusting." He chomped on a fry, starting at one end and feeding it into his mouth.

His sister, Alice, twelve, made a face. "Eww. I hate slimy food."

"That's why you're having hot dogs," Bella said. "I don't have the money to waste on lobster for you two."

As Ian headed off to the drinks table for two lemonades, I ripped open the envelope. "This must be something good, right? I mean, most creative is really special." A slip of paper fell out of the envelope. I unfolded it and read, "'Good for one oil change and tire rotation.'" I threw the paper down. "Seriously? This has to be the worst prize I've ever won." Not that I've won many. I'm not lucky that way.

The others groaned in support. Madison picked the paper up and read it front and back, in case I had missed something. Nope. "We can split it. What do you want? Oil change or rotation?"

I started laughing. "Wow. I need to think about that for a while. That's a big decision." Madison laughed too, and I knew we wouldn't forget this incident for a while. We have a lot of stories like that, fun to reminisce about and laugh over.

By the time we returned to the table with full trays holding lobster, clams, corn, and potatoes, Madison's parents had arrived. So had Lukas and Ruben. Seeing them hovering with full trays looking for a place to sit, Sophie waved them over. "I hope you don't mind," she said to us.

I shook my head, my mouth already full of sweet, tender lobster drenched in butter. No one else objected, so the professors sat down at the end, next to Zadie and Horatio.

Next to me, Ian cracked a claw, sending lobster juice

splattering. "You're dangerous with that nutcracker," I joked. "Good thing I'm wearing a bib."

"Speaking of bibs," Bella said. "Are you getting many entries for the contest?" She dipped a plump clam into butter and popped it into her mouth. Her children nudged each other and made faces. "Go on, you two. Go play." A group of their friends was running around on the grass nearby, shrieking and laughing.

"I have about six or seven entries so far," I said. "Some of them are real doozies, I can tell you that."

"We're getting a real kick out of it," Grammie said with a grin. "Each one is stranger than the next." She perused her serving of steamed clams, pouncing on an overlooked morsel hiding in its shell.

"Like the guy who wants electricity," I said. I gave them a rundown of the entrants, then said, "I can't wait to see what they come up with on the actual day."

"Neither can I," Ian said. "Sounds fun." He extracted meat from his second claw and added it to a bowl of melted butter.

"Is that how you eat a lobster?" I asked. "Pick everything out first?" I couldn't wait that long. I'd already gobbled my claws and I was now onto the tail, which had the most meat.

"Yep." Ian used his pick to press lobster meat into butter to marinate, then gathered up the empty shells and tossed them into a bucket placed nearby for that purpose. "Do all the work and then enjoy."

"I bet you ration out your Halloween candy, too," Madison said. A trace of butter made her cheeks shine. At my gesture, she grabbed a napkin and dabbed her face.

Ian laughed. "You're right. Well, I used to. My mother would throw out the leftovers every Easter, when I got fresh candy."

I leaned against his shoulder for a second. "I guess opposites attract." But eating habits aside, we were actually quite similar. Both of us were entrepreneurial, worked hard, and loved our families and friends.

A contented silence fell over the table while we worked on our dinners. I was torn between absolutely stuffing myself and eating lightly so I could dance rather than waddle. I compromised by not eating my potato and corn. Why did they bother to serve those anyway? One whole lobster and a heaping serving of steamed clams were filling enough.

I caught snatches of conversation from down the table. "It's a very innovative technology," Ruben was saying to Horatio and Zadie. "The fuel of the future." He didn't waste any time, did he? As well-off and established physicians, I'm sure they seemed like attractive prospects for investing in his seaweed biofuel company.

As Horatio leaned across the table and asked a question, the band struck up the first song. The children on the grass began to dance, some of them adding in gymnastic moves like somersaults and handstands.

"Ready to shake a leg?" Ian asked me, wiping his fingers with a moist toilette.

I leaned back to give my belly more room. "In a few. I need to let everything settle." Across the table, Sophie stiffened, then ducked her head, pretending great interest in the remains of her dinner.

"Hey, Jake," Madison called with a wave. "Thanks again for saving us today."

"Glad to do it." The lobsterman detoured to our table, looking absolutely scrumptious in faded jeans and a pale green button-down rolled to the elbows. He smiled around at all of us, his eyes lingering on Sophie, who still had her head down.

Come on, Sophie, I urged silently. *Snap out of it. This*

isn't junior high. I guess my mental-telepathy transmitter wasn't working very well because she didn't budge. She didn't even look up.

Gretchen Stolte, an attractive divorced transplant to town, got up from the next table, waving her armful of bangle bracelets to get our attention. She pointed at Jake and the dance floor in front of the band, moving her hips and pumping her fists to mimic dancing, long tawny hair swinging.

Jake studied Sophie's bent head for a long moment before give a shrug. "I guess I'm being paged. See ya." He loped off to join Gretchen and, chatting and laughing, the pair made their way through the tables toward the band.

Bella muttered an Italian swear word under her breath. "That woman. First my ex-husband and now Jake?" She gave Sophie a sharp look. "I'd go cut in if I were you."

Sophie's headshake was furious, her cheeks flaming with humiliation and suppressed anger. She leaned back in her seat and called, "Lukas? Hey, Lukas." When he turned her way, she asked, "Want to go dance?"

He scrambled out of the bench seat, excusing himself to Zadie, who he bumped with his leg. By the time he reached Sophie, she was waiting, and arm in arm, they headed off.

"This is so not good," Madison said, watching them go.

"Certainly not what I was hoping for," I said. To the rest of us, it was obvious Sophie and Jake belonged together. Would they figure that out themselves before it was too late? I sure hoped so.

CHAPTER 17

When I arrived home just before midnight, all the lights were on, which meant Grammie was still up. Good. I could use a grandmother fix.

"Iris?" she called from the dining room when I entered the kitchen. "How was the dance?" She'd left the clambake right after dessert, planning to stop by an old friend's house.

"It was fun. For the most part." I stood in the dining room doorway, looking at yards of white cotton fabric laid out on the table, pattern pieces pinned every which way. "What are you making?"

Grammie's shears flashed when she picked them up. "I wasn't sleepy so I thought I'd get a start on those little girls' aprons." The scissors cut cleanly through the cloth with a satisfying snip. "We can make two of each size and display the duplicates in the shop. Maybe we'll get some more orders that way."

"Great idea. Totally brilliant as always." I swooped in to give her a kiss on the cheek. "We can stitch them up in the side room at the store, you know." I was trying to get us used to the idea of working at the shop after years of sewing at home.

Grammie's brows rose. "Sure we can, when there isn't

a cardboard boat cluttering up the room." Her smile was teasing.

"Oh, what a disaster that turned out to be." I groaned at the memory of the race—and the discovery that some-one had sabotaged our darling catboat. "Want some hot cocoa? And are there any peanut butter cookies left?" After several hours of dancing, I was actually hungry again.

"Yes to both. Let me do a little more cutting and I'll come join you."

Hearing me clatter around in the kitchen, Quincy came to greet me with a stretch and a yawn. Of course he went right to his dish. "Seriously, Quince. Eating at this time of night?" He sat and stared at me as though saying, "You can do it, why can't I?" As always, I caved and gave him a spoonful of wet food and a few more nuggets of kibble.

I made hot chocolate the old-fashioned way, with cocoa and milk and real vanilla stirred slowly on the stovetop. After filling two mugs with the steaming brew, I put four cookies on a plate. "Cocoa's ready," I called.

Grammie left her cutting and slid onto the adjacent stool. "Thanks, dear." She picked up the mug and in-haled. "Such a comforting drink."

"It is." I sipped my cocoa, then asked, "How was your visit?" I picked up a cookie and bit into it, enjoying how well peanut butter went with chocolate. A match made in heaven.

"Wonderful. She loved the chowder I brought her. And we chatted for hours." Grammie touched her face with a laugh. "My jaw practically aches from all the gabbing." She slid a curious glance my way. "What did you mean when you said the dance was *mostly* fun?"

I told her about the scene between Jake and Sophie and

how, the rest of the night, the pair had pretended the other didn't exist. "It was almost ludicrous," I said. "I think the whole world could see that they were totally fixated on each other." Even the usually tenacious Gretchen had gotten the message and turned her attention to Ruben.

Grammie chuckled. "They'll be back together before fall, mark my words." She broke off a piece of cookie. "What I can't figure out is why your boat fell apart. I saw how hard you two worked with the glue and tape."

"That's right," I said. "You don't know what we discovered later." Where should I begin? And how much should I tell her? Although I didn't want to worry her unnecessarily, I had to mention the sabotage before she heard about it from someone else. And fill her in about Theo. She didn't know about that incident either, since she'd left the landing before I went to look for him. "Well, Grammie. Get comfortable. I've got a lot to tell you."

She listened, only asking a question or two, and when I was done, I waited for her final verdict. "Follow your instincts, Iris," she said. "I'd love to brush off the boat as a prank and Theo's mugging as unrelated to anything, but I can't do that."

"Me, neither," I said glumly. "I really hope the police crack the case soon." I attempted a smile. "I practically have Anton on speed dial."

"Perfect," Grammie said. "Anton's sharp. And he's going to solve this, I have no doubt." She stared into her mug, her expression pensive. "I can't stop thinking about Hailey. I remember when her parents died, what a loss that was to the community. They were good people. Poor Hailey was left alone to fend for herself. But sadly, from what you told me about her and Theo, it seems she went down some dark paths."

"Unfortunately, yes. She wasn't above taking an unfair advantage." And was that why someone had killed her? Or was there another motive we hadn't discovered yet?

Grammie went to bed soon after, but I was kind of wired from chocolate and sugar. I even washed the cups and pan by hand, dried them, and put them away, I was so full of energy. Normally I would have left them until morning.

Thinking that reading might help me relax, I wandered into the living room to find a magazine. Before I got started, my gaze fell on Claudia's trunk, which stood empty near the fireplace. We'd carefully wrapped the couture clothing in acid-free tissue paper and muslin, then placed the pieces in archival garment boxes. Amazingly the clothes were in excellent condition despite being stored in an attic for almost one hundred winters and summers.

But disappointingly, there had been nothing on or in the trunk to indicate that Claudia owned it or how she had traveled to the United States. But maybe I should take another look, just in case.

With Quincy looking on, I sat on the carpet and lifted the lid of the old trunk, which was lined with faded, fragile cloth. The arched top had a couple of pull-down compartments to explore. Empty. Next I pulled out the tray and set it to one side, taking a look in the main part of the trunk. There were a few fabric pockets along the walls, and I explored those with my fingers. Nothing, not even a stray bobby pin.

But in back, behind one pocket, I felt something inside the liner, where it had ripped. Working carefully so as not to cause further damage, I teased it out with my fingertips.

A postcard showing an ocean liner called the T.S.S. *Lapland*, part of the Red Star Line. I flipped it over. On the back was printed To NEW YORK AND CANADA.

Excitement hummed in my veins as I placed the card

on the carpet and reached for my cell phone. If the *Lapland* ran between Antwerp and New York, then it might well be the boat Claudia traveled on during her journey.

In less than a minute, I confirmed that the *Lapland* did indeed traverse that route, with the last voyage departing on April 29, 1932. After that, the boat sailed between London and the Mediterranean. My nerves knotted with anxious hope. If we could prove that Claudia had been on that boat or one before it, her innocence would be confirmed. At least we now had a place to start.

The next morning, I wandered out to the barn with my coffee to check on the cardboard boat. I set the mug in the grass while I unlocked the door and pushed it open, the wheels at the top squealing. Then after retrieving my cup, Quincy and I ventured inside, which still held the pleasant scents of long-departed livestock and hay.

Ian and I had draped the cardboard over sawhorses so it would dry as best it could. I touched a corner with my hand. Still damp, but better than yesterday. Of special interest was the corner in my compartment where the water had first entered, so I circled around to that spot.

Tires crunched on the gravel, and through the open door I saw Madison's Mini pull up. "Hey, lady," she called when she got out, holding a car cup. "I got your text."

"Perfect timing." I gestured for her to join me. We studied the seams of the boat in that spot and several others, coming to the same conclusion as the day before.

Someone had sliced the seams and tried to hide it with new pieces of tape. Now that the boat was drier, you could plainly see the slit in the original tape.

"Wow." I shook my head in disbelief. "What a nasty thing to do."

Madison bit her lower lip, a look of thunder in her eyes.

She pulled out her phone and punched in a number. "We are definitely reporting this. You could have drowned."

So could she, but I appreciated the sentiment, which echoed mine. *Don't mess with my people.*

"Hey, Anton," she said, a very informal greeting for our illustrious chief, I noted with amusement. "Can you swing by Iris's house? We've got something to show you. Related to the boat race yesterday." She disconnected. "He's on patrol so he'll be right here."

I didn't see Anton yesterday at the race, I realized. Or at the clambake. He'd only appeared briefly when I'd had to call 911 for Theo. No doubt he'd been busy working on the homicide case. Whenever a big case occurred in this small town, our officers often had to cover double shifts. In any event, he must have been nearby, because within five minutes, the Blueberry Cove police SUV was wheeling up the drive.

Madison tensed beside me when Anton got out and looked around. He wasn't terribly tall but he was extremely buff. He had the type of rugged features that looked good with a military haircut.

He glanced toward the barn and I knew the moment their eyes met. Seriously, I saw electricity crackling between them as a sultry Barry White song played. Hoo-boy. His gaze never left her face as he strode toward us, duty belt clanking.

"Good morning," he said as he entered the barn. He took in the cardboard sprawled over the sawhorses. "This it?"

The spell broke and we started talking, both of us explaining the situation in turn. He got the picture right away, his features grim when he saw the cuts in the cardboard. "Any idea who could have done this?"

"No," I said. "It must have happened when Ian was parked behind the library. Before that, it was at the store."

Quincy leaped up and landed right in middle of the action, a typical move. I quickly grabbed him and set him down with a gentle scolding.

"You're both okay?" His eyes were on Madison again. "No lingering aftereffects?"

She stared back, oddly mute.

I cleared my throat to get their attention. "Uh, no. Oh, we got a good soaking but we're fine. We weren't in the water long, plus we were wearing wet suits. Madison's idea."

"Good thinking," Anton said. He pulled out his tablet. "I'm going to make a report of criminal mischief. Lucky for whoever it was that neither of you were hurt or else they'd be facing other charges."

"Do you really think you can ID the person?" I asked. Unless someone came forward with an eyewitness account, I didn't see how we'd ever figure it out.

Anton shrugged. "We won't know until we try. I'll talk to the librarians and see if they saw anything." He finished entering information. "Next I'll take a few photos of the boat."

"Would you like a cup of coffee when you're done?" I asked. "Grammie made blueberry coffee cake this morning if you want a piece." Both of them looked at me with wide, eager eyes. "I'll take that as a yes."

I scooted out of the barn and across the yard to the house. It was a beautiful morning so I decided to bring the coffee cake and Anton's coffee out to the porch.

By the time I got to the porch with my tray, the two of them were strolling out of the barn, chatting. When they saw me, they changed course and came along the garden path to the porch. By their body language, I guessed things were coming along nicely.

It was about time. I'd first gotten inklings of mutual interest between them months ago. Anton wasn't her usual type, physically, but he was solid and smart and totally trustworthy. I sometimes joked that I wouldn't mind if he stopped me for a traffic violation, he was that fair-minded and respectful.

After they sat down with cake and coffee, I excused myself, pretending I needed a refill. Grammie looked up when I closed the French door. "I'm leaving the lovebirds alone." I held up two pairs of crossed fingers. "I think something's finally happening."

"About time." Grammie smiled and went back to whisking eggs in a bowl.

By the time I slowly poured coffee and added milk, Anton was standing, ready to leave. I went back out to the porch. "Heading out?" I asked.

He nodded, patting his midriff. "Thanks for the snack. But I just got another call." He glanced at Madison. "Six o'clock okay?"

"I'll be ready." Her cheeks were flaming and she had a dreamy look in her eyes. Good. Obviously leaving them alone together had done the trick.

After assuring us the department would take our report seriously, he got into the cruiser and drove away. Madison sagged back into her seat, both hands to her cheeks. "Iris, what have I done?"

I pulled out a chair and sat. "I'm guessing you accepted a date with Mr. Hot Stuff Policeman." That characterization startled a laugh, which is what I was going for. "It's one meal. What are you worried about?"

Madison used the pads of her fingers to pick up stray coffee-cake crumbs. "I don't know. That it won't work out?" She swallowed. "Or maybe that it *will*?"

Through the years, Madison had held my hand more than once during my relationship dramas. It felt really good to be able to advise her in return. "It's just dinner, Madison. Go, have fun, and then decide if you want to see him again."

"You make it sound so logical," she said with a wry smile. "I have a bad habit of thinking too far ahead."

"A lot of us do." Now it was my turn to be wry. "Imagining our wedding day before the guy even talks to us." A bit of an exaggeration, but not much. I hesitated then said, "Besides, you're perfect for each other." They were, although you might not think so at first blush. Solid, dependable Anton and adventurous, creative Madison. It could work. Plus they'd have the cutest babies ever.

She squawked and hit at me as I ducked away, laughing. "You're not helping."

"What are friends for?" I picked up my first piece of blueberry cake and took a bite.

CHAPTER 18

Grammie had an appointment this morning, so Quincy and I opened the store. This end of Main Street was quiet right now, with most people enjoying the Maine blueberry pancake breakfast and clown show down at the festival. That was fine with me, since once in a while I needed a break to catch my breath. Plus I find clowns creepy, so you wouldn't catch me anywhere near the park right now.

After the opening tasks—making coffee, turning on the point of sale system, and checking inventory of bags and wrapping tissue—I made a list. Related to the store, I still had to contact auction houses about the couture clothing and jewelry for preliminary interest. Despite several mental reminders to myself, the task had slipped to the bottom during these last few busy days.

Related to Eleanor's situation, I wanted to look for the *Lapland*'s passenger lists. And, if I had time, I wanted to google Eleanor's nephew Craig and the members of Farming the Sea. First, to help Eleanor deal with her mercenary relative; and second, to figure out who might have killed Hailey and why.

Days had gone by and no arrests had been made. Not good for the police, who liked to close cases quickly. I should have asked Anton for an update earlier but I hadn't wanted to spoil the mood between him and Madison. Without thinking too much about it, I picked up my phone and sent him a text. Maybe he would answer me. If not, I'd corner him soon.

I poured a cup of coffee then booted up my laptop. I'd already made a list of auction houses with contact names, phone numbers, and e-mail addresses. First, I called them all, but had to leave messages, which I expected. Hardly anyone actually answered the phone anymore. Then I fired off e-mails with a couple of photographs attached, a double-barreled approach. At least the pictures might convince them I had something worth looking at. And we did, I was totally confident of that.

The shop bells jingled, announcing the arrival of a customer. When I got a closer look at the newcomer, I let out a squeak of dismay. And so did Quincy. A tall adult in a loose polka-dot clown suit complete with red nose and orange wig waddled toward the counter, huge shoes flapping.

I didn't want to see the clowns, so they came to me. *Awesome.* "Welcome to Ruffles and Bows," I said in what I hoped passed for a friendly tone. "How can I help you?" Quincy, instead of running to greet a new customer as was his habit, hid under the counter near my feet. Cats know.

Painted-on red lips moved, revealing teeth that were yellow in contrast. "I understand this is where I sign up for the lobster bib contest," a deep voice said. He—I think—waved a gloved hand at the flyer I'd taped to the front of the counter.

"That's right. I have a form right here." I placed an entry form and pen on the counter. "Are you entering as your clown personality?" I asked, to be funny.

"Not this one," the clown said with disdain, as if I should have known. "I have another identity I'll be using."

"I can hardly wait," I muttered, smiling widely when the clown sent me a sharp look. "Seriously," I amended. "We are getting some great entries. It's going to be . . . um, interesting."

Pen scratching, the clown filled out the form. "Here you go." He or she slapped the pen onto the paper and pushed the whole shebang toward me. "See you then. Now I've got to go or I'll be late for the clown parade." The shoes flapped again as the costumed character clomped away.

As the door shut with a jingle, I reviewed the form. Name? *Loko the Lobster Lover.* Oh yeah, the contest was going to be interesting all right.

While I was still on Eleanor, I moved on to the *Lapland* research. Entering the search "Lapland passenger lists" surprisingly brought up a number of sites. The one with the most lists didn't have any for 1932, which was frustrating. But I sent off an e-mail to the site owner anyway, asking for help in locating the one I wanted.

My phone bleeped with a text and I picked it up, thinking it was Anton. But it was Sophie, asking if Ian and I wanted to have a picnic supper at the lighthouse with her and Lukas. She was bringing the food.

Um, yes. Although I wished Jake was going, not Lukas. But at least I could observe Sophie and Lukas together, get a read on the situation. I checked with Ian then wrote Sophie back, arranging to have them pick me up at the store. Ian was working out on the point, so we'd swing by there after.

Social plans settled, and with the doorway of the store failing to be darkened by customers, I turned to online stalking. Oh, the Internet, what would we do without it? From reading their bios, I gathered Ruben's focus was biochemistry, and Lukas was regarded as a marine biology expert. They were both all over the web, on university and professional sites and as authors of papers and presentations at conferences. I thought of the card from Château de Rochefort. Had Hailey attended a university conference there, maybe? Or had her stay been personal, perhaps a romantic getaway? I searched the hotel's site but didn't find any information on past groups, or even any coming up. They were really discreet about their guests, it seemed.

Neither professor had much presence on social media, with Ruben's posts consisting mostly of good times on holiday around Europe. Lukas posted about hiking and skiing, with shots of his suntanned face squinting into the sun.

Hailey's accounts were under lockdown, which was annoying. But I really couldn't blame her, considering the number of friend requests and followers I got from supposed ex-military officers and oil company executives. So, since there was nothing to be learned there, I moved on to Theo, her fellow teaching assistant.

Theo was much less guarded and, as I'd gathered, he liked to take photographs. His feeds held some really wonderful shots, mostly of landscapes but some of people too. Among the most recent were scenes I recognized from Blueberry Cove.

Including one of Patrick's boat, moored close to shore. I recognized the slabs of granite in the foreground. They were close to the climbing route we had taken. When we had gotten there, his boat was motoring away, toward Shorehaven.

I checked the date it was posted. The day of Hailey's death. Anton needed to see this right away.

During my first interview with the police, I'd mentioned seeing Patrick's boat near the cliffs. But without this photo, they'd probably believed the seaweed farmer when he said he hadn't seen anything, like he'd told me.

I'd also made the assumption that he hadn't stopped on the way to Shorehaven, either.

I couldn't help but ask myself: Had Patrick killed Hailey?

"See you later, Grammie," I said, heading out the store's front door. Sophie had just pulled up in front in her Subaru Forester.

"Have fun, dear," she called. "Quincy and I will be fine. We're having fresh haddock for dinner."

Lukas was in the passenger seat so I hopped into the rear. "Hey," I greeted them, clipping my seat belt. "How are you?"

"We had a great day. Place was packed." Sophie flicked her turn signal to pull out, glancing over her shoulder at oncoming traffic.

"We did too, this afternoon," I said as Sophie pulled out onto the street. "This morning was slow but I got caught up on a lot of things." Like finding Theo's photo, which I'd sent to Anton, just in case they hadn't seen it. He said thanks but hadn't given me an update. "How about you, Lukas? How are things going?"

I could see his profile as he studied the passing scene. "Not so great." He paused. "In fact I had a really bad day."

Sophie's eyes met mine in the rearview, and by her raised brows I guessed she hadn't heard this. "What's going on?" I asked, figuring that if he didn't want to talk, he wouldn't have brought it up.

"Well, where do I begin?" Another beat. "I got a call today from the head of my department. He was inquiring about my involvement in Hailey's death."

Both Sophie and I gasped. "But you're not a suspect," Sophie said. "So where did he get that?"

"I have no idea," Lukas said. "Someone obviously ran to him and filled his ears with poison. But that's not the worst thing. The police want me to come in for another interview tomorrow morning."

We both exclaimed again. "That doesn't make sense," I said. The photograph I'd sent Anton implicated Patrick, not Lukas. I almost blurted that out but managed to hold the words back. I trusted Sophie implicitly but although I liked Lukas, it was possible he would tell Patrick what I'd done. Not necessarily out of malice, but because people talk. For example, whoever went to his department head. A rival colleague, maybe?

"Well, for what it's worth," Sophie said with a sniff, "I believe you're innocent."

He reached over and patted her knee. "You are so sweet." His hand didn't linger, I was glad to note. He squared his shoulders. "I plan to cooperate fully. I want the fiend who killed Hailey caught and locked up and the key thrown away."

"Me too," I said. Pulling out my phone, I shot Anton another text. *What's up with questioning Lukas???!* He didn't answer and I really didn't expect him to. He sometimes gave me information, but only when it didn't jeopardize a case. Even though I couldn't help but be curious. And I honestly didn't want him to overstep bounds either. Even if he was my friend. And—"Guess what, Sophie? Anton and Madison are going out to dinner tonight."

"As in a date, date?" she asked. When I confirmed that, she whooped. "About time." She threw a glance at Lukas and explained the situation.

"Oh yes," he said. "I know Madison." His tone became glum. "And Anton. He's the one who asked me to come in tomorrow."

I leaned forward, between the seats. "Anton's one of the good guys. He won't railroad you or anything." Although he didn't have the final say in cases of murder. The state police had jurisdiction. So as not to spook him further, I didn't mention that. Lukas hadn't killed his student despite her difficult personality and underhanded ways, I was pretty sure.

At the intersection of Hemlock Point Road, which looped the entire peninsula, Sophie asked which way to turn. "Right," I said, checking the directions Ian had sent me. "Out near Madison's house." Our destination, the Hemlock Point Lighthouse, was at the very end, where it had stood since the 1800s.

Most of the way, the road had a view of the water, with little lanes and cul-de-sacs on both sides. Madison lived on Cranberry Circle and that was where Ian was working. When I spotted his truck parked in a wide driveway in front of a faux Colonial, I realized he was right next door to the Morris home. Their house, designed by Zadie, was a modern post and beam with cathedral ceilings and a wonderful multi-level deck perfect for entertaining. This cul-de-sac was on a rise, with enough trees cut for an ocean view, if from a distance.

I sent Ian a text to let him know we were outside. Within a minute, he came around the side of the house with a wave. "I'm almost done cleaning up my tools," he said, leaning on the edge of my rolled-down window. "Want to come in and see the job?"

"Is it okay with the owners?" I asked, although guessing he wouldn't invite us in if they didn't want visitors.

"The Grahams aren't here. And no, they won't mind. My parents stopped by last weekend, when they were up." He opened the car door for me so I could climb out.

He led us around the corner of the house, past neglected flowerbeds and a covered built-in pool. "They just bought the place a few months ago," he said. "As you can see, the previous owners let things go."

We crossed a wide deck and entered the kitchen, which featured banks of newly installed white cabinets, shiplap walls, and black soapstone countertops. The look was old-fashioned yet modern with the farmhouse sink and top-of-the-line stainless steel appliances.

"It's gorgeous," I said, rubbing my hand along a silky sandstone countertop. What a nice change from ubiquitous granite and even more ostentatious marble. "Did you design it?"

Ian rubbed the back of his neck, a pleased smile on his lips. "Well, me and the owners." Which meant he'd guided them all the way. "I'm in charge of the overall project. We had the cabinets custom built. I've been finishing up the trim and details this week."

"I'm very impressed," Lukas said, echoed by Sophie, who was practically drooling, especially over the six-burner gas stove with two ovens.

We were checking out the butler's pantry with its cupboards and shelves when a rapping sounded on the door. Dr. Horatio Morris stood on the deck, hands tucked in the rear pockets of his shorts.

"Hello, Horatio," Ian said, opening the door for Madison's father. "Come on in and join the party."

The doctor nodded at each of us while taking in the refurbished kitchen. "This has really come along," he told Ian. "The Grahams must be pleased." To us, he said, "They're good friends of mine from Dartmouth. I convinced them to buy this place." He winked. "Nice to pick your neighbors when you can."

"You're right about that," I said. One thing I loved about our farm is that we couldn't even see our neighbors, only a couple of rooftops among the trees.

Ian gave Horatio a tour of the kitchen's features while the three of us looked through the rest of the rooms on the first floor. These had received fresh paint, new built-in bookcases and cabinets, and sanded floors. We were in the double living room with its beamed ceilings and fieldstone fireplace when Horatio and Ian wandered in, still chatting.

Ian joined Lukas and Sophie while Horatio made a beeline to me. "Iris," he said, lowering his warm honey voice to almost a whisper. "I've been hoping to catch up with you."

My spine stiffened in alarm. Was he going to question me about Anton and Madison? I had no idea what he thought of the pairing and certainly didn't want to get in the middle of family matters. Especially since I'd encouraged them both. But why wouldn't he like Anton, anyway? You'd be hard pressed to find a more decent man.

Fiddling with his wristwatch band, Horatio glanced at Lukas, who was listening to Ian over by the fireplace. Lowering his voice yet another notch, he said, "The other night at the clambake, Zadie and I were approached about an investment opportunity. Biofuel."

"I've heard about that," I said to let him know I knew who and what he was talking about. Biofuel was Ruben's pet project. "Sounds like a cool idea, sustainable energy and all that."

He studied me with his large brown eyes, so like his daughter's. "It does sound promising. Seaweed is so much faster growing than wood, which is also being proposed for biofuel. But of course, I'm doing a little more due diligence before I jump in."

"That sounds wise," I said, although I wasn't exactly an expert when it came to investing in start-up companies—except our much more modest apron shop.

"I saw Anne take one of his proposals at the clambake," Horatio said. He patted my shoulder. "Let her know I'm investigating the opportunity, if she is interested. I'm available to discuss it anytime."

"Thanks, Horatio," I said. "I'll tell her. I appreciate you looking out for her." My grandmother didn't have a lot to invest, so getting good advice was crucial, as it was for any investor. But Grammie wasn't an easy mark, as others who had approached her had learned, assuming her age meant gullibility. She could run rings around most people any day.

Then I thought of someone who was much more vulnerable. Eleanor. We'd overheard Craig talking to Ruben about freeing up cash. Was he referring to Eleanor's house and other belongings? Did he want to take over her affairs so he could invest in Ruben's company?

CHAPTER 19

We found a flat granite ledge for our picnic, the lighthouse to our right, and in front of us the never-ceasing surf against the rocks. Golden light touched the rippling waves and glinted off sailboats in the bay. There were a few other visitors to the park but they were wandering around near the lighthouse.

"Let me help." I took one end of the red-and-white gingham cloth Sophie was spreading on the ground. She really knew how to do a picnic right. Once the cloth was down, we anchored the corners with rocks. The wind was calm right now but it could kick up any time down here at the shore.

"Beer in the cooler, guys," Sophie said to Lukas and Ian. Without being asked twice, they opened the smaller cooler and retrieved ice-cold cans. For us, she had a chilled bottle of white wine and glasses.

While we lounged on the cloth, enjoying our cocktails, Sophie unpacked the large cooler holding our dinner. There were chicken-and-pesto sandwiches on crusty bread, a grilled-corn and bean salad, potato salad, and a veggie platter. A bag of salty kettle chips too. We all helped ourselves, piling paper plates with food. Then we settled back and ate, enjoying the view and the warm summer evening.

I pushed all my questions and concerns to the back of my mind and tried to focus on relaxing with Ian and my friends. We chatted about the Graham house, the store, and the Bean, avoiding mention of the seaweed project as if it were a landmine.

"I might have a teaching job at the University of Connecticut." Lukas made an abrupt announcement. "They are building their aquaculture program and are very interested in my work."

I glanced at Sophie to see how she was taking this announcement that Lukas might be moving to the United States. Connecticut was only few hours away.

She seemed startled at first, followed by trepidation. But then she smiled and said warmly, "That is wonderful news. I mean, I assume you are happy about it?"

Lukas ate a last chip then set his paper plate aside. "I am. They told me I could design the program any way I want, which is huge. I would be able to expand upon what we are doing here this summer."

"Sounds like a good *career* move," I said, to reassure Sophie that he probably wasn't moving to this country for her. That would be a lot of pressure for anyone.

"It's an excellent opportunity." He waved a hand, his gaze pensive as he studied the water. "But in light of what's going on here, I'm hoping they don't withdraw the offer before I decide." No doubt, being suspected of killing a student would be a real deal-breaker for any hiring committee.

Ian gave us a puzzled look. "Did something happen I don't know about?" And just like that, the subject we'd been trying to avoid was under discussion. While Lukas filled Ian in, Sophie and I packed up the leftovers.

"This was really nice," I said. "I hope we can do some more picnics this summer." And hopefully with Jake, not

Lukas, but I tactfully didn't say that. "Next time I'll make the food."

Sophie snapped a lid on a Pyrex container. "That would be great, but I didn't mind." She gave me a mischievous smile. "I was testing new recipes on you three." She held up the bowl, which was almost empty. "And I'd say they were a success."

"I'll be your guinea pig anytime," I said lightly. "So, are we still heading down to the park?" A great band was playing tonight and we'd talked about going.

"Sure," Sophie said. "If the guys want to." As she stowed containers in the cooler, she said in a careless tone that didn't fool me, "At least I know a certain someone won't be there tonight. It's his father's birthday."

This mention meant Sophie was still mentally keeping tabs on Jake, and I chose to take that as a good sign. And I was also glad he wouldn't be there. I didn't think my nerves could take another tense situation like last night at the clambake. Ian and Lukas were still talking, so I changed the subject. "Guess what? I made some progress on the mystery of Eleanor's mother. And you're the first to know. Well, except Grammie." I hadn't even told Madison yet. We'd been caught up in the boat situation this morning and after that, talking about her dinner date with Anton.

I filled her in while we sipped a second glass of wine. "I hope someone has the passenger list I need," I concluded. "When I started this project, I had no idea you could access those."

"It is amazing, all the information people have gathered and put online." Sophie shook her head. "And most of the time it's free."

"A labor of love." Sitting with my legs crossed, sipping wine and gazing at the glorious sea, I had an inspiration.

"I think I'm going to add an apron-of-the-week feature to my website and social media. Short posts, with pictures. It's a way to share what I know, plus some really beautiful garments." I could start with the domestic aprons from Shorehaven. They'd be good for three or four posts. And some of the hostess half aprons I kept finding were too cute not to share.

"I like that," Sophie said. "I'm sure people will enjoy reading about the aprons and their histories."

Ian popped his empty beer can back into the cooler. "Ready to head out? I'd love to catch the first set down at the park."

"We are," I said. "Would you and Lukas please fold the tablecloth? Then we can go." Normally Ian was great about helping clean up so I wasn't busting him too heavily. Plus they'd been having a serious conversation and I hadn't wanted to interrupt.

We were stowing the coolers and other items in the back of Sophie's SUV when Lukas said, "Do you mind swinging by the lab for a minute? I need to pick up something."

"I don't mind," Sophie said, shutting the hatchback. "It's on the way downtown."

Ian looked at me. "Do you want to ride with me?" His truck was still parked at the jobsite. He'd loaded his tools already so we wouldn't have to wait.

"I'd love to," I said, opening the SUV's back door. I'd take any excuse to spend time with Ian, even if it was only the ride back to town.

In the end, we followed Sophie, even stopping at the old mill building where the lab was housed so we wouldn't get separated. As we pulled into the wide drive, I saw Patrick at the wheel of a late-model pickup truck, leaving the facility. He waved at both vehicles in turn before wheeling out onto the road after a brief stop. He must have traded in his old truck.

Sophie parked near the front door and we pulled into the next spot. I unrolled my window. "We're going to wait here," I told Sophie as she got out of the Forester.

"That's fine," she said. "It should only take a minute." She waited for Lukas to skirt the front of the SUV to join her.

The building's front door flew open and Jamaica ran outside. Frowning, she glanced around the parking lot, her hands resting on her hips. Was she looking for Patrick? Even from here, I could sense her distress.

"I wonder what's up." Changing my mind about getting out, I pulled on the latch. "I'm going to go find out."

"Me too," Ian said, opening his own door. As we hurried toward the entrance, Jamaica put her hands over her face and burst into tears. Now I definitely knew something was wrong. "Are you okay?" I asked, knowing it was a stupid question.

"No," she said, rubbing at her eyes. "I'm not. My ex is a jerk and even worse, my seaweed crop is ruined."

"What?" I wasn't expecting to hear that. Ian gave me a look of consternation, and Lukas and Sophie, who had now reached us, appeared equally stunned.

"Show me," Lukas said, his hand on her elbow. "Maybe we can save the plants."

We followed as Lukas escorted Jamaica into the building. Inside, Jamaica and Lukas began trotting down the hall to Jamaica's lab, the rest of us on their heels. When we arrived at the lab, the two of them were standing at the grow tank. Even a novice like me immediately saw the problem. The tubes where the brown seaweed had sprouted were now covered in green slime.

"It's contaminated," Jamaica said. She glanced around

wildly, checking gauges and equipment. "But I can't imagine how. The temps are right and the filters are still working." She groaned deeply, her hand going to her forehead. "And it couldn't have happened at a worse time. I have a big customer coming tomorrow. They want to buy my whole crop, an advance order for everything I'm growing this year."

My heart sank. And now her crop was ruined. "Can you start over?" I asked, hoping the season could be saved. The seedling seaweed went into the water in the fall, so maybe there was time.

Jamaica's eyes met mine, a bleak expression in their depths. "Maybe. But once the customer sees this mess, they won't want anything I grow." Biting her lip, she shook her head. "The timing couldn't be worse."

An inkling of suspicion trickled into my mind. Had the tanks been sabotaged? I had a hard time believing she'd made a mistake, not after hearing about the exacting processes she followed during our tour. "Do you think someone did this?" I asked.

"What?" Jamaica reared back in shock. "You mean contaminate my tanks *on purpose*? Who would do such a thing?" A heavy silence fell as the obvious answer chimed in my mind. *Patrick*. Shaking her head, Jamaica put up both hands. "No. No, he wouldn't do that. Surely he wouldn't stoop *that* low—"

"Jamaica." Lukas's voice boomed out over her torrent of words. "We can figure that out later. We need to move fast."

She whirled to face him, her expression taut with anger and anguish. "You're right. Tell me what to do."

Lukas pointed at the tank. "We need to change the water and add an additional UV sterilizer unit. We'll know overnight if it's going to work."

"Good idea. Better yet, we'll put the tubes into a new

tank and start over," Jamaica said. "I have an extra, all sterile and ready to go." The volatile emotions on her face cleared, replaced with determination.

Sophie stepped forward. "I take it you're staying here, Lukas," she said.

His brow furrowed. "If you don't mind. I want to try to save the crop."

My friend put up her hand. "Say no more. That totally makes sense. We'll hang out another night." She gave him a brief embrace, then hugged Jamaica too. "Good luck."

Jamaica laughed. "I'll need it." She smiled at each of us in turn. "Thanks for your support. I'll see you later." She and Lukas were already deep in discussion by the time we reached the lab doorway.

The three of us were silent as we trudged down the hallway, our shoes squeaking on the polished tiles. "Wow, what a bummer," Ian said as he held the front door open for us. "It would be devastating to lose a whole crop."

"I can't imagine," Sophie said. Then she added, "Well, yes I can. Last winter, during that huge ice storm, we lost everything in the walk-in because the power went out for two days." She grimaced. "Now I have a back-up generator."

"And Jamaica needs a security system," I said. "Despite her protests, I think someone sabotaged her."

Ian's gaze narrowed as he thought about that. "The timing *is* weird. The day before she meets with a big customer? I find that strangely coincidental."

"As do I," I said, glad he hadn't dismissed my theory completely. "And I think Jamaica sees it too."

Sophie moved slowly toward her car. "Who was she talking about when she said, 'He wouldn't stoop that low.'"

"I hate to say it, but Patrick, who is her ex-business partner. They have a pretty acrimonious relationship." I gave them the gist of what I'd overheard in the hallway after the lab tour.

"It all fits, sad to say." Ian studied the building. "I didn't see a security system in the lab. I'm definitely going to suggest she put one in." He put his hand on the door handle and tugged. "Right now. Be right back." He disappeared inside the building.

"He's such a good guy," Sophie said, her tone wistful. "You two seem really happy together."

"We are," I admitted. "But taking it slow . . . no more leaping before I look for this girl." Even as I said this, my innards squeezed at the lie. I was falling in love with Ian, but right now even he didn't know that, unless he could read minds. I hadn't seen any signs that he'd guessed my secret, which meant what? That he didn't feel the same way? *Grrr.* I thought I'd moved past the "Does he, doesn't he?" of high school.

Sophie smoothed a lock of long hair. "You guys were right."

"Wait, what?" I thought I'd heard what she said but my mind was still full of Ian. I finally caught up. "Right about what?"

"I love Jake," she whispered. "Ever since we broke up, it's like I'm missing a limb or something." She laughed but her eyes shone with regret. "You never know what you've got until it's gone."

I put a hand on her arm. "I don't think it's gone, Sophie. Honestly."

Ian emerged from the building. "We're going to talk tomorrow about which system to get," he told us.

"You're helping her put one in?" I asked. He was so good that way, always offering his expertise and assistance to friends. "That's so nice of you."

He shrugged at my praise. "I installed one for my parents, so I'm up-to-date on what's out there. You don't need to spend a lot of money nowadays. A couple of cameras and alarms on doors and windows are pretty inexpensive. You can even monitor the system on your phone." He reached for the driver door. "Ready to head out?"

"You know what?" Sophie said. "I'm going to go home." She tipped her head toward the building. "Lukas is busy and, well, I don't feel like dancing anymore. Or seeing people." She gave me a wan smile. "I'll see you tomorrow for dinner." Grammie and I were hosting a girls' night.

"Don't brood," I said as I climbed into the truck's passenger seat. "That's an order. And call him." She pretended not to hear me as she got into her car. But I hoped she'd take my advice.

Ian inserted the keys then paused. "You know what, Iris? I'd just as soon not go to the fest. We haven't had much time alone over the past couple of weeks."

My heart began to thud. "No, we haven't," I managed to say. *Focus on the moment, Iris.* My relationship was important too, and besides, there was nothing further I could do tonight to solve my nagging questions and concerns.

He turned in his seat and leaned closer, brushed a lock of hair out of my face. He gave me a crooked smile. "Want to hang out at my place? I've got a bottle of your favorite wine chilling. We can listen to the band from my balcony."

"Why, Ian," I said, batting my lashes. "It sounds like you've been planning this all along." My pulse thumped in my ears. I was dying for him to kiss me.

Ian shifted even closer. His mouth almost touched mine, teasing me. "Not planning," he whispered. "Hoping." And then his lips met mine.

CHAPTER 20

For our girls' night dinner, Grammie and I decided to put together a salad smorgasbord, served out on the back porch. The evening was warm, sultry even, with thunderstorms in the forecast. Hopefully they'd hold off for a couple of hours. Along with the regulars—Madison, Bella, and Sophie—I'd invited Jamaica. After her ordeal the previous night, I sensed she could use time with friends. I must have been right, because she said yes immediately and offered to bring something to share.

We set up a folding table along the wall to hold platters of fresh, local veggies, including lettuce and cucumbers from Grammie's garden. Protein included chicken, shrimp, eggs, cheeses, and ham. We also added a tray of toppings that included nuts, seeds, olives, pickled vegetables, and dried fruit, with an array of dressings.

"This looks great," I said, popping an olive into my mouth, which flooded with salty goodness. "I love big salads full of goodies."

Grammie placed a fork next to a bowl of artichoke hearts. "Me too. It's an easy way to get your five-a-day," referring to the advice to eat five helpings of vegetables and fruit each day.

Quincy tried to jump onto the table, lured by the dish of cottage cheese, which he loved. I grabbed him midleap. "What's gotten into you?" I scolded him gently. "You know better." I put him down and showed him the dish I'd made for him. It included a tiny spoonful of the creamy curds along with his regular food. I took a grilled shrimp and bit off half, then gave him the rest of that too.

"You spoil that cat," Grammie said with a fond smile. "And so do I."

Cars crunched up the drive. The ladies had arrived. Sophie and Bella rode together, and Jamaica was with Madison. As usual, everyone had brought a contribution, and while I welcomed bread and wine and dessert, I saw to my dismay that Jamaica was carrying a bowl of brown seaweed.

She noticed me studying the dish and grinned as she placed it on the laden table near the other toppings. "This is kelp salad. You slice it really thin and add vinegar, sugar, peppercorns, and coriander and mustard seeds."

Madison shot me a glance. "Sounds tasty. I can't wait to try it."

"Thanks, Jamaica," Grammie said. "You didn't have to bring anything, but we appreciate the addition." She pulled the clear wrap off the bowl and put a spoon into the seaweed.

Bella opened a bottle of wine while Sophie sliced the crusty bread she'd brought. Madison and I helped Grammie set out stacks of plates and utensils, and Jamaica filled a pitcher with ice water and slices of lemon. Then we lined up to fill our plates, commenting on all the choices. I even took a tiny bit of the seaweed, to be polite. Everyone took a seat around the table, except Sophie, who remained standing.

"Up, up," she said, holding her wine glass. "We're going to do a Belgian toast." We obeyed, and once we were standing, she said, "*Santé!*"

"*Santé*!" we echoed, lifting our glasses. Then we all laughed and sat down.

"That toast brings back memories," Sophie said. At Jamaica's questioning look, she added, "I went to college in Belgium."

Jamaica's mouth dropped open slightly and she nodded. "Now I get it. Did you know Lukas when you were there?" Eyes still on Sophie, she took a big bite of salad.

"We dated for a while," Sophie said briefly. "I was very surprised when he showed up in Blueberry Cove. We haven't been in touch for years."

"He's a good guy," Jamaica said. "I've learned tons from him already." She broke into a huge smile. "Plus he's really, really hot." The rest of us echoed that sentiment with gusto, even Grammie, who thought he could star in a James Bond movie.

"Sophie's heart is engaged elsewhere," Bella said. "So he's all yours, Jamaica, if you want him."

Jamaica sat back, a hand to her chest and a stunned expression on her face. "Oh my. Am I that obvious? Maybe I do have a teeny-tiny crush, but no." Cheeks flushed, she shook her head. "I'm not going to trespass on another woman's patch."

"It's not my patch." Sophie set her wine glass down. "For a few minutes I thought *maybe*, I admit, especially after . . . anyway, we're just friends." She picked up her fork and stabbed at her salad. "How did it go with the customer today?"

"Good, really good," Jamaica said, giving a big sigh. "I took them out to the site and they were very impressed. I don't think they were able to picture what twenty acres of water looks like until they saw it."

"Twenty acres?" Grammie buttered a thick slice of bread. "That's a good-size area. How much seaweed will you get from that?"

Jamaica had a ready answer. "About ten tons an acre, so two hundred tons." She grimaced. "If no more disasters happen. The filtration looks like it's working, so fingers crossed, the crop will be okay."

Bella and Madison hadn't heard what happened so we told them how someone had contaminated the sprouting seaweed crop and almost ruined it.

"Who would do such a thing?" Bella asked in indignation. "So mean."

My eyes met Jamaica's. I was going to let her take the lead on this one. She sighed. "I think it might have been Patrick. He's so angry with me." With an unseeing gaze, she shuddered at what must be a horrible memory.

Madison glanced at her with concern. "Don't talk about it if it's upsetting. We understand."

"No, it's okay," Jamaica said, eyes still distant as she played with one of her long braids. "I really cared about Patrick. But he's not the person I thought he was. As soon as he's opposed in any way, the knives come out." At our looks of alarm, she added, "Figuratively speaking."

"It sounds to me like you made a wise decision," Grammie said. "Selfish men make very poor partners."

"Yeah, they do," Jamaica agreed. "And we were business partners too. You know those Seascme Power Bars? That was my idea." Her mouth twisted. "But I told him to take the recipe rather than fight with him for it. He'd already called an attorney."

"That's not fair," Madison said in protest. "And no wonder they're good. You invented them, not Patrick." She folded her arms with a snort. "I'm never eating another single one." Her eyes lit. "And I'm giving them bad reviews on social media."

Jamaica gave her a wan smile. "Please don't do that, Madison. I appreciate your support but I don't want to make the situation worse."

"You're probably right," Madison said, settling back with a grumble. "But I'm boycotting them."

I didn't have to boycott the bars because a single bite had never passed my lips. "Are you going to make another product, Jamaica?" Judging by how tasty the seaweed salad was—I'd eaten all mine, to my surprise—she was a great cook.

"I might," she said. "But right now it's easier for me to sell the whole crop raw. Or dried, in bulk. Patrick had to set up a commercial kitchen to make the bars." She rubbed her thumb and two fingers together. "Big bucks for the equipment. And the packaging, marketing and so forth."

"Did Ian call you?" I asked. We'd exchanged some texts today but they were personal in nature rather than work updates. "He said he was going to help you with a security system."

"He sure did. He gave me parts of an old system his parents replaced so it's already installed and operational." Jamaica held up her phone. "I can look at the lab from anywhere." She brought up the site then passed the phone around. In the video, which had no sound, the tanks were silently bubbling away. All was well down at the lab.

"A baby seaweed monitor," Grammie quipped as she studied the screen. "How innovative."

When Jamaica got her phone back, she studied the screen with a fond expression. "You're right, Anne. They are my babies."

"Speaking of babies," I said, "how was your date last night, Madison?" She gave me a light punch to the bicep and I ducked away, laughing.

"It was fine," she said primly. Then she cracked. "Actually, we had a great time. Anton is an awesome slow dancer, did you know that?" She swayed in her seat, humming, a dreamy expression on her face.

"Eww, no. TMI," I said. "Seriously, I'm glad things went well. Good news."

Madison still wore that dreamy look. "Who would have thunk it? He's been right under my nose for years." We'd all grown up together, although Anton was a couple of years older than us.

"You're seeing him in a whole new way, dear," Grammie said. She set her fork down with a decisive click. "Who's ready for dessert?"

Sophie had brought a raspberry crisp made with local berries and rich vanilla ice cream to top the warm dessert. We dug into big bowls of the treat, making comments about how we'd saved calories by having salad for dinner. Not really.

"Lukas was supposed to go in and talk to Anton today," I said to Madison while the rest of the table was listening to Bella tell a funny story about her ex-husband. "Do you have any idea what's going on?" The threatened storms had moved in and thunder grumbled in the distance.

"You mean did we talk police business on our date?" Madison gave me a smirk. "Actually we did, a little. I got your text with the news so I asked him. But his lips were sealed."

I allowed a spoonful of raspberries and ice cream to linger on my tongue. "I wonder if Patrick said something incriminating. Remember Theo's photo of Patrick's boat moored near the cliffs? I'm sure Anton followed up about it."

"Yeah, and maybe Patrick redirected suspicion onto Lukas." Madison gnawed on her bottom lip. "I wonder if I can find out."

I laughed. "You mean use your wiles to get him to spill? I can see your relationship with the chief is going to come in handy," I joked.

Madison gave me a satisfied smile. "I could do that, couldn't I?" She thought about it for a moment then shook her head. "Unfortunately I wouldn't feel right about it. I guess lessons from my parents are too ingrained."

"Darn." I snapped my fingers, pretending to be disappointed. But really, joking aside, I didn't expect anything less. I didn't want Anton to jeopardize his position or a case because we pressured him. Or in Madison's case, seduced him into it.

Bella called to me across the table. "Are you ready for the fashion show tomorrow night?"

I had a flash of panic. I'd forgotten all about the event. "I think so," I replied, sounding anything but certain. "What do I have to do?"

"Not much," Bella said to my relief. "Why don't we meet for breakfast tomorrow around eight and go over everything? The other judges have done this before so they're all set."

"There's another blueberry pancake breakfast tomorrow," Grammie said. "I was thinking of going to that myself. It's benefiting the lighthouse museum project."

I thought about my schedule. If we met at the suggested time, I could easily eat breakfast at the park and still be at the store by nine. "I'll be there, for sure." I might even go downtown a little early and grab the folder of lobster bib entries, which were up to a dozen. Not a bad showing for the first year of an event.

Dessert over, everyone got up and started milling around, helping clean up before preparing to leave. The rumbles of thunder were closer now, accompanied by flashes of heat lightning. The storm would soon be upon us.

Jamaica slid into Madison's empty chair beside me. "Thanks for including me, Iris. I haven't had this much fun in ages." She framed her face with her hands, like blinders. "I've had tunnel vision—work, work, work."

"That's the way it is when you start a business," I said. "Ask me how I know." We laughed then I said, "I'm glad you could come. We'll hang out again soon, okay?"

"I'd like that," she said, then looked around, ready to get up. "I really should go help the others."

"Just a sec," I said. "I want to talk to you about something." When she turned attentive eyes on me, I hesitated, hoping I wouldn't blow up our brand-new friendship. "I think the police still regard Lukas as the prime suspect in Hailey's death."

She reared back, her mouth hanging open. "That's crazy. No way. Lukas wouldn't do something like that."

"I agree, it's ludicrous," I said. "Sophie thinks so too, and she's known him a long time." I paused. "So we've been wondering who it really was. And to that end, we're trying to build a better picture of Hailey's last days."

Jamaica's gaze narrowed. "You're investigating? Like private eyes or something?"

"Or something," I said. "We're certainly not trained detectives. But we notice stuff and we know people. And we don't take one piece of evidence and run with it."

"Like that jacket." Her tone was musing. "That was downright weird. As if someone was trying to pin the murder on Lukas."

"Exactly," I said. "I think so too. So." I took a deep breath. "How well did Patrick and Hailey know each other?" I put up a hasty hand. "I'm not accusing him of anything. But his boat was seen moored near the cliffs the morning she died." As she continued to stare at me, I stumbled on. "I thought maybe they'd been talking, maybe she was helping him with his project." I remembered something. "Oh, and she had one of his energy bar wrappers in her pack that morning."

"So you think he was delivering energy bars to her at the cliffs?" Jamaica's voice held a note of mockery. But then a pensive expression fell over her features. "She irritated him, I know that much. Oh, he didn't say no when she offered to hawk those bars around. He thought she was a good advertisement for them, being so cute and all." She laced her long fingers together and stretched them back and forth as she spoke. "And she was smart as a whip too. Got to give her that."

"She must have been," I said. "I'm sure there was a lot of competition for the two teaching assistant slots." At the very least, according to Theo, Hailey had been savvy about scheming her way to the top. Why depend on natural intelligence when you could seal the deal by cheating?

Jamaica gave a small groan. "Sorry," she said when I looked at her. "I still can't believe it. The whole thing is so *awful*, like a nightmare. It doesn't make sense."

"No, it doesn't," I agreed, although I was sure the killer believed what he or she had done was perfectly logical. Hailey was either a threat or had done something the killer thought deserved a death sentence.

"I was so shocked when I found out," Jamaica said. "At first I thought Theo was joking." Her mouth turned down. "But he sure wasn't."

I brought the conversation back to Patrick. "Patrick was at Shorehaven later that morning, meeting with Ruben." I hadn't seen Jamaica at Eleanor's, but maybe she had come and gone by the time I got there.

Jamaica gave an irritated snort. "Figures. I should have been there too. But I was at home, in my apartment. Drinking coffee and working on my business plan."

So Jamaica hadn't been near the cliffs in her boat that morning, like Patrick had told me after the lab tour. That weasel. Not only had he thrown Theo under the bus during that conversation, he had tried to imply that Jamaica was involved with Hailey's death. Or might have seen something important.

"Is that why the police came to the lab yesterday?" Jamaica asked. "Someone saw Patrick's boat moored at the cliffs?"

"I'm pretty sure." While I didn't have the inside track on this one, it made sense that Anton had talked to Patrick about Theo's photograph after I tipped him off. Then the next thing you know, Lukas got a call to come in. I leaned forward, feeling the need to warn her. "Be careful, okay? But if you keep your eyes open, listen to people, maybe you'll learn something important. The sooner we find out who killed Hailey, the better."

She nodded solemnly. "I'll do my best."

Everyone cleared out soon after, except Madison, who wanted to hang for a while, so Jamaica caught a ride home with Sophie. Her downtown apartment was near Sophie's. Bella owned a home on one of the side streets leading up from the harbor.

"Anyone want tea?" Grammie asked us, her hand on the kettle. "I have a nice herbal blend that's decaf."

"Sounds good," Madison said. She was admiring the small aprons Grammie had stitched, which lay over the back of a dining room chair. She fluffed the skirt of the smallest one. "This is adorable. Did I tell you Tyler and Amy are having a girl?" Madison's brother Tyler had married physician's assistant Amy last April.

"No, you didn't. Congrats to them." I was genuinely happy for the newlyweds, who were wonderful—like everyone in Madison's family. Sliding onto a stool at the kitchen island, I picked up my phone and checked my e-mail.

Outside, the wind whipped up, another sign that a storm was upon on. Thunder rolled like giants bowling in the sky, a favorite analogy when we were kids.

"Can you make me one of these aprons in a baby size?" Madison asked Grammie.

"I sure can," Grammie said. "That would be so cute." She turned to me. "Iris, we have another order already."

"That's awesome," I said, scanning my inbox. To my delight, I had a response from the site where I'd found the *Lapland* passenger lists. I quickly opened it, only to groan with disappointment. "They don't have the right passenger list for the *Lapland*. I hope we're not at a dead end." If we couldn't prove when Claudia arrived in the United States, we couldn't clear her as a suspect in her father's murder.

Grammie, pulling mugs out of the cupboard, paused. "I have an idea where to look. Hold on and I'll tell you about it after I make the tea. Go get your laptop, Iris."

After she filled the mugs with steaming water and placed them in front of us, she said, "A friend of mine was telling me the other day that she'd found her great-grandparents in the Ellis Island records."

"Ellis Island is near New York City, right?" Madison dunked her teabag up and down, using the string.

"Yes, out in the harbor," Grammie said, adding a little honey to her tea. "Many immigrants went through there to register. They also got medical checkups. There's a museum there now, I understand."

I already had the site up. "I just put Claudia's name in. Fingers crossed." I took a sip of tea while the results loaded. *Come on, come on. . . .*

The lights flickered briefly. We often lost electricity during storms out here on the fringe of town. Thunder boomed right overhead.

"Oh no. This couldn't happen at a worse time." I peered at the screen, grateful I had a battery in the laptop. But I had to wait to get online again until after the modem reconnected. I quickly hit REFRESH and the screen loaded, revealing one entry. A Claudia de Witte from Antwerp arrived in 1932, on the *Lapland*. But had it sailed before her father was murdered in Belgium?

"I found her!" I cried out. Madison and Grammie abandoned their tea and came around to stand behind my shoulder. With shaking fingers, I clicked on the entry for more information.

The voyage dates confirmed that Eleanor's mother had been on the ship when her father died. "Yes!" I shouted. "Claudia is innocent."

CHAPTER 21

Grammie clapped her hands. "Eleanor is going to be so happy to hear this news. What a relief. Not that I ever thought Claudia was guilty."

I hadn't either, though I was very glad we had conclusive proof she wasn't. "There is one thing, though." I hopped down from the stool, too excited to sit. "We never told Eleanor that her grandfather was murdered. So it's more of a good news, bad news scenario."

"It also means that Claudia was the legal owner of the jewelry," Madison pointed out. "Since the robbery happened after she left the country, she didn't run away with stolen jewels."

"True. That is very good news." I picked up my cell phone and called Eleanor. "I hope it's not too late to call." Her phone, a landline, rang and rang. "Voice mail's not picking up."

"Her power is probably out," Grammie said. "It happens a lot on that side of town." She gave us a mischievous grin. "Who wants to take a ride?"

We drove out to Eleanor's in Grammie's Jeep Grand Wagoneer Woody, the biggest, safest vehicle we had. But still, gusts buffeted the heavy SUV and rain lashed the windshield, the wipers on full speed to keep up. Thunder crashed and lightning forked across the sky. Hardly anyone was on the road, only the occasional pair of head-lights coming our way, tires splashing as they passed.

Grammie was intent at the wheel, watching the road. "I love thunderstorms. Nothing like a good one to clear the air."

"Me too," I said. Watching the lightning circle the hills was thrilling. Down on the shore, the surf must be incredible. But it was a typical summer storm, nothing that was going to uproot trees or demolish homes. Most power outages were due to a branch resting on a line. That happened frequently since the area was so wooded.

As we got closer to Cliff Road, I saw that all the houses were dark, confirming our theory that Eleanor's electricity was out. Grammie slowed when we turned onto the side road, which, with very few streetlights, was dark even under the best of conditions. Tonight only the Jeep's headlights and occasional lightning lit the gloom. Leaves and small branches patterned the gleaming black asphalt, but we didn't encounter any real obstacles.

The stone posts marking the drive loomed out of the dark, caught by our headlights. Grammie turned in and we slowly crept down toward the house, which was in almost complete darkness. A lone light shone in the up-per stories, where someone must have either lit candles or turned on battery-operated lamps.

Grammie parked near the fence, the lot empty of vehicles. The members of the seaweed project must be out, and Eleanor kept her car in the garage. Using the flashlight on my phone, we skirted the rain-dimpled pool and rapped on the French doors.

No answer. Although we were somewhat sheltered by the porch roof, the water-laden wind slapped us, sending droplets down our necks.

Two choices: go home or take a more assertive approach. Since our news was vitally important *and* I wanted to make sure Eleanor was all right, I chose the second. I boldly opened the French door and called, "Eleanor? Eleanor, are you home?"

Only a couple of thunder booms answered me as lightning flashed over the bay, which meant the storm was circling back around. I stepped into the house, the dark room briefly visible when another flash came. "Eleanor?" I called again, my voice louder. "Are you here?" Followed by Grammie and Madison, I walked through the sitting room and out into the hallway. She was probably upstairs, where I'd seen the light.

"Eleanor?" I called again. In response, a light shone and bobbed, as if someone was carrying it along the upstairs corridor. "I think she's coming."

We waited where we were, at the foot of the stairs. The lantern light grew stronger and soon we saw Eleanor on the landing. She wore a long white nightgown and in her hand, held high, was a battery lantern, the type I used while camping.

"Who's there?" she called from the top of the stairs. She must not be able to see us from that vantage point.

I moved closer, to stand right below her. "It's me, Iris. I'm here with Anne and Madison. We have news for you."

"Iris?" To my dismay, Eleanor sounded doubtful, as if she didn't know an Iris. She swung the lantern out over the railing, peering down. In the light's eerie white glow, she looked gaunt, almost skeletal. "Who's that with you?"

Grammie came up beside me. "Eleanor, dear, it's Anne. And Madison. We're here to see you. May we come up?"

Eleanor wavered, the lantern beam swinging wildly around the hall, and then she collapsed into a heap onto the floor. The lantern fell, bounced, and rolled.

After a frozen second or two, we launched into action and pounded up the staircase to her side. By the time we got there, Eleanor was sitting up, knees bent and a hand to her head. "What happened?" she asked, her voice groggy.

"You fell," Grammie said gently. She knelt down beside Eleanor. "Does anything hurt?" She mimicked using a phone then pointed at me. I pulled out my cell to call 911.

"No, nothing hurts," Eleanor said, looking up at us with dilated eyes. She patted her legs and hips. "All good." She cracked an odd, crooked smile. Had she been drinking? I didn't smell alcohol on her breath.

But at least she hadn't broken a bone, it seemed. That was such a worry with the elderly and frail. The dispatcher answered, and I asked for an ambulance, explaining that we were concerned about an older woman's condition.

Eleanor stared up into my grandmother's face. "Anne. What are you doing here?" Her voice sounded slightly slurred.

Hoo-boy. I was glad she seemed to be thinking a little more clearly. But what had caused this episode? The dispatcher assured me the ambulance would be right there and I hung up.

"We came by to make sure you were all right," Grammie said. "The storm had us concerned, with all the power outages." She didn't mention Claudia, and I thought I understood why. In Eleanor's condition, she might not comprehend what we were talking about. The news could wait.

"The electricity went out," Eleanor gestured vaguely. "It was dark."

"Iris?" Grammie gestured to me. "Do you think you and Madison could help Eleanor back to her bedroom?"

Between the two of us, we carefully maneuvered Eleanor onto her feet and helped her down the hall. She leaned heavily on us, gripping us hard with her thin, bony fingers, and stumbled along. But she was putting weight on her legs and didn't seem to be in any pain.

Grammie grabbed the lantern to light our journey and, once we entered the bedroom, she set it on the night-stand. We helped Eleanor climb into the high bed, which smelled of lavender and was made up with a set of those gorgeous sheets. A quilted satin coverlet lay folded at the foot, like something a movie star would use, and we pulled that up to cover her to the waist.

"Would you get me a glass of water?" Eleanor tugged at Madison's arm then pointed to the adjacent bathroom. Madison picked up the empty water glass and hurried off.

Grammie fussed with the sheets, smoothing them. "Are you on any medications, Eleanor? Sometimes they can cause all kinds of funny symptoms." This was a round-about way to ask whether Eleanor might have taken too much of something.

Eleanor held up a forefinger with a laugh. "I'm on one medication. One. That isn't bad for an old bird like me, is it?" She pointed to the bedside table drawer. "My pills are in there."

I opened the drawer, but instead of a medication bottle, I found one of those plastic days-of-the-week containers. Each compartment held rattling objects but I couldn't identify them through the opaque plastic.

"The rest of those are my herbs and vitamins," she said before I could ask. "I take them faithfully, every day, and they've done wonders for my health."

That was great, but two days were open, not one. Had she taken an overdose of something? Or just left a lid open? I pried open another compartment and studied the contents.

Eleanor's face screwed up in distress. "I can't imagine what's wrong with me lately. I keep leaving things where they don't belong."

Like putting her eyeglasses in the refrigerator the

other day. That had been strange, although I'd put cold milk into the cereal cupboard once. Maybe Eleanor was merely absentminded. We all were at times.

Madison returned with the water and handed the glass to Eleanor. After taking a few thirsty swallows, she went on. "And I'm so confused sometimes. I thought Craig was an intruder one morning when I walked into my office and saw him at the file cabinet."

Doing what? I glanced at Madison and Grammie, who both looked concerned.

"Let's tell the doctor all this," Anne said, patting Eleanor's shoulder in a comforting manner. "Maybe they need to change your medicine. Or the dosage."

"Maybe," Eleanor said. "Although it's only medicine for my tummy. I have reflux sometimes."

Madison drew me aside while Grammie settled Eleanor comfortably back on the pillows. "Something doesn't sound right to me," she whispered. "I'm not a doctor, but I've never heard of reflux medicine affecting people's minds. Or making their voices slur."

"Me neither." I studied Eleanor, who was lying back against the pillows, eyes closed. "But I pray it's not dementia," I said. Sometimes those symptoms could come and go, I'd heard. How tragic it would be for this bright, interesting woman to lose her mental faculties.

Lights flashing through the front windows announced the arrival of the ambulance. "I'll go down and let them in," I said, switching on my flashlight again. The electricity still wasn't back on yet. And it was pouring again, judging by the rain lashing the windows.

When I opened the front door for the EMTs, I discovered that Anton was with them. The police often answered ambulance calls as extra support. "Thanks for getting here so fast," I said, standing back to let them in.

"Hey," a voice called from the front walk. "Wait for me." Eleanor's nephew, Craig, came splashing along carrying a big black umbrella.

"Excuse me, excuse me." Craig pushed his way past Anton and the medical personnel and closed his wet umbrella with a snap, throwing drops everywhere. What an oaf. "What's going on here? Is my aunt all right? I'd also like to know why I wasn't informed."

Since time was of the essence, I ignored Craig and turned to the EMTs. "Eleanor is upstairs, first bedroom on the right in front. When we got here, she was confused and then she collapsed. No broken bones, though, thankfully."

"We'll go check her over," one EMT said. Shouldering past Craig, both EMTs flew up the stairs. Anton stayed with me, subtly blocking the way to the stairs.

"The reason I didn't call you is I don't have your number," I told Craig. "I'm sorry about that." And I was. Maybe his rude demeanor was a mask for worry. I held up my phone. "Why don't you give it to me now?"

He stared at me, his bulldog jaw working. "I don't see any reason why you should have it," he said. "You and my aunt aren't that close, are you?"

No, he was just plain rude, I decided. "Have it your way." I waved the light beam at the stairs. "Anton? Want to go up?"

Although Anton had a flashlight on his duty belt and didn't need my feeble beam, he nodded and gestured for me to precede him up the stairs. Behind me, I heard Craig give a huff and then his heavy breathing as he followed us, footsteps thumping.

In Eleanor's bedroom, the medics were checking her vital signs and questioning her about her symptoms. When Madison saw us walk in, she detached herself from the group and came over. Craig went to the foot of the bed and listened, scowling, arms folded across his chest.

Madison and Anton stared at each other for a long moment before she looked away. "I'm glad you came along tonight," she said in a low voice. "Iris and I are worried about Eleanor."

"The EMTs will figure it out," Anton said, his voice hearty with reassurance. "They'll probably take her in for observation and tests. And her doctor will be informed."

"My father is her physician, I think Eleanor said," Madison said. "But I'm hoping you can help."

Anton rested his hands on his hips, his brow furrowed. "I'm not following."

"I've seen one of Eleanor's spells before," I said. "She's confused, forgetful, in her own world. And then a while later, she snaps out of it and she's normal again." I thought of something. "But tonight her pupils were really dilated." That might have been due to the dark, though. "And her voice was slurring." That certainly wasn't due to the dark.

Anton called one of the EMTs over, speaking softly so we couldn't hear. The medic responded, nodding affirmatively, then went back to his patient.

"Okay," Anton said. "There's some . . . indication that other factors might be at play here." Meaning the EMT thought there were possible symptoms of intoxication of some sort.

I exchanged glances with Madison. "You'll want to check her bedside table drawer for a purple plastic container," I said. "She keeps her medications in there." Lowering my voice even further, I said, "Test them, will you? Something is definitely not right here."

The EMTs unfolded a gurney and began to prepare Eleanor for transport. Craig hovered around them, getting in the way. "What are you doing? Where are you taking her?"

"Move aside, sir," one of the EMTs said. "We're taking your aunt to the hospital."

"I'm all right, Craig," Eleanor said in a weak voice. "They'll take good care of me."

The other EMT patted her shoulder. "We sure will, ma'am."

Anton retrieved the pill container from the drawer while Craig, who was finally standing out of the way, watched the medical personnel wheel their patient from the room. "Maybe it's for the best, Aunt Eleanor. Maybe you shouldn't live alone anymore."

Although his words were something anyone in the same situation might say, they didn't sit right with me. Eleanor had told us that Craig wanted power of attorney. What if her illness had just provided him with the opportunity he'd been looking for to take control?

CHAPTER 22

Craig made ushering movements with his hands. "We're all done here," he told us. "Time for you to go." We moved in a bunch toward the bedroom door, except for Anton.

"Hold on a moment, Mr. Brady," Anton said. "I'd like to talk to you."

Frowning, Craig threw a glance toward the bedroom doorway. He sighed. "Will it take long? I really need to follow my aunt to the hospital."

"I'll be finished by the time she's loaded in the ambulance and ready to go," Anton said. We'd been lingering in the room but when the chief directed raised brows at us, we hurried out into the hallway, dismissed.

"I'm so glad you suggested coming over here," I said to Grammie as we moved toward the staircase. I looked over my shoulder at the hallway carpet where Eleanor had collapsed. What if she'd lain there all night? My stomach clenched. Or what if she had tumbled headlong down this long flight of stairs? The fall might have been fatal.

The front door opened and Lukas walked in. "What's going on?" he asked, seeing the three of us coming down the stairs. "I saw Eleanor being loaded into an ambulance." He took off a rain slicker and hung it on a peg near the door, then raked his fingers through his damp hair, smoothing it into place. "They wouldn't tell me anything."

"Eleanor isn't feeling well," Grammie said. "But hopefully it's nothing serious. They're being cautious and taking her in for some tests."

"Whew," Lukas said, his expression lightening. "That's a relief. I've grown really fond of her."

"So have we," I said. "And guess what? We found out that Claudia left Belgium before her father died." I knew he'd want to hear this update. "So she didn't kill him or steal the diamonds from the open safe."

"Whew again," he said. "I'm really glad to hear that."

"That's why we're here so late," Madison added. "We wanted to tell Eleanor the good news as soon as we found out. But so far, we haven't had a chance." Voices sounded on the upstairs landing, which meant Anton and Craig were coming. Madison hunched her shoulders and put a finger to her lips. "Shh."

Lukas seemed to catch on. He pasted a pleasant and neutral smile on his lips as Craig clomped down the stairs ahead of Anton, hand clutching the banister. "I'm so sorry to hear about your aunt's illness, Craig. Please extend my wishes for a speedy recovery."

Instead of thanking Lukas, Craig curled his lip in response. "You might want to seek other accommodations, de Wilde. I'm going to strongly suggest that my aunt stop taking in guests." The word "guests" sounded like an epithet.

The smile on Lukas's face wavered only briefly. "I'll wait until I talk to Eleanor, if you don't mind. We paid for the summer in advance, so should she change her mind, we'll be owed a substantial refund."

Craig's response was to mutter something intelligible, and I had the feeling he was disconcerted by the thought of having to give money back. Without saying anything else, not even good night, he stalked across the hall, picked up his umbrella, and stormed out the front door. We heard a shout as he addressed the EMTs, who were still parked in the driveway.

"Nice fellow," Lukas said under his breath. "Poor Eleanor, having to deal with him."

Poor Eleanor, indeed. I prayed that she would recover fully and be able to carry out her plan to prevent Craig from taking over her finances. I'd love to be a fly on the wall when he learned that he had been cut out of the will.

"I'm heading over to the hospital," Anton told us. "I can keep you posted, if you want." He patted his pocket, where Eleanor's medications must be. "We'll be taking a close look at everything."

"We would love to get an update when you have time," Grammie said. "As long as it's within bounds of confidentiality."

"I can do that." Anton smiled around the circle, his eyes resting on Madison for a long moment. It was as if magnets were pulling the pair together. "I'll see you all later. And good job calling it in, Iris. You can't be too careful with someone Eleanor's age." He touched his hat brim and left, closing the door softly.

The strobing lights faded from view as the ambulance and cruiser started up the drive, followed by Craig's taillights. Neither emergency vehicle put on its siren, which meant they weren't treating Eleanor's condition as an emergency. That was a huge relief. She must not be in any immediate medical danger.

"If you'll excuse me," Lukas said, "I'm going to head up to my room."

Grammie looked at us. "The excitement seems to be over for the moment. We should get going."

We said good night to Lukas, but as he started up the stairs, I thought of something. "What happened with the police?" I asked. "When you went in for questioning."

He paused on the stairs, turning to face us while gripping the banister. "They asked me again about my movements the morning Hailey was killed. According to them, a witness saw me on the cliffs near where she was found." His blue eyes blazed. "It's a total lie. Yes, I was in the state park, but I didn't even see Hailey, let alone talk to her or hurt her."

"So the witness lied, then." Was it Patrick, trying to cover his own tracks, or someone else entirely? I'd thought Patrick, due to timing, but maybe I had jumped to conclusions. "Who was it, did they say?"

Lukas made a scoffing sound. "They wouldn't tell me," he said, his words terse. "Probably afraid I would go after the person."

A chilling thought struck me. What if Lukas was lying? The case was stacking up against him—first the ripped jacket, now a witness coming forward. Uncomfortable with even toying with these thoughts, I shifted on my feet, so glad he couldn't read my mind. I'd believed Lukas was innocent all along, but now the waters were good and muddy.

"If that's all . . ." Lukas began climbing the stairs again. "Please let me know if you get news about Eleanor."

"We will," Grammie called in a cheerful voice. She obviously wasn't tormented with doubts about the professor. "Have a good night."

Outside, the rain had dwindled to occasional big drops landing with splats. We hurried across the drive to the Jeep and climbed in. I was suddenly exhausted, all the adrenaline sparked by the emergency draining away. And my brain was worn out from all the theorizing and speculating. Time to take a break.

Grammie started the Jeep, the engine catching with a throaty roar. "I'm ready for bed now, that's for sure."

"Me too," Madison said from the back seat. "This visit didn't go the way I thought it would."

"But I'm so glad we were here," I said. Despite my resolution to shut off my brain, another terrible thought chimed in my mind. Why had Craig come over tonight? Unless he had a police scanner, there was no way he would know his aunt had a medical emergency. Had he been worried about her due to the storm? Maybe, but the less-than-charitable side of me doubted it. I didn't like or trust Craig.

As if reading my mind, Grammie said, "I'm glad Craig doesn't know about Claudia's jewelry. I don't trust him an inch." In the dim light from the dashboard, I saw that her expression was sour. "I know plenty of older people who have been ripped off by family or even caregivers. Things just *happen* to disappear."

"I'll never let that happen to you, Grammie," I said, angered on behalf of her friends. "I promise."

She threw me a smile. "Not that we have many valuables worth stealing." Then we said together, "Except Quincy." We all laughed.

The three of us lapsed into silence as we rode through the warm, wet night. Overhead, the clouds dissolved, revealing a sky spangled with stars. The storm was over.

We had almost reached the farmhouse when my phone and Madison's went off in unison. "I wonder if there's news already," I said, heart in my throat. What if Eleanor had taken a turn for the worse? I picked up my cell phone and scrolled.

The text message wasn't about Eleanor, and for few seconds, I couldn't make sense of it. Then I realized it was from Jamaica. Her name wasn't in my contacts, only her number. *Alarm went off. Someone is trying to break in.*

"Did you just get a message from Jamaica?" Madison asked.

"I sure did." I swiveled in my seat. "Grammie, how do you feel about taking a detour? Someone is trying to get into Jamaica's lab."

In answer, she put her foot on the gas and the Jeep took off like a rocket, speeding past our house. I idly wondered if Quincy was watching out the window and what he would think when we kept going. He definitely knew the sound of our cars. I'd seen him go to the door before Grammie even turned up the driveway. She said he did the same when he heard Beverly's engine approaching.

Grammie took a detour around downtown, where the speed limit dipped to a frustrating twenty-five miles per hour. Instead we raced over the back roads circling town and then headed down toward the water again, to the street where the old mill building was located. Grammie had lived in Blueberry Cove all her life, and she knew every nook and cranny and shortcut.

Another text came in. *Where r u? Be there in five.* Huh. I'd expected Jamaica to get here first, since she lived closer than us. But maybe she hadn't been home when the alarm went off.

"I thought Jamaica would be here," Madison said. "Where is she?"

"I have no idea," I said. *Almost there*, I wrote back to Jamaica. Grammie slowed to pull into the entrance of the complex. *We made it*, I added.

Call 911 if you see anyone. Which meant she hadn't called already, perhaps preferring to check out the situation first rather than raise a false alarm.

Or were we walking into a trap of some sort? With a sick feeling, I recalled the lurker in the alley. The sabotage to the cardboard boat. The unknown assailant who attacked Theo.

I put a hand to my aching head. My thoughts were spiraling out of control and I was seeing danger everywhere. But what if my fears were justified? Maybe I'd been guilty of tunnel vision, eliminating suspects because I liked them. Lukas, the prime suspect. And Jamaica. Something had been off about her claim that she was in her apartment the morning Hailey died. I was pretty sure she was lying. But why? Being at home alone wasn't much of an alibi.

Grammie drove through the empty parking lot toward the building, aiming her headlights onto the front entrance. The place looked deserted, with only a safety light shining in the entrance hall. Nothing moved as we pulled to a halt.

"Let me check the front door," Madison said, slipping out of the car before I could stop her. In the glare of the headlights, she ran to the entrance and tugged at the handle. The door didn't budge. Maybe the person was gone, or if they were still inside, they had secured the door for safety reasons. It was hard to tell either way, since the labs were located in the back of the building. Along the front, the windows were dark and blank. I didn't even know who used these rooms. I hadn't paid attention to the signs during the tour.

Another thing. The locked front door must mean the intruder had a key to the building. That narrowed the possibilities to another tenant or the seaweed project team. Or, I realized, someone who worked for the college, which now owned the building.

But what if Jamaica was lying? What if there hadn't been an intruder?

Madison put her hands to the glass and peered inside.

Stepping back, she shook her head at us then hurried back to the Jeep. "The place is locked up tight," she said, climbing in. "And I didn't see any signs of life in there. No lights except the one in the entranceway."

Grammie tapped her fingers on the wheel. "The person is probably long gone. Do you still want to wait for Jamaica?"

I turned around and studied the street. No headlights were approaching from either direction. This was the perfect opportunity to evade possible trouble. But instead of telling Grammie to leave, I found myself saying, "Why don't we circle the building? Maybe they're around back." I pressed the lock button. "Lock your doors, okay?"

"Okay, oh paranoid one," Madison muttered. But I heard the click that meant she had obeyed.

Grammie backed up then drove slowly around the near side of the long building. The drive was wide on this end, probably to allow trucks to make deliveries or pick up goods at the loading docks at the rear of the mill. While we ambled along, I tried to remember exactly where the labs were.

We skirted the loading area, a bulky shed-like structure protruding from the rear, and kept going. Now we were behind the wing where the labs were housed.

Something moved and I spotted a hooded figure at one of the windows. The figure turned, putting up a hand against the bright lights shining in his face. But not before I recognized that head of curly blond hair.

Theo.

CHAPTER 23

For a long moment, there was a standoff as Theo stared at us and we stared at him. Then he broke the deadlock and bolted, arms pumping. "I'm on it." Madison tugged at her door, swore softly since it was locked, then managed to get out. She tore after him.

"Call nine-one-one," I told Grammie, unlocking my own door. Maybe Madison could run a lot faster than me and was in much better shape, but I wasn't letting her deal with Theo alone. If not heavily muscled, he was still young and wiry. I slid out of the Jeep and followed the pair across the shadowy parking lot behind the old mill.

The surface was broken and uneven, with stray chunks of tar to trip me, and I almost twisted my ankle a couple of times. Up ahead, a spotlight shone down from the corner of the building, and I saw Madison and Theo running into the illuminated area.

With bounding leaps of her long legs, Madison caught up to Theo and grabbed his hood, jerking him backward. He stumbled, arms flailing, and Madison hooked a leg around his, a neat move that used his own body weight against him. He crashed to the ground with a shout.

I put on speed, wanting to assist her as she attempted to pin him down. As I reached them, gasping for air, headlights came around the corner of the building. The spotlight shining down revealed Jamaica, at the wheel of her VW bug.

She halted the car and jumped out, racing over to join us. After fighting to subdue the thrashing young man, she and I each took hold of a foot while Madison sat right on his chest and pinned his arms. "It's no use," Madison said. "You're not going anywhere." In the dim light, I saw the quick flash of a grin. "Ask my brother and cousins if you doubt me." I recalled that her fighting skills had been honed in tussles with the unruly Morris clan.

"It's too late anyway, Theo," I added. "We called the police." At mention of the law, he tried to kick his sneakered foot up but I leaned even harder on his shin. "They'll be here any second."

"Let me up," he said, thrashing his head back and forth. "I wasn't doing anything. Just going in to do some work after hours. Get a head start on tomorrow."

"So why did you run?" Madison asked reasonably. To my admiration, she didn't even sound winded. "That looks very suspicious to me."

"Who wouldn't?" he said. "I thought that old lady was going to run me over with her Jeep."

I grit my teeth. "That old lady is my grandmother, so watch your mouth. And don't tell me you were afraid of *her*." But he should have been afraid of us, obviously.

"Why were you out here in back, anyway?" Madison asked. "That's not the usual way in, I wouldn't think."

"My key didn't work," he said, changing tactics. "So I was trying to get inside a different way."

Jamaica hooted. "It didn't work because I changed the locks. After someone messed with my seaweed crop." Her voice rose, pain and betrayal clear. "Was that you, Theo? How could you? You know how hard I worked to get those spores to sprout. You were right there, working beside me." Angry tears flooded her eyes.

The teaching assistant fell silent. Then he said in a low, almost pleading voice, "Please let me up. I promise I won't run. But there's a huge rock sticking into my spine."

"All right. But you better stay put or I'll tackle you again." Madison got off his chest, and we released his ankles. Theo rolled over and scrambled to his feet after grabbing Madison's hand for leverage. I didn't see a rock but maybe I missed it in the near dark.

Another set of headlights swooped around the corner as the Blueberry Cove police SUV came into view, Anton at the wheel. Rhonda Davis was with him this time. The SUV pulled up a short distance away and the officers climbed out, leaving the engine running. Their headlights helped illuminate the scene.

Across the lot, the driver door of the Jeep squeaked open, followed by the bouncing beam of a cell phone flashlight. Grammie was coming over to join us.

"What's going on?" Anton asked, his tone deceptively casual. His keen gaze took us all in. Grammie must have told the dispatcher the nature of the call, but he probably wanted to hear it in our own words.

Theo started to blather protests of innocence, but Jamaica said in a stern voice, "Stow it, Theo." Surprisingly, he subsided. Jamaica explained how she'd seen someone trying to get into her lab earlier, unauthorized. "I changed the locks and installed cameras after an earlier incident involving my tanks," she said. "Lukas—Dr. de Wilde— urged me to report it, but I haven't had the time."

"We'll get to that in a minute," Anton said. Standing at his side, Rhonda was taking notes. "You saw someone trying to get in tonight. Did you recognize the person?"

"No," Jamaica admitted. "The camera isn't that great plus the angle was wrong. All I saw was someone in a hooded windbreaker."

Theo's eyes lit up. "Ha," he said. "Maybe it wasn't me." He spun on his heel, ready to walk off.

"Not so fast, young man," Grammie said. "We saw you trying to open that window."

"Plus you admitted to us that you tried to get in with your key, and when that didn't work, you tried another way," Madison said. "To get a head start on work, right?" she said with a sarcastic edge.

Theo's shoulders went down at the realization he wasn't off the hook. He glared at us from under a tangle of curls, his bottom lip thrust out.

Jamaica inhaled a deep breath. "I thought about calling nine-one-one when I saw the video, but I wanted to check out what was going on first. I let Madison and Iris know, in hopes they could get here faster than me."

"Where were you?" I asked. Last I'd known, Sophie had dropped her off at her apartment downtown, only blocks from here.

"I was out at the Sunrise Resort," she said. "After I got home earlier, I was too restless to go to bed. So I headed out there to listen to music." The resort was north of town, about five miles up Route One. She was right, our house was much closer to the mill, and so was Shorehaven, although Jamaica didn't know we'd gone to see Eleanor. The tension I'd been holding eased, as did the suspicions I'd been harboring about Jamaica. For now, at least.

Anton was listening intently, his eyes darting from face to face. "Who got here first then?" He never jumped to conclusions, I noticed. I should follow his example.

"We did," I said. "We didn't see anyone in the front of the building so we came around here to check. And then we saw Theo, standing at the lab's back window and trying to open it." I pointed to the Jeep, still parked where Grammie had left it. "When he saw us," I continued, "he ran off. Madison chased him and took him down.

I helped stop him from getting away, and then Jamaica showed up."

"Took him down?" Brief amusement curled Anton's lips. He glanced at Madison, who shrugged, then at Jamaica. "Did Mr. Nesbitt have permission to enter your lab tonight?"

Jamaica folded her arms. "No, he did not. If I'd wanted him to have access, I would have given him a new key."

"But you didn't tell me that," Theo sputtered. "I've gone in before, with my old key." I hated to admit it, but he had a point.

"Yeah," Jamaica said, "after I gave you an assignment." Her eyes drilled into him. "Do you have one from me right now?"

Theo's answer was to duck his head and toe his sneaker into the cracked tar.

"Mr. Nesbitt." Anton's voice was soft but somehow infused with authority, a compelling combination. I wished I could sound like that. "Why were you here?"

The teaching assistant shivered, a series of emotions running over his face. Then the words poured out of him. "I was supposed to turn off the breakers to the lab." He gestured toward the sky. "Make it look as if they flipped due to a spike from the storm. No one would find out until morning, when it would be too late." He slid a glance at Jamaica. "And I put dirty water into your tanks, before. That's what made the algae grow on the spores."

"You little—" Jamaica leaped forward, her hands outstretched. But before she could hit Theo, or maybe strangle him, Anton neatly inserted his larger bulk between the farmer and Theo. Frustrated, Jamaica yelled, "Why? Why would you do that?"

Theo had a sick, sheepish expression on his face. "He paid me to. I needed the money so I could go to Europe and do that fellowship."

There were so many things wrong with this picture, I didn't know where to begin. Talk about the complete and utter lack of intellectual integrity required to sabotage a Farming the Sea project. Not to mention that trying to ruin someone's business was a criminal offense. Malicious mischief, once again. Had Theo sliced our cardboard boat?

"And now you'll be doing a fellowship at the men's prison," Madison said, standing with arms crossed. She looked as disgusted as I felt.

"Who paid you, Theo?" Anton asked.

Good point. I'd been so broadsided by his confession I hadn't considered that aspect of it. Theo hadn't done this of his own volition. He was working under someone's direction. Someone who wanted Jamaica to fail.

Theo swallowed visibly, his Adam's apple bobbing. He glanced both ways as if afraid of being caught squealing. "It was Patrick," he said, his voice croaking.

Jamaica let out a screech of frustration and rage. "Seriously? It wasn't enough that he stole my recipe, he's trying to put me out of business?" Again she lurched toward Theo, who stepped back hastily. "How could you do this?"

"Don't let her get me," Theo said, real fear in his voice, cowering behind Anton.

Jamaica halted, eyes blazing, then pivoted on her heel and stalked away, muttering. Grammie hurried to her side. "Let's take a walk, Jamaica." The pair began to circle the parking lot, Grammie steering her out in a large circle to give her more territory to cover—and more time to calm down.

Anton began reading Theo his rights, telling him that he was under arrest for various charges. I walked a short distance away with Madison. Jamaica and Grammie were still circling the parking lot, their voices drifting our way.

"Wow," I said. "I totally wasn't expecting that. I thought we would find Patrick trying to get into Jamaica's lab, not Theo."

Madison stared at the arrest underway with narrowed eyes. "Me too. What a fool Theo is for doing Patrick's dirty work. He really blew it."

Rhonda was helping a handcuffed Theo get into the cruiser's back seat. "I wonder what else Theo did for Patrick?" Even as I said the words, my heart jumped with a new and terrible idea. Had he pushed his colleague off a cliff for money? Maybe Hailey had caught onto Patrick's plans to destroy Jamaica's business.

Madison's mouth opened in horror. "Do you think *Theo* killed Hailey?" she whispered, her voice rising to a squeak.

"I don't know. He was up there. He had access to the jacket." I raised my hands helplessly. "I'm not sure what to think."

"We need to talk to Anton." She trotted across the lot, trying to intercept him before he drove away. Rhonda was already in the cruiser. She whistled and waved, drawing his attention.

He turned and waited for us. "Is there something else?" he asked.

"Come over here a second," I said, indicating that he should move out of earshot of the SUV. When we were far enough away, I said, "You need to question Theo about Hailey." When he started to stay something, I interrupted. "Again, I mean. I know he was questioned once—we were there, remember? But I wonder if she was killed because of what Patrick was up to. Maybe she found out. Or maybe Theo wanted to eliminate her from competition for the fellowship." I paused to gulp in a breath, feeling as though I needed to hurry. I was sure Anton wanted to get back to the station to process Theo's arrest. "I know it sounds farfetched but I never would have guessed he'd betray Jamaica this way, either."

He was listening to me, I could tell by the expression on his normally stoic features. Encouraged, I went on. "And Patrick. He was at the cliffs that morning. I don't know what he said about Lukas"—that earned a sharp glance of surprise—"but he has obviously been up to something, as we now know. Hailey was working with him closely to try and sell those energy bars. Which Jamaica invented, by the way. So maybe Patrick killed her." I was kind of contradicting my earlier statement about Theo, but I really thought they should come down a little harder on Patrick. Especially now.

Anton gave us a brusque nod. "Thanks for your thoughts, Iris. We are putting out a BOLO on Patrick Chance, by the way. He's got a lot to answer for already." BOLO stood for "be on the lookout." He started to turn away, then paused. "Be careful, both of you, all right? Until we have Mr. Chance in custody, I don't want you taking any foolish risks."

Like responding to news of a break-in without backup, maybe? "Point taken," I said. I thought of a couple of other things I wanted to clear up. "Oh, just as a favor to us, can you ask Theo if he sliced up our boat? Or if he was the one lurking outside Ruffles and Bows the other night? Someone was."

Anton put his hands on his hips. "Is there anything else you haven't told me?"

"I'm sorry," I said. "It didn't seem worth reporting at the time. I didn't actually see anyone, but a garbage can was knocked over. An empty one. Why would an animal go after an empty can? And . . . I thought I heard something. But I honestly assumed it was just my mind playing tricks on me."

"Good point," Anton said. "I'll ask him." His eyes lit.

"By the way, I have good news. It looks like Eleanor is going to be okay. They're keeping her for a couple of days to do tests, but she's not in any immediate danger."

Madison and I let out huge sighs of relief. "Thanks for telling us that," I said. "I'm going to sleep a whole lot better now."

"Me too," Madison said. "I was really worried."

Anton motioned toward the cruiser. "I'd better get going. See you later." He trotted toward the SUV.

The cruiser had disappeared around the building by the time Jamaica and Grammie joined us again. "They're putting out a BOLO for Patrick," I told them. "And guess what, Grammie? Eleanor is okay. Still in the hospital but not in danger."

"Oh, I'm so relieved to hear that," Grammie said. "Jamaica, when we went to see Eleanor tonight, we discovered she was quite ill. So she went to the hospital to be checked out."

"Good news on both counts, then. Eleanor is great. And I'm so glad they're going after Patrick." Jamaica wrapped her arms around her lean middle, glancing at her laboratory windows with a shiver. "Maybe this nightmare will soon be over. I'm so glad we put in that security system. Otherwise I would have lost my whole crop."

Grammie gave the farmer a hug. "Hang in there, Jamaica. We're a phone call away if you need us."

"Thank you so much." Jamaica's eyes closed briefly as she returned the embrace. "I don't know what would have happened tonight without your help."

Theo would have gotten away, that's what. And probably returned another day to literally pull the plug on Jamaica's seaweed. Maybe catching Theo would be the thread that unraveled the rest of this puzzling case. I could only hope.

CHAPTER 24

The aroma of frying bacon and sausage guided me through the festival grounds toward the pancake breakfast tent, where lines had formed. This was the last day of the festival, but judging by the throngs of people milling around, it was still going strong.

No doubt the excellent weather all week had helped make the event a success. There hadn't been a drop of rain until last night. And now the thunderstorms had blown away, leaving the sky over the glittering bay a deep, rich blue without a single cloud. I was thankful no storms were in the forecast for tonight, when the outdoor fashion show was being held. The stage and catwalk were already up in readiness, and workers were stringing lights and testing the sound system. Jake was helping with the lights, and so was Ian's dad. I didn't see Ian, though. He must be at the job site already.

A familiar figure was right in the middle of the action, giving orders—Bella. I wasn't surprised, since the fashion show was her baby. She considered it her mission to make sure we were all well dressed here in the hinterlands of Maine. Flannel shirts and clumsy rubber-soled boots hadn't made the cut for the show, I was pretty sure, unless she found fashionable versions.

I changed course and headed toward the stage, hoping I

could drag her away for breakfast. The meeting had been her idea, after all, and I was starving. As I approached, Bella and Jake detached themselves from the other workers to confer over Bella's clipboard.

"Hi, guys," I said, walking up behind them. "Beautiful day, isn't it?"

They turned to me with smiles. "It sure is," Bella said. "And what a relief, after last night. I was worried the rain might hang on."

Jake tipped his head back and studied the sky. "Nope. A high pressure front pushed it all out of here."

Bella's dainty brows knotted as she studied my face. "Madison told me what happened last night, over at the seaweed lab. Did she really tackle Theo like a football player?"

"She sure did," I said. "And I helped hold him down, along with Jamaica, until the police got there."

Jake laughed. "I can just picture that. Why were the police involved?"

I realized that Jake really had been out of the loop since he and Sophie had broken up. We hadn't seen him much, which I regretted. I really liked Jake.

"Theo was trying to break into the building." I gave them a condensed version, hitting only the highlights. "There's a BOLO out for Patrick Chance, if you see him, Jake," I concluded. "He owns an old lobster boat, painted pale green."

"I know that boat," Jake said. "It used to belong to a lobsterman who's now retired. One of the old-timers." He pointed a finger at me. "And I think I might have seen Jamaica down at the docks, too."

"Probably," I said. "She's quite stunning." I gave him a brief description of her.

"Oh yeah," Jake said. "That's her. She runs a little white skiff, sixteen-footer." He laughed. "One morning

I thought she and I were going to crash right into each other, she was moving so fast." He made a whining noise while gesturing with his hand and laughed again. "I blinked and there she was, coming right at me. It can be hard to see a small boat at that time of day."

"When was that, Jake?" I asked, almost afraid to hear the answer. My intuition already knew. But maybe it was wrong.

"Hmm." He scratched his cheek, thinking. "When was that?" Light dawned in his eyes. "It was the day before the festival. I remember because I was thinking about how many lobsters we were going to need." He laughed. "A lot more than usual."

The morning Hailey was killed. Jamaica had plainly told me that she had been at home drinking coffee. But instead, Jake had seen her racing across the bay in her boat. "Which way was she going?" I asked, barely able to force the words past the lump of disappointment and sorrow in my throat. I knew the answer to that too.

He looked puzzled at my question but he answered. "I was cutting across the mouth of the harbor, headed south. She was coming the other way."

Toward the cliffs at the state park. Jamaica had lied to me. She had been at the crime scene that day, not at her apartment.

"Are you okay, Iris?" Bella asked in concern when I let out a little groan.

I shook my head, not wanting to verbalize my fears in this very public spot. "I'll be all right." Once I got over my shock. "Do you still have time for breakfast? I understand if you're too busy."

"Yes, I do. We really need to talk about tonight." Bella flipped through the clipboard then handed it to Jake. "Do you mind taking over supervision duties for a while? Everything is in pretty good shape."

He took the clipboard and waved it at us. "Go, eat. We'll be fine."

Bella and I started walking toward the breakfast tent, where I noticed with gratitude that the line had shortened. Although after hearing about Jamaica, my appetite was pretty much gone. Bella didn't press me for explanations. Instead she burbled on about the upcoming show, her light chatter giving me time to regroup, for which I was grateful.

We joined the back of the line and as we slowly moved toward the food, a little of my appetite came back. It all smelled so good. At one long griddle, a cook was expertly turning golden disks studded with fresh blueberries. Beside him, another cook used tongs to turn strips of bacon and link sausage.

After we handed over tickets, the cooks served plates holding three pancakes and three pieces of our choice, bacon or sausage. I chose sausage, then collected pats of butter, tubs of maple syrup, napkin-wrapped silverware, a cup of coffee, and orange juice. Huh. A lot of food for someone who wasn't really hungry.

We found seats at one of the long tables, sitting across from each other. Bella unrolled her napkin and picked up a fork, which she used to scoop butter from the tiny containers onto her pancakes. "Madison texted me about last night." She picked up a second pat. "Sounds like you guys were really busy. And I'm so, so happy that Eleanor is okay."

When we'd gotten home last night, I'd gone right to bed, not even thinking to text Bella and Sophie with all the news. I was pleased that Madison had done it, since I hated leaving our friends out of the loop, even inadvertently.

"Me too." I spread butter over my pancakes, watching it melt. "Grammie and I plan to go over to the hospital later and visit her." Grammie was going to pick up flowers at the local florist for us to bring.

"Wish I could join you," Bella said. "But with the show . . ." She ripped open a maple syrup tub and poured the sweet liquid onto her pancakes. "Please give her my best wishes."

"I sure will." I took the first bite of pancake, along with a piece of sausage. Mouthwatering maple goodness. "So, tell me what I need to do tonight."

Bella explained that for the regular portion of the show, I would sit on a panel of judges. The models participating represented various local organizations and had put together outfits for different categories. Some of the clothing had come from Bella's and other stores, while some was homemade, vintage, or otherwise sourced.

"We're having Rich Hammond from the Grille do the announcing," she said. "He's going to describe each outfit and what pieces went into it. Then you and the other judges pick winners." She showed me the scoring sheet. We would choose best in a category—say, summer sportswear—and then most creative, funniest, and best accessories for each category. There were a lot of opportunities for the models to win prizes.

"We used to just model outfits from various stores," Bella went on. "But everyone got bored with that. This way it's a lot of fun, and people come out to cheer on family and friends who are modeling."

"It does sound fun," I said. If the entries in the regular fashion show were anywhere near as creative as the lobster bib ones, it would be a hoot. "So, how is it going to work for the lobster bib portion?"

Bella chased a piece of pancake around her plate, mopping up syrup. "You're the only judge, so you will pick the top three winners."

That made sense, but I guess I hadn't thought that part

through. All eyes would be on me—well, once they could tear them away from those wild and wacky outfits. "Wow, that's a lot of responsibility."

"Don't worry. There's also audience voting, using a phone poll we're setting up. So we'll have the people's choice for the top three as well."

"Does that mean a mob won't come after me if I don't pick their favorite for the grand prize?" I was only half joking. I'd witnessed how vocal and riled up people could be when they disagreed with a decision, even if the stakes might seem small to many.

"We're going to have Rich pull names for the prizes," Bella said. "Once the six winners are chosen."

This was all very elaborate for such a small contest, but I didn't argue. Some of the people entering were going all out from what I could see, so we needed to give them full consideration.

Once we finished eating, we cleared our dishes to make way for the next wave of pancake eaters. Bella gave me a hug. "See you tonight, Iris. It's going to be fun."

"I think so too." I watched as she bustled back toward the stage, thinking I might take a stroll along the shore before going to the store. It was such a lovely morning.

The noise and activity of the festival receded as I walked along the shore path, passing the library and then a row of historic homes along the waterfront. If I went far enough, I'd reach the yacht club, located on a spit of land extending into the harbor.

This was lovely, the breeze ruffling my hair and the warm sun on my face. Gulls cried and the incoming tide lapped gently against the rocky shore. Halfway along the spit, I saw a man sitting on a bench. When I got closer, I recognized Lukas.

But this wasn't the groomed and gorgeous European

dream I'd met only days ago. This Lukas was unshaven, his face gray and drawn, his broad shoulders slumped.

"Lukas," I said, standing in front of him. "How are you?"

He looked up at me with bloodshot eyes. "Not so good, Iris. Ever see your whole world implode right before your eyes?"

Without invitation, I sat beside him on the bench, smoothing my skirts. I was already dressed for work in a pale blue dress and white pinafore. "Yes," I answered simply. My parents' deaths of course, then the loss of my beloved grandfather last winter. Oh, and being laid off from a job I loved, that had stung too, but paled in the light of greater losses.

"I've lost both my teaching assistants, one tragically, the other stupidly, my teaching career is on the line, and one of my seaweed farmers is wanted by the police." His lips twisted. "Oh, all of it is nothing compared to what Hailey lost, but seriously, my life is a train wreck."

It did sound dire when he put it that way. "You still have Jamaica," I pointed out. "She's doing okay." Then my heart squeezed. She'd lied to me. I bit back further assurances, hating it when I got them from people who were well-meaning but basically minimizing the situation. "Honestly?" I said. "You're screwed."

That blunt statement startled a bark of laugher out of him and then he was roaring, doubled over, tears streaming. So was I, the belly laughter a huge release of the anxiety and tension I'd been stuffing down for days.

We slumped back against the bench as the laughter drained away. "I needed that." I discovered clean tissues in my apron pocket and handing him one.

"Me too." He wiped his eyes and blew his nose. "Thanks, Iris. You're a good friend."

I warmed at the compliment as we sat side by side

for a few minutes watching small waves ruffle the shore. Far out in the bay, a tanker made its way toward Belfast. No sign of a pale green lobster boat. Where had Patrick gone? He couldn't hide forever, could he?

Faint music drifted from loudspeakers at the festival as the first rides began to move. Tomorrow cleanup would begin and by evening, tents, rides, and booths would be gone. The park would be back to normal until the next event.

Would Lukas's life ever be back to normal? I sure hoped so.

"Iris," he said in a musing voice, "remember the matchbook from Chateau de Mount-Gauthier?"

It took me a second to catch up. "Yes, I do. Did you find out why Hailey had it?"

"Not quite," he said. "But I did remember that Ruben attended a conference there. He was presenting his bio-fuel concept to a small group of industry experts."

"And maybe Hailey was there, too?" If so, I hoped it was on a professional basis. The thought that Ruben might have been involved with a student disgusted me.

"I'm not sure if she went," he said. "I didn't see a list of attendees. But sometimes professors invite students along as a learning experience. She would have met some top names in biofuel that weekend."

"Thanks, Lukas. I guess it's more than we knew before." But not much more. The matchbook might be merely a memento of a nice trip. Or maybe it wasn't even hers. She might have picked it up somewhere.

Dead end or vital clue? Right now I had no idea.

CHAPTER 25

A small but modern hospital, Blueberry Cove Medical Center was located on the crest of the hill overlooking downtown and the harbor. I drove us up there in Beverly, Grammie cradling the bouquet she had bought earlier for Eleanor.

"Are you nervous about tonight?" she asked me as I turned into the hospital lot.

"A little," I said, acknowledging the knot of excited trepidation in my gut. It was a familiar feeling, one I experienced every time I had to speak in public.

The fashion show was two hours from now, giving me barely enough time to visit Eleanor before going home to shower and change. After the show, I was planning to attend the semi-formal dinner and dance under the stars with Ian as my date. I could hardly wait for that part of the evening. We almost never dressed up, so it should be fun.

Ian looked great in a dinner jacket. With a sigh, this time of anticipation, I pulled into the visitor slot and turned off the car. We gathered our handbags and the flowers and made our way to the lobby.

Both of us faltered slightly when the big doors swished open, inviting us to step inside. We hadn't been to the hospital since last winter, before Papa Joe died. Thankfully they'd released him under the hospice program and he had spent his last days in his own home. But the mingled aroma of disinfectant and floor wax was still all too familiar.

Then Grammie lifted her chin and charged across the squeaky clean floor to the front desk. "Good evening," she said to the attendant. "Eleanor Brady's room, please." Judging by her pleasant, steady tone, one would never know the heartbreak she had experienced in this place.

We took the elevator to the second floor, to the unit where Eleanor was staying. At the station, a nurse directed us to her room. "Miss Eleanor is doing great," he said. "We're going to miss her around here."

I took away two things from his comment. Eleanor was well-liked by the staff *and* she was being discharged soon. Thanking him for his help, we continued down the corridor and found Eleanor's room. The door was open, but we knocked. A pulled curtain was blocking our view of the bed.

"Come in," Eleanor called. My heart lifted with joy. She sounded so much stronger and clearer than the last time we had seen her.

She was propped in bed, reading a magazine, her eyeglasses up on her head. To her left, the curtains were open, revealing a view of the harbor. Not bad at all for a hospital room.

Grammie set the extravagant bouquet on the wide windowsill, next to a few others. Eleanor exclaimed in delight. "Those are lovely. Thank you."

We both gave her a kiss on the cheek, then settled to visit. Grammie sat in a chair and I leaned up against the windowsill.

"I understand you're getting out of here soon," Grammie said. "Well, the nurse didn't say that explicitly but we read between the lines."

Eleanor closed the magazine and scooted upright a little more. "I'm being discharged tomorrow afternoon. And though everyone has been wonderful here, I'm eager to get home." She glanced in the direction of the room door. "Do you mind closing the door, Iris?"

I hurried to comply, wondering what she didn't want anyone to overhear. I shut the door gently and returned to my perch.

Eleanor's expression was grave. "They found Valium in my blood work. Someone has been drugging me, and three guesses who."

We both gasped at the news, although we'd suspected something like this all along. "Valium can cause confusion, can't it?" Grammie said. "I know there are some medications that affect us even more when we get older."

Eleanor lifted a brow, a glint of humor in her eyes. "You mean when you're as ancient as me? But you're right, Anne. The doctor explained it to me." She leaned forward slightly, dropping her voice. "And it was in my herb supplements, the ones in capsules. Isn't that a dirty trick?"

"It sure is," I said, angry at whoever had done such a heinous thing. It had to be Craig Brady, the only person I knew with something to gain—all of Eleanor's property, including the diamonds he didn't even know about. That reminded me of the other reason why we were here.

"The police have been informed," Eleanor said. "I don't know how they can prove anything, but it's certainly been a warning for me. And I'm taking steps."

"Good for you," Grammie said. "We're here if you need anything." She turned to look at me. "Do you want to do the honors?"

"I'd love to." I slid off the sill and moved closer to the bed. Then I wasn't sure how to begin. Eleanor didn't even know about her grandfather's horrible death. "Lukas helped us do some research into Claudia's life. It was easier for him since he can read Flemish, French, and German."

Eleanor was listening intently, her gaze never leaving my face. "What a nice young man he is," she commented. "How fortuitous he was here to help."

"It was," I said. "He soon learned that Claudia did come from a noble family. Her father was a baron."

Her mouth dropped open slightly. "Wow. That is not what I was expecting to hear. I'm related to European royalty?" Her laugh was disbelieving.

"We could always tell," Grammie joked. "You're so queenly."

"Bossy, you mean," Eleanor said, smiling at her friend. "Don't hold back, Anne."

After they were done laughing, I cleared my throat. "There's more, Eleanor. And I'm afraid it's a tragic story."

Her face sobered as she clasped her hands together in her lap. "Go on."

"Your grandfather was killed in 1932, during a robbery, they think. He was a diamond dealer." I hurried to tell her the rest. "Claudia had left the country before it happened. She was on the *Lapland* when he died." I didn't bother to connect the dots. Eleanor was capable of doing that for herself. "Lukas found an engagement announcement. She was supposed to marry another baron."

Eleanor thought for a long moment, her eyes distant. "She must have been very unhappy," she said, "to leave her luxurious lifestyle and become a nursery maid, of all things. Poor Mama. I'm glad she at least had us." She paused. "Now I know why she never spoke of Belgium or her family. She wanted to put it all behind her."

Maybe the murder was why Claudia had kept a low profile in the United States. She didn't want to be dragged into the scandal. Or found by her fiancé. Without any real evidence, I sensed she'd been running away from him. Maybe it had been an arranged marriage.

"And then she had a fairy-tale ending to her story," Grammie said softly. "She met and married a handsome prince and had a darling daughter."

Eleanor greeted Grammie's fanciful words with a snort, but she was smiling. "I'd like to think she had a happy ending. We all deserve that. Well, most of us, anyway."

On the other hand, I couldn't help thinking, some of us deserved jail time, including Craig Brady. A gentle knocking sounded on the room door, and I went to answer, thinking it was a nurse. But Cookie Abernathy, attorney-at-law, stood there, holding a buttery leather tote. "May I come in, Iris?" she asked with a smile. Cookie had been Grammie's attorney when Grammie was a murder suspect earlier this year. Not that Cookie's practice was confined to criminal law. Like many rural attorneys, she served clients in a number of ways.

"Please do," I said, standing back to let her into the room. I closed the door again, figuring that other people didn't need to know Eleanor's business with Cookie. And in fact, Grammie and I should excuse ourselves so they could talk in privacy.

"Eleanor. How are you?" Cookie shook her client's hand gently. Grammie had risen from the chair and Cookie sat, setting the bag by her feet.

"I'm fine, thank you," Eleanor said. "I got the word that they're going to spring me from this place tomorrow." She and Cookie laughed, but then fear flickered in Eleanor's eyes. "I want to make sure everything is written in stone before I take a step out of this room."

"We can do that." Cookie pulled a sheaf of documents from her bag. "I have what we discussed right here." She handed a document to Eleanor. "If you're happy with that, you can sign." She glanced up at us. "Do you mind hanging around for a few minutes? We need two witnesses to Eleanor's will."

"We'd be happy to do that," Grammie said. "Why don't we step out into the hall, Iris? Cookie, let us know when you're ready for us."

At home, I took a leisurely shower and dried my hair, then padded about in a robe getting my outfit ready. Curled in the middle of my bed, Quincy looked on. "What do you think, Quince?" I held up the vintage coral semi-formal dress I'd bought to wear tonight. The bodice was ruched and fitted, the skirt a froth of organza. A pair of matching T-strap pumps and a clutch bag completed the outfit.

My phone rang, and expecting Ian or Bella, I picked it up to look. Lars Lavely? With a sigh, I answered. Otherwise he'd continue to call or worse, stalk me at the fashion show. I might as well get it over with.

"Hello, Lars," I said. "What's up? I'm kind of busy getting ready for tonight."

"Oh, yeah, the fashion show." Computer keys clattered. "I'll only keep you a minute. I understand you were at the scene when Theo Nesbitt was arrested. How did you happen to be at the lab?"

I plopped down on the bed, not wanting to answer his question at all. But if I blew him off, I would lose the opportunity to find out what he knew. The paper might have updates from the state police.

"Well," I said slowly, reaching out to rub Quincy's chin. "Jamaica asked us to swing by because she got a security alert and we were closer to the lab than she was. She didn't know if her new system was working. But it works great. Make sure to put that in the article."

He grunted. "You do get yourself right in the middle of things, Iris. Ever think about being a reporter?"

"Not really," I said honestly. But I probably would make a good one. I was nosy enough and yes, I did have a knack for finding trouble. "So, I have a question for you. Any updates on the BOLO for Patrick Chance?"

"Bunch of unconfirmed sightings," he said. "Both his truck and boat are missing, which is a neat trick when you think about it."

"He must have an accomplice," I blurted. Then, realizing I'd said that out loud, I quickly added, "That's off the record, by the way."

"It's the obvious conclusion," Lars said loftily. "Nesbitt was released on bail this morning. No one has seen him since." Keys clattered again. "Want a preview of my article about the BOLO? I found a great picture of Patrick to use."

"Sure," I said. "Send it over." Now Lars was treating me like a colleague. Odd, but I ran with it. "I'm always impressed with your articles, Lars." Though not always in a good way, Mr. Tabloid Man.

"Lay it on, Iris, lay it on," he muttered. "Sent it. Take a look."

The picture of Patrick made me bark a laugh. He stared wide-eyed into the camera, unshaven and his hair a mess, looking completely unhinged. Lars had framed it with BOLO—WANTED.

"Wow. Where'd you find that?" I could hear the door and window locks clicking shut all over town.

Lars gave a satisfied chuckle. "Social media. Taken during a binge, I reckon. I cropped out the beer bottles in both hands." He chuckled again. "When are people going to learn?"

Maybe after Lars featured their worst moments in the *Blueberry Cove Herald*. But tactful me didn't say that, and I signed off, reminding him I had to get ready. My stomach clenched with anxiety again. I really didn't like speaking in public, especially into microphones. Quincy butted my hand with his head, a signal to keep patting him. "But it will be over soon," I told him. "Only a couple of hours and I'll be off the hook."

CHAPTER 26

As a judge, a parking spot had been reserved for me at the park, a perk I really appreciated. The evening was warm but I had grabbed a white mohair wrap for later. The dinner dance was also being held outside, and as I hurried along the sidewalk, heels clicking, I heard the strains of "I Only Have Eyes for You" drifting from the music stage. The band must be warming up.

The models were getting ready in a large tent behind the catwalk stage, so I went there first. All was pandemonium inside, with people popping in and out of makeshift dressing rooms. I saw my grandmother's hairstylist, Moriah, dashing around with a giant can of hairspray and a determined look on her face.

"Iris, there you are." Bella checked off my arrival on her ever-present clipboard. "You can go ahead and take a seat onstage, if you want." A gaggle of teens pushed past us with their garment bags, yelling to one another. "It'll be a little quieter."

"Okay," I said. "See you soon." I dodged a woman pulling a makeup case on wheels and got out of there. Bella had her work cut out for her, creating order out of that chaos. And she somehow would, I had no doubt.

Besides me, the fashion-show judges included Ian's mother, Fiona Stewart; Zadie Morris; and Sophie, who looked great in a blue sheath dress with a matching bolero.

"Sophie," I cried. "I didn't know you were judging." I hoped Jake would come tonight, and that they would finally make up and put the rest of us out of our misery.

She laughed. "I didn't either. But someone dropped out and I was recruited. You know how hard it is to say no to Bella."

"I sure do," I said, pulling out a chair as I greeted Fiona and Zadie. We were seated behind a table at one side of the stage, where we would have an excellent view of the models. From here, we could also see the chairs filling up fast on both sides of the catwalk. "Looks like we're getting a good turnout," I said to Sophie.

"We are," Sophie said. "I heard they sold out."

"That's great news." Even though people could view the stage from different spots in the park, for a really good look they had to buy a ticket for a seat. Most people were happy to do so, since the five-dollar fee was benefiting the festival's chosen charities.

Horatio Morris bounced up the side stairs to the stage. "I came to wish the judges well," he said. "We've broken our funding goals this year by quite a margin." Horatio was on the finance committee for the festival.

"We were just talking about that," I said. "Awesome."

"It sure is," he said, bending to give his wife a quick kiss. "I'll see you after. Save the first dance for me, dear."

"You bet I will," Zadie said with a laugh. "See you later."

Before leaving the stage, Horatio came over and hunkered down beside me, his expression serious. "Remember the matter we were discussing the other day, at the Grahams?"

"I sure do." Horatio had mentioned the biofuel investment Ruben was promoting, said he was looking into it.

Horatio pressed his lips together as if reluctant to say more. Then he sighed. "I hate to say this, and it's for your ears only, but the proposal is far from solid. Another group of scientists is planning to process seaweed using an almost identical process they've already patented. The two are similar enough that there will probably be legal challenges for Ruben if he goes ahead."

"Got it," I said. Not that I was an expert in how technology start-ups worked, but whoever held patents held the power. Patent infringement was a big no-no. "Thanks for the info."

He rose to his feet and tapped the tabletop. "I'll leave you to it, then. Thought you should know." He strode away with a wave.

Music blared as Bella and Rich walked out onstage. "Good evening, everyone," Bella said into the microphone. "Welcome to the Blueberry Cove Fashion Show." Spotlights danced across the stage as the music struck up again. The audience clapped and cheered.

I pushed thoughts of Ruben's investment away and focused on my judging duties. It was showtime.

The fashion show was really fun, with great outfits in a number of categories. Models of all ages swung tennis rackets and golf clubs, carried tiny dogs in handbags, and clomped across the stage in hiking boots. Master of ceremonies Rich Hammond displayed a great sense of humor as he commentated, making the audience laugh. We tabulated votes, selected winners, and then it was time.

The band struck up "Under the Sea" as the other judges slipped off the stage and Bella motioned for me to come forward. Praying I wouldn't trip and fall flat on my face in front of hundreds of onlookers, I picked my way across the stage to her side. The lights were blinding, preventing much of a view of the audience, but I did see Grammie right by the stage. She was holding Quincy, who was leashed. She'd said she might bring him. The sight of those I loved best gave me a huge boost, and I was able to smile into the bright void straight ahead.

"Don't leave your seats yet," Bella said. "We have a very special treat for you tonight. Our first annual Lobster Bib contest." She paused for clapping. "As owner of Ruffles and Bows, which specializes in aprons, Iris kindly agreed to judge this portion for us. So please, sit back and relax."

Then she handed the mic to me. *Eek.* "Hel . . . hello everyone," I said, not used to hearing my voice boom out like that. "I'm so excited to be here." As if agreeing, my voice rose to a squeak. "We've got some very creative entries tonight. These are not your mother's lobster bibs, folks. So without further ado, let's begin."

There. I was done, for now. I handed the mic to Rich, who held a paper with information about our dozen entrants, and hurried back to my chair. A glass of water waited there for me, refilled by someone, and I took a sip. Then I almost spit out the water when the first competitor strolled onto the stage.

The contestant wore a huge stuffed lobster attached to her front, and even stranger, a hat shaped like a lobster's head, antennas and all.

"Now that's what I call a lobster bib," Rich said, letting out a rolling chuckle. "Let's give our first entry a big round of applause."

The crowd went wild as each contestant strolled out onstage. The man who wanted electricity wore lights that flashed in the shape of a lobster. "Don't try this at home," Rich said, to laughs. Another woman's bib apron was trimmed with mini lobster buoys, which was very cute, and the clown, at least I think it was him, wore a hazmat suit, complete with booties. Another wore a doctor's mask and carried a scalpel. They were ridiculous and over the top and really fun.

After tabulating votes—the lighted outfit won hands down—and handing out prizes, my duties were finally done.

I was climbing down from the stage when one of the contestants approached. "I want you to have this," she said, thrusting the lobster-buoy apron at me. "Maybe you can display it in your store."

"Seriously?" I said. "A lot of work went into this." It would go in the window on a mannequin, I decided, if she really wanted me to have it.

She nodded. "Yes, it's a gift." She started to back away. "And I love your store by the way. So glad you opened it."

That was nice to hear. "Thanks," I called. "Have a good night." I glanced around the stage area, which was practically deserted. Everyone had moved over to the dinner tent. I didn't want to carry the apron all night, so I decided to pop over to my car and leave it there. But before I went, I called Anton to tell him the latest about Ruben. He didn't answer so I left a message. Maybe he was with Madison at the dance.

I skirted the festival grounds, now quiet, and headed to the parking lot. On the way there, I heard the throb of an engine down near the wharf. Only a few boats used that part of the harbor since the ferries docked at the wharf.

In the sodium glow of security lights I saw a lobster boat, one of the old-fashioned wooden ones. Like Patrick's. But it was white, not pale green.

"Iris? Is that you?" a man's voice said from up the path. "How are you tonight?"

Great. I recognized that accent. "Ruben," I said. "What are you doing here?"

The professor sauntered out of the dark toward me,

a big grin on his face. "I'm on my way to the dance." He snapped his fingers, moving his hips back and forth. "Hoped I'd see you tonight."

Oh, brother. "I have a boyfriend, Ruben. I thought you knew that." I gestured toward the parking lot still a distance away. "Now if you'll excuse me, I need to get going."

In a flash, his friendly demeanor dropped. "You're not going anywhere," he said, his voice a snarl.

I yelped when I saw he had a gun, pointed right at me. "What are you doing?" My hands went up and my car keys and the apron fell to the pavement. Thankfully my tiny clutch, which held my phone and a lipstick, was in my pocket. Gotta love those pockets in '50s dresses.

"Move," he said, gesturing me down the path. "We're taking a little ride."

I moved as slowly as possible, trying to figure out how to get away from him. I thought of screaming, but he now had the gun jabbed right into my kidneys. A distance away at the park, the band struck up a lively swing tune with horns and drums. No one could hear anything over that.

"Iris?" A soft voice called behind me. "Wait up." Heels clattered along the pavement. Oh no. Sophie.

"Welcome," Ruben said. "Come along or your friend will die. Okay?"

Keeping the gun trained on our backs, he forced us to walk down to the waterfront, where the lobster boat still sat, engines running.

"Why are you doing this?" I asked. Then I knew, the truth flashing over me like icy water. "You killed Hailey."

"Keep moving." He prodded me with the gun again, hard. Sophie whimpered. "And the little witch deserved it. Threatening to ruin me and all I've worked for."

"But why go after me? I haven't done anything." I'd

barely had a chance to digest what Horatio had told me about Ruben's company, that it was on shaky ground.

"Craig Brady," was his answer. "He warned me about your nosing around. About your attempts to drive a wedge between him and his aunt so he won't get his due."

Craig was a crook, complaining about me to try and justify how he was trying to cheat his elderly aunt. And so was Ruben. "You're using technology from those other scientists, aren't you? Your company is a fraud."

Ruben laughed. "Amateurs borrow but professionals steal. Isn't that the saying? Of course I used it, changed a few little minor details. Everyone does it."

Next to me, Sophie stumbled and I saw how scared she looked. I reached out and took her hand, squeezing it. We'd get out of this somehow. *Failure is not an option.* The thought of one of Grammie's favorite sayings heartened me.

Surely people must be wondering where we were by now. Ian was expecting me to join him at dinner, for one thing. Horns blatted in the bandstand again and I tried to send him a telepathic message. *Need you. Send help.* If I could get to my phone somehow, I'd send a real message.

We went down the ramp to the lobster boat. "I've got a couple of passengers for you," Ruben called.

Patrick stepped out from under the canopy, his grin wolfish. "Mission accomplished, huh? Climb aboard."

Another figure ducked out from the shelter, and my heart sank. Theo. He was in this up to his eyeballs, obviously making a bad situation worse for himself.

I hesitated. Should we make a break for it? I could jump into the water and maybe Sophie could run . . . but the grip of Ruben's hand on my arm defeated those thoughts. Patrick had gotten out of the boat and grabbed Sophie, and despite her struggles, he managed to push her over the gunwale. I was next, landing in a heap on my knees on the hard wood planks. I covertly patted my skirt, relieved that I still had my clutch, then crawled over to Sophie. She leaned against me and we huddled together.

The engines spooled up as Patrick backed away from the dock. With a spin of the controls, we were facing out into the harbor. "Next stop, Canada," he called. Theo whooped.

They were taking us to Canada? But that spark of hope quickly died when Ruben spoke. "We have one stop to make first," he said. "Two passengers are disembarking."

Uh-oh. Sophie's body went rigid. "You can't kill us," I said. "They'll chase you down until you die." I knew Anton would. My fingers curled into claws. Before things got that far, I would fight for my friend's life. I wasn't going down without a battle.

The men exchanged smug glances. "They won't go after us," Patrick said. "Not if it's pinned on Jamaica." He laughed. "She was so dumb to chase me down that day and beg me to come back to her. I said no, babe, that ship has sailed." He puffed out his chest with a laugh. "And then she went and lied to the police about it."

"Sweet, sweet Jamaica," Ruben said. "She's taking the big fall."

Oh, Jamaica. But I'd been there, making a last-ditch effort for a relationship that truly shouldn't be saved. She'd obviously been too humiliated to tell anyone, and backtracking on her alibi would only make her look guilty. But Jake had seen her, so it was sure to come out now, once—no, we couldn't let that happen.

I closed my eyes and tried to picture my phone screen. Edging even closer to Sophie so they couldn't see my movements, I slipped my fingers into the clutch and touched the screen. It wasn't locked, thank goodness. But I really needed to look at it so I could send a text.

The boat rocked in the wake of a larger ship farther out, and that gave me an idea. With a groan I rolled over onto my stomach. "I feel sick. I always get so, so seasick." So, so big a lie. I groaned again, more deeply this time, and began retching, my whole body convulsing.

"Don't throw up on the deck," Patrick said with alarm. "Do it over the rail." We were out in the harbor now, far from the lights of shore.

"Okay," I whimpered. "I'll try to make it." Gagging and retching, I crawled to the transom in the rear and leaned over the rail. My great acting job kept them all far away, I noticed with satisfaction. While I was curled over, still pretending to throw up, I slid my phone onto my lap. First I turned off the ringer. I didn't want them to hear ringing if someone tried to call. I texted Ian and Anton. *Send help. Patrick's boat Jamaica's seaweed farm Ruben gun.* Without waiting for a reply, I put my phone on record and slipped it into my pocket. After retching a couple more times, I crawled back to Sophie.

"Ugh," I said, making a show of wiping my mouth. "That was awful." I almost laughed at how absurdly disgusted they looked. Thinking of my phone busily recording away, I said loudly, "So you're taking us to Jamaica's seaweed farm, I'm guessing."

"Quit guessing," Ruben said with a snarl. "And stop talking. You're about the nosiest woman I've ever met."

"You know, I really didn't suspect you, *Ruben*," I said, practically shouting his name for the phone's benefit. Sophie threw me a strange look. "I thought Patrick killed Hailey. Or even Jamaica." I looked at Theo. "Or you." I knew there wasn't much chance Ruben would have a change of heart and let us go even if he had jumped to conclusions falsely, but it was a worth a try. And oh, how I hoped someone would hear this someday.

Ruben chuckled, as if reminiscing. "It wasn't really

planned. I followed her out to the cliffs that morning to see if I could talk sense into her. But good luck with that. If I didn't pay her a huge sum of money, she was going to blow the whistle to the other scientists and my investors. I couldn't believe it. She was my top student and I even took her to a premier event at Chateau de Mount-Gauthier." He pushed one palm forward. "So, pow. Over she went."

Picturing the scene, my belly lurched, the feigned sickness about to become real. "And you pinned it on Lukas by using his jacket." Maybe if it hadn't gotten ripped, Ruben would have left it at the scene. Anything to point the finger at someone else.

"Why not?" Ruben said. "He didn't like her either. If she didn't get the fellowship, she was going to claim discrimination. She had a letter to the dean all drafted. I saw it when I searched her pack."

I hated to say it, but Hailey really had gone to the dark side in her struggles to get ahead. Not that she deserved death for it, though. Maybe getting kicked out of school and a little jail time for attempted blackmail.

"She tried to blackmail me, too," Patrick said, his tone heavy with disgust. "She was going to tell Jamaica my plans to push her out of the seaweed business. I planned to have Theo take over her lease."

"Seriously, Theo?" Even I could hear the disgust in my voice. "You were helping these crooks?"

In response, Theo's shoulders hunched and he looked scared. As he should. Sabotaging plants was one thing. Aiding and abetting our murders, quite another. Figuring he was the weakest link, I decided to try and break him.

Cliffs loomed out of the dark, which meant we were almost to Jamaica's seaweed farm. I stared back at the harbor, praying that someone had gotten my text and was raising the alarm. My glance fell on a box of Patrick's

Seaseme Bars. "Can I have one?" I asked, pointing. "Theo, would you bring me one?"

He looked at Patrick, at the wheel, and at Ruben, sitting on a bulkhead with his gun. Patrick jerked his head in answer, as if telling Theo to go ahead. Bracing his legs against the movement of the boat, Theo went to the box of bars and pulled out a few. He brought them over to us.

When he handed me one, I took hold of it and whispered, "Help us." I put everything into those two words, trying to convey that it wasn't too late for him but soon would be.

He stared back at me with glassy eyes and I couldn't tell if he got the message or accepted it. But I didn't say anything further. I couldn't, because Ruben was watching us. I ripped the wrapper and took a bite. Hmm. Not as bad as I expected. If I didn't know there was seaweed in them, I wouldn't be able to tell.

Lights moved across the water. Someone coming to help us or just random boats? I prayed it was help coming. Patrick cut the engine and we drifted, water lapping against the sides. Mooring balls floated in the water, marking the seaweed-growing area.

A tense silence fell over the boat. This was it, the moment when they disposed of inconvenient us. My mind whirled with possibilities for self-defense as I glanced wildly around the boat. We weren't going down— literally—without a struggle.

Then Theo darted forward. What was he doing? Going after that oar to hit us? But instead he picked up a flare gun. With a loud bang, the gun went off, releasing a burst of orange light that could be seen for miles.

"What did you do that for?" Patrick left the wheel and launched himself on Theo, punching him. The two men, locked together, staggered back and forth. Ruben entered the fray, trying to help Patrick after Theo landed a good one on his jaw.

Sophie jumped up and ran to the wheel. Of course. She knew how to pilot a lobster boat, because of Jake. She throttled up the engines and took off toward the harbor, sending the men flying. Patrick and Theo fell to the deck, Patrick hitting his head hard. Theo managed to sit up, but blood was gushing from his nose.

Ruben pointed the gun at Sophie. "Stop, right now," he ordered. I grabbed the oar and whacked him right in the back, hard enough that the gun flew into the air, over the side of the boat, and, *plop*, sank without a trace.

Ruben tried to pull Sophie away, so I hit him again. Another boat loomed up out of the night.

Jake and Ian, in Jake's lobster boat. My heart stuttered then soared with joy and relief. I'd never been so glad to see anyone in my life. The two of them were tall and handsome and magnificent.

"Coast Guard and Marine Patrol are on their way," Ian called. "It's over." As if underscoring his words, two other, much larger, boats came around the point. Jake cut his engine and brought his boat around alongside Patrick's.

Ruben grabbed Sophie, his arm around her neck. "Let us go or I'll hurt her." When I waved the oar at him, he tightened his arm, making her choke.

Jake's eyes frosted over. "It's too late, Ruben. You'll never get away. The Coast Guard is already in formation." He reached under the console, where I knew he kept a shotgun. All the lobstermen did, in case they ran into trouble on the water. But the gun would be no use with Ruben using Sophie as a shield.

Then a familiar little orange face popped up over Jake's rail. Quincy? What was he doing here? With a magnificent leap, he cleared the slice of open water and landed on our boat, then launched himself at Ruben, spitting, hissing, scratching, and snarling like a bobcat. With a shriek of pain, Ruben fell back, releasing Sophie. "Get him off me!" he shouted, putting his hands over his face as Quincy climbed him like a tree.

Holding a hand to her throat, Sophie snatched the key out of the ignition and threw it overboard. No one was going anywhere now.

"Iris!" Ian called. "Over here." He stretched a hand to me and I clambered into Jake's boat. He gathered me tight, his arms like iron bands around me. "I was so worried about you." He swallowed audibly. "I thought"—his voice grew husky—"I thought I might have lost you."

With my face mashed against his shirtfront, I murmured, "I take it you got my text?" I felt laughter rumble in his chest. Something soft brushed my calf. Quincy was back, his mission complete. He wound through our legs in a figure eight while purring up a storm. I picked him up and snuggled him between us, the three of us warm and safe.

"How did Quincy get here, anyway?" I asked. "Last time I saw him, he was with Grammie."

Ian laughed. "While we were looking for you, he somehow got out of his harness and followed us. He found the apron you dropped, by the way, which was our first clue. Then somehow he sneaked onto Jake's boat without us noticing him."

"That sounds like him." I kissed my cat's head. "I love you both so much," I whispered. Then I froze. Had I really said that out loud? So much for my resolve to stay in the slow lane this time. Ian hugged me harder but didn't say anything. Maybe he hadn't heard me.

The Coast Guard and Marine Patrol arrived right then with engines roaring, lights flashing, and orders shouted through bullhorns. Officers, including Anton, boarded Patrick's boat, taking over from Jake, who was holding the trio of baddies at bay with his shotgun.

Sophie was seated in Jake's captain's chair, sipping from a bottle of water. Jake bent to put the gun away, then turned to his ex-girlfriend. I peeked at them, heart in my throat, as I waited to see what would happen next.

Jake gently took the bottle of water from her and set it aside. With a sob, he put his arms out, his chest heaving with emotion. Tears streamed down Sophie's face as she threw herself into his arms. "I love you, Jake. Please forgive me."

He bent over her, smoothing her hair with one large hand. "There's nothing to forgive. It was all my fault." He kissed her on the head. "I love you too, babe. It's okay, it's all going to be okay."

I glanced at my guys, who were also watching this touching reconciliation. It *is* going to be okay, I thought as I reached a hand up to Ian's neck and pulled his lips to mine. It most certainly is.

CHAPTER 27

G in and tonic, Iris?" Brendan asked as he held out a tray containing tall and frosty drinks. He was one of several servers hired for Eleanor's garden party a week later, which had turned into quite the bash. Grammie, Ian, and I were seated at a table next to the pool, waiting for Madison and Sophie to arrive, while Bella watched from a lounge chair as her children frolicked in the pool.

"I'd love one." With a smile, I selected a glass, lifting it in a toast of thanks. Now that the mystery of Hailey's death had been solved, a weight seemed to have lifted from Brendan's shoulders. He returned the smile, seeming so much freer with them now, and offered Grammie a drink. Ian was sipping from a bottle of beer.

I settled back in my chair with a sigh. What a treat this was. The weather was perfect: warm and dry with a gentle breeze off the bay. A jazz group played on the veranda, and under a big white tent on the lawn, tables groaned with a cold salad and seafood buffet. Huge grills nearby sent clouds of delicious smoke into the air. Our hostess was flitting around the terrace saying hello to all her guests and making sure that everyone had enough to eat and drink.

"Eleanor is doing so much better," Grammie said,

watching her laugh at something Horatio Morris said. "It's like she's a different person."

Grammie was right. The confusion was gone, she had more energy, and she was much less stressed now that Craig was totally out of the picture. In fact, he'd been arrested for spiking Eleanor's herbal capsules with Valium. We'd also figured out that he had been playing tricks on her, like putting her eyeglasses in the refrigerator and claiming she must have done it. Gaslighting 101.

"I wonder what the big announcement is," I said, taking a sip of tart and tangy gin, so refreshing on a hot afternoon. "I tried to get her to tell me but she wouldn't say a peep." The auction houses had finally responded to my queries, and we had auctions lined up for the clothing and the jewels. The expected proceeds would allow Eleanor to make some major repairs on the house and still have enough for a sizable nest egg. She and Cookie had been cloistered off and on for the past week, working on something top secret.

Lukas and Jamaica sat at a nearby table, deep in conversation. He had decided to take the university job in Connecticut and would be moving later in the summer. As the pair laughed together, I had a feeling we'd be seeing him in town now and then.

Regarding Jamaica, I had been so relieved when my suspicions turned out to be unfounded. She'd come clean to the police about chasing Patrick down the day of Hailey's death in her boat, an impulse she soon regretted. They'd talked before Patrick encountered Hailey on the shore, so fortunately she hadn't been withholding anything really relevant to the case. Later she had told me how relieved she was that he didn't want her back, especially after his illicit activities came to light. Releasing her from their toxic cycle was about the only nice thing he had done. She'd learned her lesson, she'd said, and would pay attention to any red flags next time.

Patrick had finally confessed to this meeting at the cliffs with Hailey right before her death. She had caught him in Jamaica's lab after hours and threatened exposure—unless he paid her. Soon after they parted, Patrick saw Ruben and Hailey together on the cliffs from his boat, and watched Ruben push Hailey to her untimely death. In return for his silence, Ruben promised Patrick a stake in his new company. In his confession, Patrick also cleared up a couple of troubling incidents. He had stalked me outside the store and had sliced our boat. He was trying to scare me, to stop me from asking questions.

Ruben was now facing murder-one charges in Hailey's death, as well as kidnapping and attempted-murder charges for forcing Sophie and me onto Patrick's boat. As I'd thought, the fact that he was wearing Lukas's jacket when he committed the crime and then left it in Lukas's room had boosted the charges to premeditation. If he hadn't tried to frame Lukas, he might have been charged only with manslaughter.

Ruben had mugged Theo to get his camera, worried that the student might have taken an incriminating photograph that morning. But there was nothing, only the photograph of Patrick's boat, which the police hadn't thought much of at first. After the BOLO went out, Patrick had painted the boat white and given it a new hull number, which is why he had been able to slip into the harbor undetected.

As for Theo, his decision to help us on the boat followed by an offer to testify against Patrick and Ruben would probably mitigate the jail time he was facing. Although he had willingly agreed to sabotage Jamaica's lab, he soon found himself in over his head with the evil pair. He'd been afraid they would kill him too, which was why he was even there when Ruben kidnapped us.

"When is everyone else getting here?" Ian asked me, his hand reaching for mine under the table. Ever since that night a week ago, we'd been closer than ever. But although I was now pretty sure he'd heard me, he hadn't returned the words. I was fine with that, I decided after a brief bout of hurt feelings. I didn't want either of us to make decisions based on the heat of the moment. Been there, done that, lived to regret it.

I glanced at my phone. No new texts. "They're probably on their way." Over at the pool, a deeply tanned man with super-white teeth lowered himself into a chair next to Bella. He said something and she laughed, tossing back her long hair. Go, Bella.

Grammie had noticed him as well. "That's the dentist's son, Lance Pedersen. He's quite the sailing champion, as you probably know." Lance was an Olympic medalist adored by the media for his good looks and charismatic personality.

"He's back in town?" Ian's brows lifted in interest. He studied Lance, who had been three or four years ahead of us in school. "I've always enjoyed following his career."

"Me, too," I said. As a long-time patient of Dr. Oslo Pederson, Lance's father, I'd heard plenty about his celebrity son.

"Here they come." Grammie waved as Madison, Anton, Sophie, and Jake came through the gate onto the terrace.

"I'll get another couple of chairs," Ian said, jumping up to grab empty ones from nearby tables.

Sophie and Jake were holding hands, looking totally blissed out. Over the past few days, I'd often thought about our ordeal on Patrick's boat, marveling at the bravery we had displayed. I know my focus on saving Sophie had been responsible for allowing me to keep a relatively cool head. When we compared notes, she said the same thing, that all she could think about was fighting to save me. We'd always been good friends, but now our bond was even deeper.

"Great party," Madison said, glancing around. She waved at her parents then bent to kiss Grammie's cheek. She hugged me then sat in the chair Anton held out for her. After she was settled, he bent to kiss her before taking his own seat. Looks like *that* was going well. Madison, my bestie partner in crime, was happy, which made me ecstatic.

Sophie and Jake remained standing, still holding hands. When we looked at them with curiosity, Jake said, "Sophie and I have something to tell you."

She smiled up at him. "We just came from the attorney's office. Jake and his dad signed papers about the transition of the business."

Using two fingers, Madison whistled. "Good news," she said. "About time."

Sophie and Jake were still smiling at each other, making no move to join us at the table. My heart thumped and I just knew. "But wait, there's more," I said. "Hang on a sec, okay?" I stood and waved to catch Bella's eye, then gestured her over.

"What's going on?" she asked after hurrying around the pool. Her gaze fell on Sophie and Jake, and a speculative expression crossed her face. She grinned in anticipation.

Sophie held up their entwined hands, turning them so we could clearly see the ring on her third finger. "We're engaged."

"Getting married next June," Jake added, his face flaming red with pride and pleasure under his freckles.

We hooted and cheered, stomped our feet and jumped up to exchange hugs. The word spread through the rest of the party like wildfire and the other guests applauded and called out good wishes.

Eleanor came over and greeted the happy couple, taking Sophie's hand in hers. "I'm thrilled for you both," she said. "And I'm honored you're sharing the announcement here at Shorehaven."

"Thank you, Eleanor," Sophie said. "We certainly couldn't have picked a better place."

Our hostess released Sophie's hand. "Why don't you have a seat? I think it's time for me to make my own announcements." She nodded at Jamaica and Lukas, who rose from their seats. The trio walked to the veranda and gathered in a spot where everyone could see them. Brendan said something to the musicians and they stopped playing.

"Good afternoon, everyone," Eleanor said. "I'm so glad you all could join me today. Are you having a good time?" The crowd shouted affirmatives. "Today isn't only a celebration of friendship, although that was the main reason I decided to throw a party. I also want to share a very important decision I've made." She paused. "I'm donating Shorehaven to College of the Isles. This house will become an aquaculture study center, under the direction of PhD student and entrepreneur Jamaica Jones and Dr. Lukas de Wilde, from the University of Connecticut. Their aim is to develop sustainable business models while protecting our precious marine environment."

Again applause broke out, the guests exchanging delighted looks and smiles. I was thrilled for Jamaica, who had been waiting for acceptance in a PhD program.

"What wonderful news," Grammie said. "Eleanor's gift will make a big difference to the people of Maine."

Jake nodded in agreement. "Anything that helps our coastal economy while preserving the environment is a win-win."

Jamaica held up a hand. "But wait. There's more." She nodded at Eleanor to continue.

"We all know how important financial aid is to help worthy students without means," Eleanor said. "So as part of this new initiative, I'm endowing a scholarship in the name of Hailey Piper."

It took a second but then everyone caught on and began applauding, a wave of emotion flowing over the crowd. Tears burned in my eyes, and when I glanced at Grammie, I saw her swipe at her eyes. Although Hailey had made some major mistakes in her all-too-short life, Eleanor's scholarship meant she would be remembered for her brilliance and commitment to aquaculture instead.

That concluded Eleanor's presentation, and the party resumed, guests taking turns to approach the terrace and speak to her and the codirectors of the new program. The musicians launched into "What a Wonderful World," including vocals. I loved that song.

"We never did get a chance to dance the other night," Ian said, holding out his hand. "Shall we?"

"I'd love to." I took his hand and allowed him to help me up. He put an arm around my shoulders and guided me toward the lawn, where other couples were already dancing barefoot. As we went, I noticed a couple arriving, an older man walking with a cane, accompanied by a younger woman who watched him closely. His daughter, I guessed.

I tugged on Ian's arm to halt him. "They're here. The Belgian cousins."

He followed my gaze. "That's great they made it. What a perfect day for a reunion."

Warm satisfaction glowed in my heart. We'd done this, helped Eleanor reconnect with her long-lost relatives. I was thrilled for her.

We began walking again, and at the edge of the make-shift dance floor, we paused to kick off our shoes.

Ian placed one arm around my waist, pulling me close, and clasped my hand with his. I put a hand on his shoulder, enjoying how warm and solid he was. He smiled down at me, eyes crinkling. "Ready?"

We began to move, my full-skirted frock swaying with each step, the grass soft under our feet, a salty breeze teasing our skin. Overhead, the pale disk of a daylight moon shone in the sky, like an extra special decoration hung just for us.

My world was wonderful, indeed.

THE END

Read on for an excerpt from

BODIES AND BOWS

THE NEXT INSTALLMENT iN ELIZABETH PENNEY'S APRON SHOP SERIES—

Available soon from St. Martin's Paperbacks!

A loud bloop bloop from the fish tank made me jump, the three-year-old *Reader's Digest* almost slipping from my grip. But the pretty angelfish still swam serenely in their underwater lair, showing no concern for any of the humans waiting to be tortured.

I was at the dentist's office, alone in the waiting room except for the fish, on a gorgeous morning made for anything but this. Through the big window facing downtown, I could see a deep blue bay dotted with islands. Sailboats and lobster boats tracked across the water, leaving creamy froth in their wake. Summer was almost over, I realized wistfully, and I'd barely had a chance to enjoy it. For good reasons, but still.

A child screamed in a back room, followed by pleading reassurances from his mother and the lower, calmer tones of Dr. Pedersen. "This won't hurt a bit, Timmy. I'm just going to take a peek. Open wide, there's a good boy."

"You'll get a lollipop if you listen to the dentist," his mother said.

Twenty years ago, that could have been me, cowering in the big chair and staring wide-eyed at the tray of scary-sharp implements. Dr. Oslo Pedersen had been taking care of my teeth since I moved to Blueberry Cove at age eight, to live with my grandparents after my parents tragically died in a car accident. I put a hand to my cheek, wondering if the filling that had landed like a chunk of tinfoil on my breakfast plate was one of Dr. Pedersen's. I don't have many fillings, fortunately, mainly because my grandmother had limited sweets and stood over me until she could trust me to brush and floss.

Instead of turning back to the magazine, I thought about my to-do list. At nine, Grammie would open Ruffles & Bows, the vintage apron and linens shop we owned together on Main Street. We had fall inventory to unpack, and then, after the shop closed, volunteer duties at the lighthouse.

Tonight, a group of us planned to go through old trunks left behind by the last keepers, who left in the early 1950s, when the light was automated. The new lighthouse museum was scheduled to open on Labor Day weekend, thanks to various local fundraisers. Our committee was in charge of creating exhibits depicting life as a lighthouse keeper, and it was shaping up to be a really fun project.

"Iris?" a voice inquired from the doorway.

I looked over to see Gretchen Stolte, dressed in a smock and pants uniform. "Hi, Gretchen. I didn't know you worked here." Not that I knew her well. She was a recent transplant to the area, an attractive woman with tawny hair and green eyes.

She gave a soft snort as we started walking down the hallway to the examination rooms. "I'm a licensed dental hygienist," she said. "Over ten years of experience."

"Wonderful," I said, feeling scolded for my innocuous remark. She was one of those prickly people who took offense easily, I remembered.

My glance fell on a photograph depicting a small sailboat heeling over in tumultuous seas, one of many lining the hallway.

"Dr. Pedersen must be so glad to have Lance back in town," I said, attempting another pleasantry. His son, a world-class sailor and Olympian, had recently retired from the pro circuit with a great deal of fanfare. With his good looks, bad boy reputation, and outstanding performance, Lance was a media—and local—darling. My friend Bella Ricci had gone on a few dates with him this summer, and the rest of our posse was vicariously enjoying the situation.

Her shoulders stiffened and she sped up, forcing me to race-walk down the carpet. Oops. I'd done it again. Too late I recalled that Gretchen didn't like Bella, therefore any mention of Lance would salt the wound. She had gone out with Bella's ex-husband, Alan, for a while, and when they broke up, she blamed my friend, which was totally unfair. But people were rarely rational in matters of the heart, I had learned.

"Have a seat," Gretchen ordered when we entered the tiny treatment room. She sat at a narrow desk that held a computer while I set down my handbag and climbed into the big chair. "What brings you here today?"

Why do we always have to repeat medical information despite relaying the problem while making an appointment? With a sigh, I leaned back in the chair and studied the ceiling panels, which displayed an aerial map of the Maine coast. "I lost part of a filling from a right bottom molar this morning. While I was eating breakfast."

Gretchen clicked keys, bringing up my chart and studying it. "You have one restoration in that quadrant."

"That's it." I obediently opened my mouth when she came to take a peek. I also closed my eyes against the bright light she pulled down to shine right into my face.

She studied my tooth for a long moment and then I felt the heat of the lamp move away. "Dr. Pedersen will be with you shortly. Dr. *Peter* Pedersen."

"Oh. I usually have Dr. Oslo," I said, disconcerted by this news.

"Dr. Peter is taking over the practice due to Dr. Oslo's pending retirement," she said, that snippy tone back in her voice. "We're gradually transferring all the patients over." That made sense, since Dr. Oslo was well into his seventies. He'd seemed ancient to me when I'd started coming here.

She bustled out and I was left to wait, my anxiety building with every moment. Even staring at the map on the ceiling trying to find landmarks didn't calm me. I wanted the procedure to be over so I could get out of here. Lollipop or not.

Finally I heard footsteps approaching. A tall man with cropped dirty blond hair and a goatee, dressed in a white coat, strode in. *Dr. Pedersen, I presume.* He resembled his famous brother in height and facial structure, but while Lance dazzled the eye, the same features were merely ordinary on Peter.

He peered at my chart then at me. "Iris? I'm Dr. Pedersen." Without waiting for an answer, he handed the chart to Gretchen then reached for the lamp. "Open wide for me."

I closed my eyes again and so it began. After examining me with hums and muttered exclamations, he injected my gum with something that numbed the whole right side of my mouth. Saliva pooled immediately, and I prayed I wouldn't choke on my own spit. How often did that happen, I wondered.

"So, Iris, where do you work?" He asked this and a variety of other questions I couldn't answer while he fiddled about, drilling and packing and probing.

When I finally dared to open my eyes, they were both staring down at me with almost identical expressions of concern. "Am I okay?" I asked, trying to push myself up-right.

Dr. Pedersen patted my shoulder. "You're fine. Lovely set of teeth." He handed me a piece of articulating paper. "Bite for me, please."

Soon after, I staggered out into the sunshine, blinking, my mouth still numb and my bank account quite a bit lighter. Halfway across the parking lot to my car, I noticed Lance, shirtless and in shorts, rinsing down his Porsche with a hose. The Pedersens lived on the property, with the dentist office in one wing of a huge Colonial house. At the back of the paved area used for parking stood a former carriage house, now a four-car garage.

With a grin, he shut off the spray. "Hey, Iris. Beautiful day, isn't it?"

I mumbled something, my lips still not working right. But between my mouth gaping open and the drool, I probably looked like 95% of the women he encountered. Trying to smile, I fumbled for the keys to Beverly, the white '63 Ford Falcon my late grandfather had restored for me.

Lance whistled. "Nice car. Maybe you can take me for a spin some time."

My face flamed with heat, despite knowing that he was only being friendly. It wasn't his fault that he was sex on a stick, as my bestie Madison called him. Plus I was very happily seeing someone, a gorgeous carpenter named Ian Stewart. Rather than respond, I settled for a wave and climbed into my car. By the time I was backing out of my space, he had the hose spray on again and was intent on washing down the headlights.

Bella lived down the street from the Pedersens in a cute Craftsman bungalow. As I approached, I saw a tow truck from Quimby's garage in the driveway, with Bella's gray Volvo wagon up on the flatbed. Oh no. That wasn't good.

I signaled and pulled over to park on the side of the road, then shut the car off and hopped out. Bella was standing on the lawn watching Derek, the tow truck driver, finish raising the flat bed to level. Noticing me, she gestured me over.

"What a bummer," I said, trotting across the grass. "What's wrong?"

Bella grimaced. "I don't know yet. It wouldn't start." She folded her arms across her slim body, the ocean breeze lifting a lock of her long brown hair. "But whatever it is, I'm sure it will be expensive. And take a while. Good thing Derek can give me a loaner."

I groaned in sympathy. Car repair bills always seemed to strike when you could least afford them, both financially and time-wise. "Need a ride to the garage?"

Her face lit up. "Would you? Derek offered me a lift but . . ."

"Say no more." Derek Quimby was a talented mechanic but a total slob. I'd seen the inside of his tow truck, and it was a mess of fast food wrappers, old coffee cups, and random paperwork. Bella must have been on her way to work at her boutique, and she was wearing a pink silk skirt and matching top, with an open-front fine-knit cardigan over it. I wouldn't trust that outfit to Derek's truck either.

A man of medium height and about our age came around the hedge from the adjoining house, a Victorian that had been made into apartments. He had tousled dark hair and a heavy beard, and was wiping greasy hands on a rag. "Hey, Bella. Putting Derek to work, are you?"

"Not by choice," Bella said. "Kyle Quimby, this is my friend, Iris Buckley. Kyle teaches sailing down at the yacht club. Derek is his cousin."

"Nice to meet you," I said, noticing Kyle's great tan and an athletic build set off by faded jeans and a tight t-shirt. Both were as grease-stained as his rag. "Are Bella's kids in your class?" Alice and Connor were taking sailing lessons at the club this summer, a rite of passage for many local children.

"They are." He gave me a white pirate grin. "Naturals, both of them." He turned to Bella and gestured with his rag. "Need a ride? Give me a minute to clean up and I can take you on my way to the club." The grin flashed again. "Bella's not the only one with car troubles. My '74 TR-6 is giving me fits, as usual."

Thanks to my grandfather, I actually knew what a TR-6 was, a small sports car made by Triumph between the years of 1968 and 1976. "It has a 2.5 liter in-line six engine and a manual transmission, right? Those babies are fast."

His dark eyes held mingled surprise and respect. "You got it. Come take a look if you want. We can go for a ride some time."

"I'd love to. But right now I'm taking Bella to the garage. And then I have to get to the shop." At his quizzical expression, I added, "I own Ruffles & Bows, the apron shop on Main Street."

"Oh yeah, I've seen it," he said. "Nice place." He looked at Bella. "So you're all set, I take it?"

"I am, Kyle, but thank you," Bella said. "Iris and I have a lot to talk about."

We did? All I had to share was my Lance sighting a few minutes ago. Other than that I thought Bella and I were up to date. The members of the posse—Bella, Madison, Sophie, Grammie, and me—either spoke to or saw each other every day.

"That's cool," Kyle said. "But if you ever need my help, you know where I live." How nice that Bella had such a considerate neighbor. I also thought that he might have a crush on her, which would be totally understandable.

A native of Milan, Italy, Bella had natural elegance, olive skin, and the face of a Renaissance Madonna.

The whining noise from the tow truck hydraulics finally ceased, restoring blessed silence to the neighborhood. Derek checked to be sure the Volvo was secure, then walked over to join us. He greeted Kyle and me with a nod. "We're all set, Bella. Ready to head out?" Like his cousin, Derek was dark-haired, although clean-shaven with a fade, and he was about the same height and weight.

"Iris is giving me a ride to the garage," Bella said. "We'll meet you there."

Derek nodded. "All righty then. See you in a few." As he headed for the tow truck, Kyle tagged along to give him the update on the TR-6.

"Let me grab my things and we'll go," Bella said. I waited on the lawn while she dashed into the house, but when Kyle went back around the hedge, I strolled up the sidewalk to check out his TR-6. The British racing green paint job and tan interior appeared to be in mint condition, and I could imagine the joy of racing along winding roads in that sporty little beauty.

Behind the wheel of the tow truck, Derek gave a honk and began to pull slowly down the drive. Bella emerged from the house as he turned onto the street, and I hurried to meet her at Beverly. Enough daydreaming.

Quimby's garage was located on the state route that skirted town, so rather than go down to Main Street and out that way, I decided to cut through residential side streets up here on the hill.

"Guess who I saw at the dentist office?" I asked as we set off. I couldn't repress a grin. "Lance. He was washing his Porsche."

Bella continued to look straight ahead but a tint of pink flushed her cheeks. "We went for a ride in the Porsche last night, after we had dinner at the Lighthouse Grille." The

Grille was one of the best restaurants around, with excellent food and a romantic atmosphere. "It was fun."

"I'll bet. How are things going with him?" I was curious, not only because he was a sports celebrity, but because she hadn't really dated since her divorce. After ten years of marriage, she'd caught her husband cheating and immediately thrown him out. She'd barely recovered from the life-disrupting trauma.

She lifted one shoulder in a shrug. "They're fine." She threw me a smile. "Keeping it casual." The smile faltered slightly. "Did I tell you that Alan is staying in town this week?" Her ex-husband.

"Get out of here. Why? And where?" Horror swept over me. "Not with you, I hope." Usually the children went to his place in Rockland on alternate weekends and school vacations.

Bella laughed. "Iris, calm down. He's staying at the Sunrise Resort with his grandmother so they can both spend time with the kids. And by the way, I just found out that Florence used to live at the lighthouse. Her maiden name was Bailey."

"Seriously? That's fantastic. I hope she'll let us interview her." We'd been hoping to track down members of the Bailey family, but after almost sixty years the likelihood was slim, we had thought. Florence coming to town right now was a gift. "How old is she?"

"Eighty-five and still going strong. She told me that she's very excited about the lighthouse museum. She even brought photo albums with her."

I groaned in excitement. "Pictures of the lighthouse in the 1950s? I can hardly wait to see them." Our exhibits would have so much more depth if we could talk to Florence and find out what life in the lighthouse was really like. Maybe she'd even let us film an interview. We could set up a monitor and play it on a loop.

We had reached the intersection with U.S. Route 1, and naturally had to wait for passing traffic to thin before pulling out. Summer traffic on the Maine coast was horrendous, which we locals resented but welcomed at the same time. Catering to tourists was how most of us made a living. Grammie and I had sold a lot of aprons and linens to visitors this summer, and better yet, we had captured their emails for future marketing efforts. Customers could order from our online store—or ask us to stitch up custom aprons. That new sideline was taking off.

"Iris, there is something I need to tell you." Bella's tone was tentative.

I jerked my head around to face her, fear making my heart lurch. "What is it? Are you okay? Are the kids okay?"

She gave a little laugh. "No, it's nothing like that. We're totally healthy." She pressed her lips together, studying me and obviously thinking about how to tell me whatever it was.

A horn beeped behind me. Now, of course, traffic was clear but I couldn't focus on Bella and driving at the same time. I waved for the driver to go around us.

"It's Alan," she finally said, as the other vehicle roared past. "He wants to give our marriage another try."